SOLDIER SWORN

THE TERALIN SWORD

D.K. HOLMBERG

ASH PUBLISHING

If you want to be notified when D.K. Holmberg's next novel is released and get free stories and occasional other promotions, please sign up for his mailing list by going here. Your email address will never be shared and you can unsubscribe at any time.

www.dkholmberg.com

MAP

1

Endric rode toward the northern mountain range, staring at peaks that seemed no closer than they had the day before. The sky held a hint of rain, something that it had so often as of late. There was another scent to it, one that held the vague memory of rot mixed with the fetid scent of decay, so that Endric continually thought he would find some carcass, but he never did.

"How much farther do you think we'll have to ride?" he asked Brohmin.

The younger man, the one the Conclave referred to as the Hunter, shook his head. "The Antrilii wander. They're found throughout most of the northern mountains, but there's nothing predictable about where we'll find them. I suspect when we come across them, they'll have known about us far longer than we will about them."

The longer they rode, the more Endric questioned himself. They had managed to stop Urik and his plan. He had managed to prevent war in the north, where Urik had intended to force the Denraen into opposition with the Ur and with the band of Ravers, soldiers for hire who wandered the north. Urik had intended to use teralin, thinking to use its strange influence when it was charged in a specific way, and Endric felt lucky that they had managed to prevent full-scale war. What more would have been lost if they hadn't prevented it?

Still, they had lost much. Listain, the leader of the Denraen spy network, had been killed, brought down through Urik's machinations. Another of the en'raen had been lost while trying to reach Dendril. So much of the Denraen now had turned over, leaving Dendril as the one constant, and now Endric—new to his role—ventured north. Was seeking to understand where he came from, learning about his father's past and the people he was descended from, worth so much that he should be willing to sacrifice the Denraen?

Endric wasn't certain. That was the reason for his hesitation and the reason he felt a growing reluctance despite the slight thrill that worked through him every time he thought about seeing his cousin once more.

"You knew Dentoun?" Endric asked. His uncle had died during the Deshmahne attack, destroyed when Endric had begun to finally accept his fate. His uncle had been a skilled swordsman, one with talent that was nothing like what Endric had ever faced. The Antrilii were the reason that the Deshmahne were halted during their attack, prevented from reaching their goal in Vasha. Perhaps his father could learn exactly what Urik had intended now that the other man was in the Denraen custody.

"I have traveled with the Antrilii many times. Each time, I

learn something new," Brohmin said. "Now that Dentoun has been lost, I doubt I will be as welcomed as I was."

"Why would it matter?"

"I was young and foolish once."

Endric glanced over. Brohmin had wisdom in his eyes that belied his age, raising the question of how old he actually was. There seemed to be knowledge that a man in his twenties should not possess, and yet it seemed Brohmin did. That, combined with the impressive sword work he had demonstrated, made Endric question whether he had him pegged correctly.

Maybe Brohmin was older than he appeared. He was a part of the Conclave. And from what Endric had been able to ascertain, Brohmin was a *valued* part of the Conclave.

"I would prefer to think that we're both still young."

Brohmin tipped his head, a motion that Endric had come to realize was his way of shrugging. "Some of us more than others."

Endric smiled, waiting for Brohmin to say more, but there was nothing.

The mountains rose in the distance, growing ever more impressive the longer they rode. The northern mountain chain towered higher than those in the west, with peaks that would have towered over those around Vasha.

To the north, snowcapped peaks rose well into the clouds, disappearing so that Endric could no longer even see the tops. He imagined standing atop one of those distant mountains, staring at the world around him, and could practically envision himself as one of the gods of old before they had departed the earth. Ascended. That was what the Urmahne believed, and Endric thought the old gods really *were* found in places like that, places like the Lashiin ruins in Vasha, or dozens of other ruins they'd come across in his journeys.

"What do you hope to gain by visiting the Antrilii?" Endric asked.

Brohmin tipped his head once more, another shrug. "Perhaps nothing."

"There's something you seek. Otherwise, I doubt you would come with me."

Brohmin arched a brow. "Really? You think that you know me so well after only a few weeks riding with me?"

It was Endric's turn to shrug. They *had* been riding for several weeks, and it had passed uneventfully. Days were spent in the saddle, evenings spent making a quick hunt for something to eat, sitting by a fire, and often, Endric working with Brohmin to practice his sword work.

Before traveling with Brohmin, Endric had known the man was a skilled swordsman. That had been clear the first time that Endric had seen him. If he had not been, he would not have been able to withstand the brutality of the Deshmahne attack. Not only withstand it, but he had been able to stop many of the dark warrior priests, while others struggled with even a single priest.

Endric had wondered how Brohmin's skill would match up to his own. How would it compare to Endric's father? Dendril had been the most impressive swordsman Endric had ever faced before, but Brohmin demonstrated forms and techniques that Endric had not learned that made him at least the equal to Dendril.

How could he be so skilled *and* so young?

That was the question that lingered in Endric's mind each time they sparred, the question Endric never managed to have an answer to. Perhaps he was not meant to have those answers.

"Maybe I don't know you that well, but I know you're searching for something."

"There's a hunch I have that's troubled me since Urik appeared. With the Deshmahne growing stronger in the south, I fear something has changed."

"I think the Denraen would agree with you."

Brohmin shook his head. "Nothing quite so dramatic. But we have known peace for many years. Now, these warrior priests challenge that peace. If we're not careful, it may lead to outright war."

"So you come north, thinking to learn about what's happening in the south?"

Brohmin tapped the side of his head. "Exactly."

They fell silent, riding toward the distant mountain range. The closer they came, the more Endric began to wonder whether they would be forced to cross the mountains before reaching the Antrilii but suspected that they would. Otherwise, wouldn't they have heard more about the Antrilii from the villages they'd passed?

They were mysterious, a people known to wander the north, segregated from the rest of the world. What little Endric knew of them told him that they believed they had some divine mission they were called to perform.

Could they have some mission assigned to them by the gods? He didn't see how that was possible, but perhaps they had some way of speaking to them that was like the Magi.

Toward evening, Endric noted a small village in the distance. He tipped his head toward it and pointed, trying to draw Brohmin's attention. So far in their journey, Brohmin had them avoiding most other villages. They had worked with the supplies they had carried with them when they left the Denraen and had managed to hunt and collect what else they needed, but Brohmin seemed interested in avoiding the villages altogether.

Tonight was no different.

Endric frowned but said nothing. He wouldn't push, not wanting to create strain between himself and Brohmin, but it would be nice to sleep in a bed. He'd been on the road now for the better part of two months, first on a planned trip south and then facing the Ravers before finally going after Urik. He no longer knew what the comfort of a bed would feel like. His father would probably laugh at him for such thoughts and think him soft. Perhaps that did make Endric soft.

Worse, he suspected that when—and if—they found the Antrilii, there would be no comfort there either. He'd seen the Antrilii and how they traveled and slept under the open sky. What sort of comfort would men like that demand?

Perhaps he needed to be hardened in that way. Perhaps that was why his father had encouraged him to head north.

No, that wasn't quite right. Dendril hadn't encouraged him to travel north but had not denied him the freedom to leave. Dendril seemed to understand what Endric needed and seemed to understand that he couldn't become the soldier he needed to be if he remained with the Denraen and didn't take the time to learn where he came from.

"Why don't you want to stop in a village?" Endric asked as they passed, continuing northward with the night beginning to grow thick and dark around them.

"If we stop in a village, we limit the chance that we might come across the Antrilii."

"Are we far enough north that we should find them?"

A soft howl pierced the night, and Endric perked up, listening to see if it sounded like one of the merahl. If it were, should he be more nervous? They were creatures that had a specific ability to hunt groeliin, creatures Endric doubted he could see, let alone fight. Now that he knew he was descended from them, maybe he *could*.

"We near the edge of where we might begin to see signs of them," Brohmin said. "When we do reach them, I think you need to be ready for the real possibility that they won't welcome you."

"Even though I traveled with Nahrsin?"

"Nahrsin might have led after his father died, or another may have taken his place. I'm not exactly certain how the Antrilii determine who rules. All I know is that Dentoun had led for many years. The Antrilii would mourn his loss."

Endric wondered whether the Antrilii would refuse him. He was effectively family, wasn't he? They had returned to help in Vasha and had fought—and helped to eliminate—the threat of the Deshmahne. Those weren't the actions of a people who would abandon him, were they?

But what did Endric know of them?

After a while, Brohmin motioned for them to stop. They had reached a narrow stream that would be a good place to camp. Endric paused and drank the cold water. Despite the days in the saddle, there was something invigorating about making his way north that felt exciting about searching for answers at the urging of one of the Magi—and another of the Conclave.

Mage Tresten was right. Endric *did* have to know where he had come from so that he could know what he could become. For now, he no longer knew what that was. With Listain's death, would it mean that he would ultimately end up succeeding his father?

For so long, Endric had wanted only to be a soldier—to do nothing more than fight—and now that he had assumed a position of command, taking a role where he was expected to lead, he was no longer certain what he wanted. Fighting—especially now that he had been forced to fight and kill more than once—no longer had the same appeal. Now that he had lost those who were close to him, Endric thought he understood the desire for peace.

It was his turn to make a small cookfire while Brohmin wandered off on a hunt. Endric barely had the small fire blazing before Brohmin returned, a pair of small hares clutched in his hand. Endric found it impressive that the man could hunt rabbit with only sword and knife. It wasn't the first time that Brohmin had managed to snag such creatures, and he doubted that he would ever discover the Hunter's secret.

While Endric tended the fire, Brohmin skinned the rabbits, spitted them, and began to roast the meat. Endric sat back, caught up in the moment.

Because of that, he somehow missed the sounds of movement around him.

Shadows suddenly appeared.

A large, catlike creature sat next to Brohmin, watching him with deeply intelligent eyes.

"The merahl found us," Endric said.

Brohmin nodded. He seemed reluctant to move and simply sat there, watching the merahl and letting the creature watch him as well.

"What is it, Brohmin?" Endric asked.

"I think... I think this one is not too fond of me."

The merahl blinked, almost as if acknowledging Brohmin's claim.

Endric found himself smiling. "Why would the merahl not like you?"

"The same reason the Antrilii didn't care for me at first."

It was Endric's turn to arch his brow. "What aren't you telling me?"

The merahl lunged forward and slammed Brohmin back with one of his massive claws, settling on Brohmin's chest. The merahl flashed sharp fangs that glittered in the firelight.

Endric stood and started toward Brohmin, but the other man raised his hand.

Brohmin stared at the merahl, meeting the creature's gaze. If Endric didn't know better, he would almost believe that something passed between them, some sort of soundless communication, but then it was gone. The merahl sat, keeping two of its massive paws resting on Brohmin's chest, unwilling to move.

"What should we do?" Endric asked.

"We wait."

"Wait for what? For the merahl to decide whether or not it wants to kill you?"

Without looking toward him, Brohmin answered, "Yes."

2

It seemed as if moments stretched into hours. Endric stood, watching helplessly while Brohmin remained trapped beneath the merahl's massive paw. The creature refused to budge, and Brohmin seemed unwilling to even attempt to throw him off. Endric wondered whether Brohmin would even be able to, or if the creature was too massive. Maybe Brohmin couldn't even move him.

"How long will we have to wait?" Endric asked.

Brohmin shook his head, keeping his gaze fixed on the merahl's bright-eyed, intelligent stare. "Hopefully not much longer. He's heavy." Brohmin's voice had taken on a breathy quality.

It seemed as if the merahl relaxed, easing some of the pressure off Brohmin, though he still didn't remove his paw from the other man's chest.

Had the merahl understood what Brohmin had said?

He knew the creatures to be intelligent, but that seemed to

be attributing an uncomfortable amount of intelligence to them. What other explanation was there?

Endric thought for a moment and decided to try something, regardless of how foolish it might make him seem. The only one here to witness it would be Brohmin, and if Endric failed, then it wouldn't matter.

"I am Endric, son of Dendril, descendant of the Antrilii. My uncle was Dentoun, first of the Antrilii, and his son is Nahrsin, a hunter of the Antrilii," Endric added. The last part seemed fitting, though he didn't know how accurate it was.

The merahl turned its massive head toward him. The creature had a blunted jaw, bright eyes with oblong irises, and sharp, pointed ears. The ears were the most responsive, swiveling at every sound, but the merahl also sniffed the air, noticing everything. Stripes of silver worked along otherwise reddish brown fur. There was something distinguished about the creature that matched its bright intelligence. How had he never heard of the merahl before coming across them with the Antrilii?

"I come north seeking to understand the Antrilii," Endric went on. It felt less ridiculous the more he spoke to the creature. Could the merahl actually understand, or was he simply being foolish? "The man you have captured comes with me. He means no harm to the Antrilii, and he means no harm to the merahl."

The merahl shifted, pressing down more with its heavy paw.

Had Endric said something that offended him?

"I don't think it worked," Brohmin said with a grunt.

"Please," Endric begged. "Let us meet with the Antrilii before you decide his fate."

The merahl flicked its ears before setting its large head down in something like a nod.

That had to be his imagination, didn't it? No creature would nod. That was a human gesture, nothing like what he would expect from any animal, regardless of how intelligent it might be.

Yet the merahl removed his paw from Brohmin's chest and sat crouched next to him. Endric had the impression that the merahl would pounce at any moment were Brohmin to make the mistake of attacking.

Brohmin sat up, gingerly rubbing his chest. He maintained eye contact with the merahl, but he said nothing.

"Thank you," Endric said.

The merahl studied him a moment before, with a dangerous grace, bounding off and disappearing into the darkness.

"Where do you think it's gone?" he asked Brohmin.

"There aren't many men willing to speak to the merahl," a voice said behind him.

Endric spun, his hand reaching for the hilt of his sword before freezing. There would be no benefits in attempting to attack, especially if this were one of the Antrilii. They were who he hoped to reach, not a people he should attack.

Standing before him was a tall man dressed in dark black leathers. A fur-lined cloak covered his shoulders. His face was painted in streaks of red and black, making him terrifying in the darkness. The light from the flames flickered off his face, making it even more terrifying. Endric did not recognize this man, though he had only traveled with a handful of Antrilii. Endric steadied his breathing and tipped his head respectfully in a nod toward the Antrilii. "I am Endric, son of Dendril—"

"I heard what you said."

Endric waited for the Antrilii to say something more, to perhaps share that Endric had no reason to fear him or that he would call off the merahl from attacking Brohmin, but the Antrilii said nothing. He simply stared, his eyes weighing Endric.

"I come in search of the Antrilii, wanting to know of my heritage."

The Antrilii grunted. "If you are interested in that, you would have come long ago."

He waved a hand, motioning toward the south. "Return, Endric, son of Dendril. Go back to your home and the safety of the south. Leave the north to those who have not forgotten their vows."

The man whistled, and his brow creased in a frown before he ran into the darkness after the merahl with a swift gait—swifter than Endric would have expected—and also disappeared into the darkness.

Endric stared after him, frowning. "What was that?"

Brohmin coughed, and Endric looked over to see him rubbing his chest and shaking his head. "I'm not certain. I thought I was the one the Antrilii wouldn't want to see." He looked over at Endric, a hint of a smile on his face. "Glad to see there's another they are equally annoyed with. It takes some of the burden off of my shoulders."

"What do you think he means by *return to the south?*"

"I thought that part was pretty clear. The other parts of it were less so."

"You mean the part about abandoning vows?" Endric asked.

Brohmin tipped his head, shrugging. "That. The disgust he seemed to have with your father. I suspect they're tied together." Brohmin turned and looked toward the north, into the darkness where the Antrilii had disappeared. "It seems your father leaving the Antrilii wasn't appreciated," Brohmin said.

Endric could only nod, though he had no idea why. What reason would the Antrilii have for being upset with Dendril? The Antrilii he'd met had seemed willing to help, but then again, those Antrilii had been family.

What sort of political situation had he come into?

Had his father known what he would encounter?

Endric didn't know the last time his father had been north and visited the Antrilii. Had he abandoned some vow that offended them? Was there something more to what his father had chosen by serving the Denraen?

Brohmin pointed to the fire. "Come on. We still need to eat. In the morning, we can continue north, see if we can find other Antrilii, maybe some who your father hasn't pissed off." He said the last with a hint of a smile. "Though, I wonder if there are any like that. Maybe your father has angered all the Antrilii other than those he was related to."

"You're not helping."

Brohmin reached for the spit and pulled the rabbits away from the fire. The meat had blackened, left longer than they had intended during the merahl attack and then the Antrilii appearance. Brohmin frowned as he pulled a chunk of meat off the rabbit, chewing it slowly. "I might not be helping, but neither is this." He spat next to him, then tore another hunk of meat off, tried that instead.

Endric sighed and had no choice but to sit next to him and try to force himself to eat while pushing away questions about his father and the Antrilii, and what it meant for him.

Endric awoke before the sun crested the horizon. The clouds had dissipated, leaving a clear sky with a hint of gray. It was nothing like it had been for the last few days. It had cleared without raining, leaving it so that Endric could make out the peaks of the mountains in the distance. In the growing light of the morning, the mountains appeared even more impressive. Fog trailed around the upper levels of the mountains and snow stretched far closer to the ground here in the north than it did in the mountains around Vasha.

Endric made quick work of cleaning up the campsite, burying the remains of the fire and smoothing over the earth so that they wouldn't leave any sign of their passing. It was habit, ingrained into him from his Denraen training. Brohmin, as he often did, touched the ground after Endric was finished, as if he were dissatisfied with Endric's work. Endric couldn't deny the fact that he always seemed to make it less obvious that they had been here. They mounted and continued northward without so much as a word.

Endric still struggled with the Antrilii appearance the night before. Even when he had been frustrated with his father's lack of action, he had always thought of him as an honorable man, though perhaps a little hesitant to act. The Antrilii comment about abandoning vows made Endric wonder if perhaps his father weren't as honorable as he liked to believe.

By midday, Brohmin called them to a halt, stopping them near the edge of the stream they had been following. He crouched near the ground, staring at it while Endric took a drink, allowing his horse to drink as well.

"What is it?" Endric asked.

Brohmin shook his head. "Tracks. But they're inconsistent."

They had been expecting to see signs of the passing merahl

or even the Antrilii, but so far, they had not managed to do so. If they had found tracks, this would be the first time. "Merahl? Horse? Man?"

Brohmin shook his head. "None of the above. These are old, and something I haven't seen for over a year."

Endric wiped his hands on his pants, drying them off, before crouching beside Brohmin. It was dry. Despite the thick clouds and the threat of rain, there'd been none. Endric studied the tracks, trying to make sense of what he saw. They were shallow and strangely shaped. There was a sharp point toward the heel and a wide, almost claw like feature to the toes.

"What is it?" Endric asked. "It doesn't look like any animal I've ever seen."

Brohmin shook his head. "No," he said. "Probably not like any animal that you've seen. Though, if you are really descended from the Antrilii, it wouldn't surprise me if you would be able to see it."

Endric frowned. "I'm not sure what you mean by that."

"Pray that you don't have to understand."

Brohmin stood and dusted himself off. He reached for the reins of his horse and climbed into the saddle, motioning them forward.

They rode for another hour or so before Brohmin paused, his brow knitted in a deep frown. He leaped from the saddle and crouched down, looking at the ground intently.

Endric climbed carefully from his own saddle and came alongside Brohmin, studying the ground with the same interest. Much like the last place that he had studied, there was a strange animal print. This one was like the last, though if Endric didn't know any better, it would be more recent.

"How old do you think this is?" Endric asked Brohmin.

Brohmin shook his head. "Several days. At least now I understand why the Antrilii had been through here."

"Antrilii? You think he was—"

"On a hunt. We're too far south for the Antrilii to have come this way for no other reason."

Endric turned his attention back to the animal print. If the Antrilii had been hunting, then the only reason would be for the possibility of the groeliin. Was that what Brohmin had meant about him seeing the creatures?

He looked at Brohmin, but the man almost intentionally ignored him.

"Come on," Brohmin said. "If the Antrilii have come through here on a hunt, we can follow them and maybe we can find someone a little more accommodating than the man we encountered last night."

"And if we don't?"

"Then you might have to keep searching until we reach your cousin." Brohmin glanced over at him, and he shrugged. "The Antrilii will hunt. And you want to know about your people."

"What do you want, Brohmin?"

He offered a hint of a smile. "Something I doubt the Antrilii can provide."

3

They reached the lower hills of the northern mountain chain. Brohmin stopped several times, staring at the earth as if he would find some answer that Endric didn't understand. During one of the stops, Brohmin ran his hands along the earth, mumbling something under his breath. The print they followed seemed slightly clearer when he did, almost like the mumbling had made a difference and clarified what they were tracking.

Each time they paused, Endric felt a surge of hope that they might be closer to discovering the Antrilii. Other than the night when the merahl had appeared, there had been no other evidence of the Antrilii. They had heard no cries of the merahl either.

By midmorning on the third day after the merahl had attacked Brohmin, Endric stared up at the mountains. They were close enough that he could feel the cool wind whispering out of the north, an icy breeze that skimmed across his cheeks.

He pulled his cloak closer, feeling no warmer with it on than with it off. He was not dressed appropriately for the weather and had prayed that they would reach the Antrilii before they hit true winter, or he might freeze in the search. Brohmin seemed less concerned about the cold, seemingly ignoring the chill that gusted in on the breeze.

"Are we getting any closer?" Endric asked.

Brohmin sniffed the ground. For a moment, it appeared as if he almost licked the ground, though Endric suspected that was more his imagination.

"Closer, yes. But we're not any closer to seeing evidence of groeliin."

What would happen if they encountered one of the creatures without the Antrilii there to face it? Dentoun had made it seem as if they was something only the Antrilii could hunt, and even they had relied upon the presence of the merahl. Would he and Brohmin be able to resist if it came to that?

"Have you seen any other sign of the Antrilii?" Endric asked.

Brohmin glanced up. His hand rested atop the print. "How long did you study with the Denraen?"

"All my life."

"And you don't have any ability with tracking?"

Endric shrugged. "Tracking was never my area of expertise."

Brohmin stood and dusted his hands across his pants. He reached for the reins of his horse so that he could climb back into the saddle. "Tell me, Endric. What *was* your area of expertise?"

"Unfortunately, fighting. I spent most of my life thinking that I was a skilled fighter."

Endric climbed into his saddle, his gaze fixed on the mountains. That was part of the reason he wanted to find them. If he could find Nahrsin, and if he could discover what the Antrilii knew about swordsmanship, maybe—just maybe—he might be able to fight the way they could. Endric hated that it drove him, but there was no denying the fact that he was motivated by a desire to improve and not be outclassed by another swordsman.

"What you mean unfortunately?" Brohmin asked. They continued north, this time angling along the foothills. They hadn't yet begun to cross into the steeper portion of the mountains, and Endric wondered if Brohmin were leading them north along the trail of the groeliin, thinking that they would encounter the Antrilii, or whether he was avoiding the mountains altogether, or maybe there was another reason. Maybe there was a mountain pass.

"While I was growing up, I knew I was a skilled fighter." Endric glanced over at Brohmin and saw that the other man was watching him. "My brother taught me, though some of the other soldiers contributed. It's because of Andril that I learned most of what I know."

"I've heard your brother was a skilled swordsman. You could have done worse than learning from him."

"Not skilled enough," Endric said.

Brohmin nodded slowly. "He was part of the Denraen party that was attacked by the Deshmahne. I had forgotten."

Endric swallowed. "When he was lost, I blamed my father. I thought he didn't take the Deshmahne seriously enough. I thought that he didn't know and wasn't willing to discover the true extent of the threat."

"Your father has been a part of the Conclave long enough to know the nature of the Deshmahne threat."

Endric nodded. "I know that now. At the time, I didn't. I was foolish. I challenged my father, and I lost."

Brohmin smiled widely. "You challenged Dendril? That would mean were you to have won—"

Endric nodded. "Were I to have won. But I didn't. I didn't come close. It was the first time I had truly felt outclassed with the sword." They rode silently for a while, Endric lost in his thoughts. Brohmin allowed him to sit in that silence, not pressing him, and for that, Endric was grateful. "When I came upon the Antrilii—or when they came upon me—I began to realize there were others with even more skill than me. Men like Dentoun, and Nahrsin, and—"

"Most of the Antrilii are quite skilled," Brohmin said.

"They are. And then there was you."

Brohmin tipped his head. "I don't think it's fair for you to compare yourself to me."

Endric shook his head. "We're similar ages. I think it's a reasonable comparison."

Brohmin had a strange smile on his face. "I'm older than you would think," he said.

They continued, and after a while, Brohmin paused, jumping from his saddle to examine another track before climbing back atop his horse.

"What changed?" Brohmin asked. "You failed in your challenge, but the Denraen welcomed you back following the attack?"

"When I returned to Vasha, I was determined to learn whatever I could from my father. I trained with Dendril and any others who were willing to work with me, wanting to improve, not wanting to face the same overwhelming sense of being outclassed I felt at that time."

Brohmin nodded. "I think that you succeeded. You survived against Urik when even your father would have fallen."

Was that enough for him, or was there some greater purpose? That was what motivated him now. He didn't know what he was meant to do, and whether it only involved fighting or whether he would need to do something more.

That seemed to be where Tresten was guiding him, the Mage prompting him to learn more about himself, to learn more about where he came from so that he could understand his purpose. Was it only about fighting? Was that what he was meant to do? If it was, he wanted to be the most skilled fighter possible. He did not want anyone to be able to defeat him.

Yet Endric felt there had to be more for him than only fighting.

Brohmin pointed toward the mountains. "There's a pass up here that will lead us through."

"You think the Antrilii on the other side of the mountains?"

Brohmin tipped his head. "Eventually they come south, but they rarely remain here. I was surprised we came across the man the other night. That is unusual for them, unusual even to see merahl outside of the far north or the Great Forest."

"There are merahl in the Great Forest?"

"Some. Those that are found in the Great Forest have a different purpose. They're not there to hunt groeliin. They are not trained the way the merahl in the north are trained."

How did Brohmin know all of this?

They veered into the mountains and Brohmin guided them steadily through the narrow pass. It was close to evening when he paused and jumped from the saddle, unsheathing as he did.

Endric hurriedly copied him. "What is it? What do you see?"

Brohmin raised a finger to his lips. "It's not so much what I see. It's what I feel."

"I don't feel anything."

Brohmin glanced over. "If you are descended from the Antrilii, then you should notice something. Focus on it. I might need your assistance."

"Assistance?"

"Your hard-earned skill with the sword."

Endric scanned the rocks around them, searching up the mountainside, and then back behind him. He saw no evidence of anything that would raise Brohmin's concern. There was nothing that drew his attention. The mountains were nothing but barren rock with a few small shrubs, an occasional evergreen tree, and a few other plants, but here the rock was more barren than other places.

As he prepared to tell Brohmin that he detected nothing, he realized there *was* something.

It was a strange sense of foulness that pressed against him in a way that he could not completely explain. Endric squeezed the hilt of his sword. This was a teralin blade, one with a polarity he had changed, and there was something about the sword that augmented his ability, but not in the same way that the dark teralin swords had helped the Deshmahne. As he held the hilt, he felt a surge of power.

Strangely enough, it pressed against him.

It was a wave of foulness, something like the dark energy he detected from the Deshmahne. He heard a noise on the rocks above him.

Endric looked up and, at first, he saw nothing.

Then it seemed as if his eyes began to adjust and a dark shape began to appear.

Not only a single dark shape, but several. They moved toward him and Brohmin.

"Is that groeliin?" he whispered.

Brohmin placed himself between the creatures and the horses. He shifted his stance, getting into a ready position. "It's good that you can see them. There are several, which may be more than I can handle on my own."

"I thought the Antrilii hunted them. I thought they would prevent them from moving too far south," Endric said.

Brohmin nodded. "They do. And they will. But the Antrilii haven't reached them yet. And we are here."

Endric slid around his horse, standing ready. He stared at the creatures as they made their way down the rock, noting that they had what appeared to be some sort of strange energy around them. It was a darkness that Endric could not completely explain.

He couldn't see them clearly, though he'd never seen them alive. When he'd traveled with the Antrilii before, he had seen the groeliin, but only from a distance, and only when dead. He was under the understanding that he shouldn't be able to see them while alive. What did it mean that he did?

Was *this* why Tresten had wanted him to travel north?

The nearest creature reached Brohmin, and he darted into a quick attack, beheading the creature in one swift motion.

As he did, their attack changed, and the groeliin swarmed off the rocks, heading toward them. There were nearly a dozen of the creatures. They carried clubs and attacked with claws and had an odor to them. They were like nothing he had ever faced.

How was he to fight these things?

"*Now*, Endric," Brohmin urged more calmly than Endric would have managed.

Endric focused on his patterns, trying to keep the catahs in his mind, staying as focused as he could. It was both easier and more difficult to attack these creatures than he had expected. Fighting the Deshmahne or the Ravers was one thing. They were men, and he had struggled against years of Urmahne teachings demanding peace. With these creatures, he felt no such remorse.

And yet, Endric felt as if he were not going to be enough. As if in spite of all the skill that he possessed, in spite of all the training he had, there were too many for him to face.

Brohmin slipped and fell, one of the groeliin's clubs swinging toward him.

Endric swung around, slicing through the creature's thick hide, keeping Brohmin alive.

A groeliin club struck Endric in the back, sending him staggering forward.

He fell onto the rock, losing his grip on his sword.

He felt the creatures approach and suspected that he wouldn't be quick enough to turn. Now that he was prone, unable to stand and no longer in possession of a sword, the creatures would tear through him. He had seen the way they destroyed when he had traveled with the Antrilii. He had no false beliefs that he might be able to survive their attack. If the groeliin reached him—and there was nothing now that would stop them—he would be killed.

Where was his sword?

As he scrambled for it, he found it trapped beneath one of the horse's hooves.

Endric reached for his boot knives. They had saved him once before, and without his sword, it was all the hope he had.

Endric took a knife in each hand and leaped to his feet.

Two of the creatures stood on either side of him. Endric spun, twisting his arms in the form he had learned from Senda, borrowing from her staff techniques. He had found those patterns useful more times than he'd expected.

He cut two of the groeliin down, but there were still too many remaining.

And where was Brohmin?

Had he fallen?

Endric's back burned where the club had hit him. At least he still had movement and sensation in his hands and feet.

The creatures circled him. Endric put his back to the horse, knowing that it might end up requiring him to sacrifice his ride. The horse whinnied loudly and kicked out with powerful strikes of its rear hooves. Only one of the strikes connected.

Endric lunged toward the nearest creature, but it shifted back, anticipating his attack.

"Brohmin?"

Had he come all this way, had he learned all that he had, only to fail now? It seemed a cruel twist of fate for him to fall to these creatures, creatures that the Antrilii—people he descended from—actively hunted.

The Antrilii that he'd encountered had been right. He was no Antrilii. His father had abandoned whatever vows that he had, and now left Endric unprepared for what he faced.

Endric lunged forward, catching one of the groeliin.

His horse cried out and fell.

Endric spun and saw Brohmin's horse collapse as well.

The groeliin had taken out the horses. Now, even if he were to survive, he would face a long journey by foot either back to Vasha or the attempt to cross through the mountains. Either way would be difficult. And that was only if he managed to survive.

Endric shook those thoughts from his head. He focused on what he could do now. He focused on survival.

He felt rather than saw two of the creatures near him.

Endric focused on the forms he knew, thinking of what he had learned from everyone he had trained with. He dipped, dropping his shoulder as he swung up the knife, catching one of the creatures in the chest before spinning around, stabbing at the next.

He surged forward, trying to reach the next groeliin, but pain surged through his spine. He slammed forward, and another club struck his shoulder.

Endric screamed.

His vision began to blur. He rolled, trying to bring his knives around, not wanting to die without putting up as much of a fight as he could, but saw no sign of the groeliin in front of him.

But he felt something.

Endric started to turn. Another club struck his leg.

The pain was immense.

He sat up, stabbing almost involuntarily with his knife before he fell backward.

His vision continued to fade. This time, he suspected there would be no coming back.

As he began to pass out, he heard a soft scream.

Was that Brohmin?

No. The sound wasn't a scream. It was a howl.

Endric had heard it before and had appreciated the sound then.

He laughed bitterly to himself. The merahl came too late to help him.

4

E ndric jostled awake.

He was alive. Somehow, he was alive.

He didn't know how.

Pain surged through his body, the kind of pain he'd known after losing to his father. It was the kind of pain that told him that he still might not survive even though he had lived through the initial encounter. The pain was so intense that he could barely keep his mind focused.

He hurt everywhere. He felt a throbbing pain in both his back, his leg, his head, and even his arms. Were they dragging him to wherever they lived? Would Endric see the home of the groeliin? He couldn't even imagine the horrors of that place. If it came to it, he might need to take his own life.

He sniffed, noting a familiar scent. Smoke.

Did the groeliin know how to light fires?

If they did, would they roast him? Perhaps they thought to eat him rather than simply destroy him. Maybe Brohmin was with him. If that were the case, then he would need to find the strength to fight. Somehow, he would have to get free. Somehow, he would have to help the man so that they didn't fall to the groeliin together. One of them needed to get free.

He tried opening his eyes, but it didn't work. He moved his hands, and as he did, pain shot through him. His legs ached with a fire that reminded him of when he had been flayed open by his father's greatsword, Trill.

How many wounds had he taken? Was this even something he could survive?

Endric moaned.

The sound escaped his lips almost involuntarily. It sounded muted, hollow.

Something touched his arms, then his head, then his legs. Endric wanted to kick, wanted to struggle, but there was no use. His body didn't respond as it should. In that, he was much like he had been when he had faced his father. And he was equally weakened as he had been then.

A muted voice carried to him. "Careful."

Voices? That didn't seem like what he would expect from the groeliin. Voices meant men.

A memory of the howl that he had heard before passing out came back to him.

He had heard the merahl but thought that the creature had come too late. There should have been no way for him to have survived long enough for the Antrilii to reach him. There had been too many groeliin, too many of the horrible creatures for him to face. But maybe somehow, he *had* survived.

"I *am* being careful, Nessa."

Nessa. That wasn't the name of a groeliin. That was a female name. That was a female voice.

Endric tried opening his eyes again, and this time they seemed to respond. He managed to see shades of light, enough that he realized that he was in some sort of room.

A room with smoke? That meant a hearth. That meant a home.

He moaned again.

He had been trying to say something, trying to create words, but his mouth didn't seem to function the way it should.

"Shush," he heard. "Don't try to talk. Let your body mend."

"Where?" He managed to make the one word and allowed himself to feel that minor victory, satisfied in the fact that he had succeeded that much.

"You're safe," the voice said.

Endric shivered. The feeling came on almost involuntarily. There seemed to be nothing he could do about it. As he did, pain surged through him anew.

He felt something rub along his skin, and the burning increased again. A pungent aroma came to his nose, and it reminded him of the salves that Dentoun had used on him when he was trying to heal him after finding him on the plains, saving him from death by the laca.

"Antrilii?" Once again, he felt a surge of victory that he managed even to say that much. The word was hard to form and came out almost like a mumbled, mixed-up sound, but it was enough—he hoped it was enough—for Nessa to know what he said.

"Antrilii, yes. You have reached us."

Endric breathed out heavily, and another moan escaped his lips. This time, he did not attempt to suppress it. How could he, when he finally had reached the people he sought?

"Groeliin?"

"See? He could see them." This was a different voice, not Nessa, and sounded younger, more urgent.

"None but the Antrilii can see them. That's our gift from the gods." This was Nessa. She spoke in a hushed voice and seemed to keep her attention away from Endric, as if she didn't want him to hear what she said.

"Me. Antrilii."

It wasn't entirely true, and it wasn't really what Endric and wanted to say, but his mouth and body didn't work well enough for him to form the proper words. There was no way for him to explain who he was, who he had descended from, and no way for him to explain that his father was not an oath breaker. He didn't know if it even mattered to Nessa or the other Antrilii who were with her.

"Which tribe do you think he's from?" the other voice asked.

"He's not of the people. Did you see his clothes? Did you see how he was found?"

"But if he sees them—"

"That's what he tells us."

"But you know how many groeliin he was found near."

"How. Many?" Endric managed.

He blinked his eyes, trying to clear them, trying to be able to see Nessa or the other person with her. All he saw were gradations of shadows. The last time when he had come around, healed by the Antrilii, there had been a more pleasant welcome from them. Then again, his father had been the one who had arranged the Antrilii assistance.

A face loomed into view, although Endric couldn't make out the details. He thought he saw strands of dark hair braided together and slung over her shoulder, but it could just as easily have been thick bands of rope. There was no sign of a painted face, no evidence of anything else that he would traditionally attribute to the Antrilii. There was only the word of the women here and the scent of the stuff they used on him that made him believe that they really were Antrilii.

"You were found near seven dead groeliin. What happened to the Antrilii warriors who killed them? Did the rest of the brood take them?"

Endric blinked again, confusion washing through him. His mind throbbed, and it was difficult for him to process what she was saying.

"Brood?" he managed to ask.

"Yes. The seven would've been part of a larger brood. Where were the Antrilii who slaughtered the beasts?" Nessa asked.

Endric took a breath. Pain still surged through him, but it was lessened, nothing quite like it had been. Whatever salves she had used on him had at least taken that much away. Was it possible that he might actually survive the attack?

Considering how he had felt when he had awoken, and what he remembered of the injuries he sustained while facing the groeliin, it seemed impossible that he would be able to survive it.

"You were beaten, nearly destroyed by the groeliin," Nessa went on. "Only by the luck of the merahl and Antrilii arriving did you manage to survive."

"No Antrilii. Me."

It was progress putting three words together. Hopefully, he would be able to carry on an actual conversation soon.

"Impossible," Nessa said. "None other than the Antrilii can kill these creatures."

Endric knew that not to be true. Brohmin had been able to see them and fight them, and he was not Antrilii. That meant there were others. Was that some special gift of the Conclave? Was it the reason he was able to have such skill with the sword? Endric didn't know and didn't know that it mattered.

He decided to change tactics. He was getting nowhere with Nessa when discussing the Antrilii and the dead groeliin. But he could find out more about what happened to him, and perhaps he could find out more about whether something had happened to Brohmin.

"How bad?" he asked.

Nessa leaned closer, and he could see the faint outline of her eyes. Definitely no paint on her face, not like the rest of the Antrilii he had encountered.

"Bad wounds. Clubs. Some of them were spiked. Good thing this group doesn't seem to have poisoned their weapons. That's not always a given," Nessa said. She leaned away, leaving Endric staring upward.

He could make out canvas overhead and realized that he'd been wrong about his initial assessment. Now that his vision had cleared, he saw that they were in some sort of tent. He felt softness beneath him and wondered if he finally had managed to find a bed. It had only taken him nearly dying to do so.

"Will I live?" Endric asked.

Nessa snorted. "Will you live? The gods don't provide me with my medicines for you to die, outlander."

That was a term he had not heard before. If Nessa was the one who had mixed the medicines, that made her a healer of the Antrilii. Given what Endric had seen of Dentoun's medicines, and how effective they had been at keeping him alive, it gave him the first surge of hope that he felt since awakening that he might actually live through this ordeal. And now that he had found the Antrilii, he might actually live to learn what he'd come to the north to find.

"There was another," Endric said.

Nessa leaned toward him, and he saw her face more clearly. She had heavy lines around her eyes but a distinctive face, and the dark hair that he'd seen braided and hanging off to each side of her head was definitely there. She had strands of color woven into it. A mixture of red and burnt orange that reminded Endric of the paint the men had worn on their faces. Did the women of the Antrilii fight?

They were questions he hadn't asked. Even in the Denraen, women soldiers were rare. Senda was a scholar first, though she was incredibly skilled with the staff. There were other women soldiers, but it was relatively rare. Most remained as scholars. A part of him thought that might be a better life than living as a soldier, risking yourself in certain death over and over again. As much as he had learned of Senda, he wondered why she subjected herself to that.

"There was no other. None but you."

Endric steadied his breathing. "There was another with me. He fell when we were fighting."

"You were fighting this man?" Nessa asked.

Endric started to shake his head but had a surge of pain that split his skull when he did. He stopped the movement, trying to control the rolling wave of nausea that worked through him. He might survive this, but it would take time for him to recover. "Not fighting this man. Fighting groeliin."

"As I said, that's not possible. Only Antrilii face the groeliin."

"Nessa—"

"Shush, girl. Run along and let me continue fixing him."

Endric sighed. What was there to say? What was there that

he could do to convince Nessa that he could see the groeliin? Likely, it didn't even matter that he convinced her. He'd come to find the Antrilii so that he could understand more about himself. He could focus only on that, and convincing them of what he did or did not see wouldn't really matter.

But finding Brohmin did.

"The other. There was another with me. Did you find him too?" he asked again.

"I didn't find you. Hunters did."

Hunters. The word sent a twinge of sadness through him. Brohmin was the Hunter. And if Brohmin had not survived this, what impact would that have on the Conclave? Did they require the Hunter among them?

"Where am I?"

Nessa continued to minister to him, rubbing her hands over his arms and legs, and pain flared up anew. This time, the salves smelled different. There was less of a pungent odor to them and more of a floral scent. As the burning pain faded, it was replaced by a cooling sensation, a warmth that seemed to start deep within his muscles and work its way outward. As she rubbed along his legs and moved to his arms, the cooling sensation continued. It seemed as if she healed him as she went, but that was something only the Magi would claim.

"Where are you?" Nessa said as she worked. She huffed briefly and turned her attention back to rubbing his shoulders. She placed her hands on either side of his face, and Endric felt a flare of pain through his cheeks that washed up into his head. The pain lasted for a moment, long enough for him to bite back a scream, yet a moan still escaped his lips. When the pain passed, so did the discomfort in his skull. The nausea eased. Whatever it was that she was doing seemed to be working. Endric needed to be thankful of that.

"You are in Farsea," Nessa said.

Endric racked his brain to remember the maps that he had studied during his time with the Denraen. Part of his studies as a soldier had required him to learn geography. That had only intensified when he had taken up the mantle of en'raen, forcing him to learn even more about the geography of the lands. Endric struggled to come up with where he might be.

"I'm not familiar with Farsea."

Nessa grunted. She started again on his feet, working her hands up his legs. This time there was no burning pain; there was only a cooling sense. The scent of the salves she used changed again, neither pungent nor floral, now minty, reminding him of the teas some men drank in Vasha.

"No surprise that you don't know Farsea," Nessa said.

"Why? Where is Farsea?"

Nessa grunted again. "Farsea is an Antrilii city."

Endric's breath caught. Antrilii city? The Antrilii didn't have cities. They were nomadic wanderers. If they had cities, that meant they were something else. That meant they were more than the nomads they were rumored to be.

How much of this had his father known? How much had Tresten? Was this why the Mage wanted him to learn about the Antrilii?

"How did I get to Farsea?"

Nessa squeezed his head between her hands, and the pain surged once more before fading. "Rest, then we can talk. Then you can tell us more about how you know of the groeliin, how you know of the creatures only the Antrilii know."

5

E ndric awoke to less pain than he had felt when he had fallen asleep. Muscles ached, but with none of the same agony they had had before. Now it was more of a stiffness, something that he felt as similar to the type of stiffness after a long ride, or after practicing with the sword for long periods of time. This was not the same pain, the searing, burning kind of pain that he had experienced when he had first awoken.

Endric moved his head cautiously, hesitant to sit up. When he last tried to move his head, he had felt waves of nausea, but those seemed to have passed. He was left with a memory of it, but none of the same horrible sensation that he had experienced when he tried moving while sitting with Nessa.

Now that he could turn his head, he looked around. Walls of canvas surrounded him. Surprisingly, Endric noted that they were brightly colored, not drab as he would've expected. The Denraen preferred browns and grays for their tents. This was orange and red, colors that reminded him of the sunrise. A hole cut in the roof allowed for a trail of smoke to drift outward.

Carefully, Endric sat up, rubbing his arms, trying to bring feeling back into them. He found a thick, pasty ointment on his arms, and when he sniffed at it, he noted a hint of the same mint that he had smelled when he last remembered Nessa working on him.

There were no injuries, nothing that he could find that was obvious, only patches of pink skin. Pale flesh that appeared as if it had once been ripped open and had somehow healed in the time that he'd been here.

How long *had* he been here? Could it be that he had been here long enough to fully heal? Had he been unconscious for most of it? That seemed both blessing and a curse. It would be a blessing not to remember the pain of his wounds healing, remembering all too well what it had been like when he had recovered after the folly that was his attempt to challenge his father. Yet he worried about how long he had been out. If he had been unconscious for the weeks that it would take for him to fully heal, what had happened to Brohmin in that timeframe?

Could he have survived?

Nessa had seemed surprised that there were as many dead groeliin around him as there must've been. Endric remembered how many he had killed, knowing that he had struck them with both sword and knife, resorting to using his boot knives before he completely passed out.

Endric bent his legs, pulling them into his chest. They were bare, much like his arms, and covered in the same white ointment as his arms. Endric ran hands along his legs, feeling for injury, but felt only the same achiness that he felt throughout the rest of his body. There was the stiffness, soreness that came from a hard day's work, but nothing more than that.

How was it possible that he had survived this attack with little more than stiff muscles? Could the Antrilii healing be that skilled?

That seemed unlikely. The Antrilii were nomads. They didn't have the same knowledge and scholarship found in places like Vasha or Thealon. More likely than not, he wasn't as injured as he had first suspected.

Endric stood, cautiously testing his legs, trying to determine whether they would hold him. A surprising amount of strength remained, and he was able to bounce on his heels, feeling the stiffness slowly resolve. He continued to balance, shaking his arms, drawing strength back into himself.

He looked around the space he was in. They had laid him on a flat, elevated cot. The sheet that had been used to cover him now rested on the ground, likely tossed during his restless sleep.

But *had* it been restless?

Endric felt more refreshed than he had in some time. Maybe the stiff muscles and pain that he felt came from the fact that he'd been sleeping as long as he must've been.

A folding table rested near the head of the cot, and on top of the table were several jars of creams. Endric picked up the first jar, a wide-mouthed one, and twisted the top off, bringing it to his nose. It was a brownish-white paste and stunk, carrying the same pungent aroma that he remembered from when Dentoun had healed him on the plains. This was the first salve that they had used on him, and the first cream Nessa had used to help him recover.

Endric replaced the top and swapped it for the next one. As

he opened it, he noted the same floral aroma that he recalled. That ointment had left his flesh burning but then had followed with a soothing sense. It was pale white, almost milky in appearance, and seemed greasier than the other.

Endric replaced the top to this jar and moved on to the next. As he lifted it, he expected the minty-scented salve that he had noticed when Nessa had rubbed it on his face and arms, but this was not that one. This had a distinctly bitter aroma to it. The ointment was not white or even brownish white; this was gray, verging on black, and there was something vaguely unsettling about it. Endric sniffed at it and debated reaching in to touch it, but held back.

He set the jar back on the table, leaving it next to the other.

He scanned the others, but each of them was smaller than those three main jars. Most were a similar shade to the others, all white or creamy in appearance. On the shelf below the table, Endric noted a roll of leather, so he unfolded it, noting that it contained a neat line of needles.

Had they stitched him? Had his wounds require that much repair?

Dentoun had stitched him when injured the last time and had done so with a steady hand. There didn't seem to be the same pain—or itchiness—that Endric would expect were he to have required his recent wounds to have been stitched.

He made his way toward the opening of the tent. As he did, he realized that he was dressed only in his small clothes. If he was in the north and in Antrilii territory, he expected it to be cold. Surprisingly, Endric was not. The air had a warmth, almost a heat to it that came from more than the fire glowing to the one side of the tent could account for.

Endric grabbed the sheet that had fallen to the ground at the end of the bed and wrapped it around his waist.

Where was his sword? If the Antrilii had found him, would they have found his weapon? After what he'd been through, everything that he had faced while dealing with Urik, he valued the teralin sword.

And he felt naked without his boot knives. Well, he felt naked without any of his weapons or clothes. Wrapped in only the sheet, he felt unprepared for whatever he might face on the other side of the tent flap.

Endric untied it, pushing out, and ducked his head through it.

He was taken aback at what he saw.

The Denraen didn't possess maps beyond the northern mountain range. Most considered the lands uninhabitable, nothing but ice and emptiness all the way to the sea. It was much like the lack of maps detailing the Unknown Lands.

This was nothing like what he had expected. There was a city around him. Wooden buildings that were simply—but stoutly—made were arranged in a neat and orderly fashion. A few trees dotted the spaces between the buildings. Lush, thick-bladed grass covered the ground, slightly browned but still with enough green to told Endric that the season hadn't fully changed here. In the distance, he saw the mountains stretching higher and higher before reaching the snow-peaked tops. Wispy bands of clouds surrounded the mountaintops. The sun was out, but only as a smear of yellow.

Had they drawn him back south?

If they had, why would the Antrilii settle south of the mountains? How would they have avoided detection there?

Endric shook his head. That didn't make sense. They

wouldn't have been able to avoid detection there. That meant that rather than south of the mountains, he was north of them. Which meant that as he stared toward those peaks, he was staring south.

As he looked around, he wondered how that was possible. How could there be such lushness this far to the north? How was it that these lands had been unexplored, lands that clearly were habitable but seemed untouched by any other than the Antrilii?

Footsteps approached, and Endric turned. A young girl, possibly no older than ten or eleven, looked at him with wide eyes. She had dark hair braided much like Nessa's. She was dressed in simple leathers, and Endric recognized them as the same type of leathers Dentoun and Nahrsin had worn.

"You shouldn't be out."

Endric attempted to smile, hoping that he could disarm the girl, but felt as if his smile only looked like a frown. "No? Where should I be?"

"In the healing tent. You haven't fully recovered."

Endric glanced back, looking at the tent. Considering all the buildings—and the permanence—that he saw around him, the tents seemed surprising. Why had they healed him in a tent rather than in one of the buildings?

"I'm better. Otherwise, I wouldn't have managed to make my way out," Endric said.

The girl watched him and then went running off.

Endric stared after her, wondering whether she was the same girl he had overheard in the tent when he was recovering. He decided that it didn't matter. All that mattered now was figuring out where he was, and then... then he needed to see what he could learn about the Antrilii. That was his entire reason for coming here.

Yet, even with that understanding, a part of him worried. If Brohmin had not been found with him, that meant he had either been captured and dragged off by the groeliin, or he had not been as injured as Endric had thought. Maybe he had escaped. But if he had escaped, why hadn't he brought Endric with him?

There were too many questions for him. It left him unsettled, not knowing what he needed—and should—be doing.

He considered wandering through the town, but that felt like a violation of the Antrilii trust. They already were skeptical of him. He had gathered that from the fact that they were suspicious he had faced the groeliin, as well as the strange reaction from the Antrilii they'd encountered to the south of the mountains. But he didn't understand why.

Maybe the best answer would be for him to simply return to the healing tents and wait for Nessa to return. She was his only contact in Farsea so far, though from what he could tell of the town, there were many Antrilii here. Would they all view him with the same skepticism as Nessa? Worse, if he revealed who he was and where he came from, would they all view him as the same as the Antrilii they had encountered out near the lower foothills?

As Endric stood there, he became aware of sounds within the village.

There were no sounds like he expected in a village, nothing like the hammering of a blacksmith, the playful running of children, or even the stream of merchants. Since Endric hadn't known that Farsea existed, he suspected merchants didn't either. Even if they did, how would they reach a place like this on the other side of the mountains? Doing so would be incredibly difficult.

He turned in a slow circle, and when he completed his circle, a woman stood in front of him. She wore an orange dress striped with red and yellow. Deep black hair was braided into three thick braids that went over each shoulder and down her back. Colorful ribbons were woven into the braids. Endric recognized her eyes, the dark, deeply lined eyes that watched him.

"Nessa," he said.

"Lynn tells me that you have recovered. That you think that you are well enough to leave the tent."

Endric shook his head. "I'm not sure how much I've recovered, but I feel well enough to be out of that tent."

Nessa grunted. "Perhaps. Or perhaps you have not fully recovered, and you should remain resting. You were severely injured. A man like that requires time. You are not as robust as the Antrilii."

Endric thought that a strange comment. What did it mean that he wasn't as robust? He didn't feel as if he were less robust.

"As I've told you, I am Antrilii."

Nessa laughed, a sound that seemed both amused and mocking at the same time. "You? Antrilii? When you were saying that when injured, I thought it a statement of a delirious and injured mind."

"Maybe delirious. Definitely injured. But it's true."

Nessa eyed him a moment and then motioned him forward. They started through the streets and passed by some of the buildings. As they did, Endric began to see movement within them. He heard boots along floorboards in one. As he passed another, he smelled the smoky aroma of meats and breads being baked. In another, he heard steady hammering, that of a blacksmith he hadn't noticed before. He saw only one other person besides Nessa, and that was another young girl, her hair braided much like the first—Lynn—and wearing similar leathers.

"This is Farsea. Few men"—and Nessa seemed to make sure to emphasize the word men—"have ever reached Farsea. The mountains are too difficult to cross, and those who do manage to reach the pass find that the way is often blocked with unpleasantness."

"You mean the groeliin."

Nessa glanced over at him, a hint of a question flashing in her eyes. "Yes. The groeliin. Most who attempt to come through the mountain passes find the groeliin descending on them and pray for death when that happens."

"Why would they pray for death?"

"Because the alternative is worse."

They stopped near what must be the edge of the city, and Endric looked inward, noting how neatly organized the row of houses and buildings were. Each seemed placed perfectly. From here, the ground sloped gradually away, overlooking the village itself. As he did, he realized this was not a city that would rival anything like Vasha or Thealon, but was far larger than anything he could have imagined. How many people lived here? How many Antrilii were there?

"Then again, you would have known that, were you Antrilii." Nessa crossed her arms and looked at him.

Endric had a sense that what he said next would determine his fate. If he said something wrong, he suspected that she would banish him from Farsea. Without a horse, without a sword or knives, he doubted he would make it very far on his own. And if what she said about crossing through the mountain pass was true—and he had little reason to doubt that it was not —he didn't like his chances of survival.

She watched him, an unreadable expression on her face.

He hesitated only because of what the first Antrilii had said to him. If they didn't care for Dendril, what would they make of the fact that he had come here? Would they allow him to stay?

This was a woman who had healed him, who had brought him back from injuries that should have taken his life. Endric owed her an explanation, even if it was one that he feared would bring some sort of backlash and more questions.

And without sharing with her, and without telling her the reason that he came, he wasn't certain that he would learn what he needed.

Wasn't the reason that he had come this way to discover more about his people?

It had been, up until the point when he met the Antrilii on the near foothills. That had made Endric begin the question and worry that perhaps he needed to be more cautious with what he shared.

"I come looking for an Antrilii by the name of Nahrsin," Endric said.

Nessa's eyes twitched, barely at all, but enough that he could tell that she recognized the name. "How is it that you know Nahrsin?"

"Nahrsin helped me once when I was gravely injured."

Nessa shook her head. "That happens to you often?"

Endric laughed. "Not often, but he was there the last time."

"It must be more than that, outlander. Why is it that you seek Nahrsin?"

"Because," Endric began, his gaze surveying the Antrilii

homes. If the village of Farsea were transported anywhere else, set down in the planes of Saeline, or even outside of Thealon, he would have been at home there. Farsea could have been any other northern town. "His father, Dentoun, is my uncle."

Nessa's eyes wrinkled deeper. "That would make you Dendril's son. The oathbreaker."

There it was again. It was the same word the Antrilii they had encountered outside the mountains had said. What did it mean for him? What did it mean for his father?

What would Nessa do?

Endric nodded, waiting for her reaction, worried what it might be.

Nessa took a deep breath, a heavy sigh escaping her lips. "Come on then."

Nessa started back into Farsea, and Endric hurried after her, wondering what he didn't know about his father, and how that impacted his visit.

6

The inside of the building was filled with long rows of tables. It was no more ornately decorated on the inside than it was on the outside. The walls were paneled wood, painted a faint orange, leaving Endric wondering why the Antrilii preferred such bright colors. Everywhere he went, he seemed to see the same bright colors. Was there something about those colors that appealed to them? Was there some meaning to them?

He took a bite of the flatbread that was on the plate in front of him. It had an interesting texture and a sweet taste to it. On either side of him were two young girls. One was Lynn, the young girl he had encountered on the street and who he had now learned was either Nessa's daughter nor her assistant. He had thought her ten or eleven, and that was mostly because of her height but had learned that she was only eight. The girl was tall, though. Then again, all the Antrilii he had met were tall.

Inside the dining hall, there seemed to be an order to where people ate. Nessa sat toward the center of the dining hall along a table that ran perpendicular to the three other long tables. The hall was filled with women. Endric was the only man present.

"You need to eat, to gain your strength," Lynn said. She watched him with her hands resting on the table, an earnestness to her face that would be amusing if not for the fact that Endric suspected that she spoke on Nessa's behalf.

"I am eating," he said. "Are all meals spent like this?" When Nessa had taken them through the village, he had observed nothing more than the rows of buildings. She had brought them back to the healing tent, administering another salve over his skin, this one the minty-smelling one. She had paused when she did, checking the tops of the jars of each, eyeing him strangely, seeming to know that he had inspected them as well. The ointment felt cool on his skin and left him invigorated. It was a strange and yet refreshing sense.

The Denraen could use a similar healing balm. He could imagine applying something like this when he was injured after a particularly violent battle, or even after a particularly vigorous sparring session. It would allow him to recover more quickly and not suffer the same aches and pains that he had known during his sparring sessions.

"All meals while the hunters are away," Lynn said.

Endric surveyed the inside of the dining hall, looking at each of the women. They were of all different ages. They were dressed in various ways, as well. The younger ones seemed to prefer leathers, much like Lynn did. The older women seem to prefer brightly colored dresses, much like what he saw on Nessa. Others wore a combination, leather breeches beneath their dress.

Each Antrilii had almost uniformly dark hair. Most of them had dark eyes. Most of the women wore their hair long and braided, though there were a few with short, close-cropped hair. None were plump. All seemed fit, as if they were battle-hardened warriors themselves.

They also seemed as if they didn't know what to make of him. When Nessa had brought him to the dining hall, the conversation had stopped. They had turned to him, staring, the younger ones watching more openly, though Endric had seen even the older women watching with interest. He wondered what they thought. He had come, openly claiming that he was Antrilii. Had Lynn or Nessa shared with them that he had killed the groeliin? That seemed impressive to them, though he had nearly died in the process.

"Where are the hunters?" Endric asked. He turned his gaze back to Lynn and saw her chewing on a long stock of a dark green vegetable that Endric wasn't familiar with, but it was set on his plate as well. He took a bite of it, finding the skin chewy, with stringy veins running through it. It was not unpleasant but had little flavor.

"The hunters are hunting."

Next to him, the girl on the other side started laughing. Lynn shot her a look, and the girl cut off, covering her mouth with her hand.

"Groeliin?"

Lynn nodded. "They seek the Chisln—"

The other girl shot Lynn a heated glare, and she cut off. Endric glanced between them. What was he missing here? "What's the Chisln?"

"It's nothing," Lynn said. She took a quite bite, filling her mouth so she didn't have to say anything more. "What really happened with the groeliin?" she asked between bites.

Endric shrugged, taking another bite of the long green vegetable. "I'm not exactly certain. I was coming north through the pass. The man coming with me noticed them making their way down the mountainside. There were nearly a dozen."

"That's not many," the girl next to him said.

"Hush, Jenna." Lynn shot her another warning glance before looking at Endric once more. "Who is this man you are with? How was he able to see the groeliin?"

"He has some ability to see them."

"He is Antrilii?" Lynn asked.

Endric shook his head.

"Then he was gifted from the gods. Like the Antrilii."

Endric fell into silence while eating. He finished the green vegetable before moving on to the strangely shaped meat on his plate. He hadn't seen any animals, or livestock, and wondered what they had served him. He started into it hesitantly but found the meat flavorful and juicy. It tasted somewhat like beef, though there was a gamey flavor to it. He ate quickly, taking bites of his bread in between, before wiping the remains of his flatbread across his plate, cleaning up the remaining juices and finishing the bread.

Lynn watched him, a satisfied look on her face.

"When will the hunters return?" Endric asked.

Lynn shook her head. "They return when the hunt is over. That's the only time they can return."

Endric frowned. "What do you do while they're gone?"

"We prepare. We protect the village."

"Protect the village? From what?"

Lynn's eyes darkened. "It's not only men who can fight,

outlander," Lynn said. "Men are good for only one thing, while we're able to do much more."

"I didn't —"

A hand tapped on his shoulder, and he looked back to see Nessa watching him.

"Come, outlander. It's time to visit with the Yahinv."

"The Yahinv?"

Nessa nodded, and Endric stood, tipping his head toward Lynn and Jenna. Jenna giggled softly, but Lynn only watched him, her eyes with an intensity that an eight-year-old should not possess. As Nessa led him away, Endric shook his head. "That one is precocious, isn't she?"

Nessa huffed. "Precocious would be fitting for her. She is talented, which gives her confidence."

"What kind of talent?"

Nessa glanced over. "The kind that allows you to live, outlander."

Endric looked back at Lynn. "She was the one who healed me?"

Nessa shook her head. "Not her. But she made the liniments that allowed you to live. She was the one who suggested that we heal you. Were it up to me, you would've been left to see if you could survive without healing."

They left the building, and Endric cast another glance back at Lynn, letting it linger on the young girl. He would have to thank her the next time he saw her. He had thought that Nessa had been the one who had saved him, but if it hadn't been her, then he needed to express his gratitude to Lynn. Endric had no doubt that he would not have survived without the ministrations of the Antrilii healers. He could easily recall the pain, the agony, that he had experienced when he had awoken.

"Where are you taking me?" Endric asked as they passed beyond the edge of the village. They made their way north, beyond the edge of the city where Endric had been before. From here, the ground sloped away, the hills around Farsea abrupt, concealing much.

"As I said, it is time that you visit with the Yahinv."

Nessa led him away. The sun had begun to set, leaving a colorful sky in its wake. Streaks of color filled the sky, and Endric found himself staring at it, marveling at its simple beauty. It seemed clearer here than it did in the south. The clouds that he had noticed over the last few months were not present here, and the air had a surprising warmth. There was none of the chill he had experienced in the foothills, or even through the first stages of the pass through the mountains. Endric found that the most surprising of all. Why was it so warm here? This far to the north, he expected it to be colder and thought there should be snow or ice on the ground.

"How long have the Antrilii lived in these lands?" Endric asked, trying to keep pace with Nessa. She moved quickly, and Endric couldn't see where they were heading. They followed a slightly worn path that wasn't quite a road, but the grasses were trampled, making it easy enough to follow.

"The Antrilii have lived in these lands for over a thousand years."

Endric blinked. How could that be possible? "Farsea didn't appear that old," he said.

Nessa shook her head. "Farsea is only a few hundred years old. There are others."

"Are the other Antrilii villages like it?"

"Are you always this foolish, outlander?"

"What does that mean?"

"Do you not have other cities in your southlands?"

In the distance, he saw what appeared to be a turret rising above the hill they headed up. Nessa guided them in that direction, slowly veering toward it. Was that the Yahinv?

"There are other cities in the south. I just didn't know how many cities the Antrilii had."

Nessa said, "The Antrilii are several distinct tribes. Each tribe has its own home. But each tribe comes together to face the groeliin threat."

"Like when Dentoun led the Antrilii south after the groeliin?"

Nessa stopped and crossed her arms over her chest as she considered him. "Tell me about that experience, outlander."

Endric shrugged. "I don't know much about the groeliin attack. I was… found… by the Antrilii east of Vasha. Dentoun led a band of Antrilii south, chasing groeliin. There were five merahl hunting with him."

He wasn't sure whether to tell Nessa about how the Antrilii had faced the Deshmahne, not certain whether that mattered, and not certain whether she would believe him or whether she would question him again. "That is too far south for the groeliin," Nessa said.

"That is what Dentoun thought as well. They chased the groeliin on a hunt."

"And that is where he perished? He was killed by groeliin?"

Endric studied her. Now he thought he understood. Had Nahrsin not shared what happened? Had Nahrsin not told the rest of the Antrilii how his father had died? If he hadn't, what did that mean for his tribe?

Unless Nahrsin came from a different tribe. Which meant that Farsea was not Nahrsin's home.

"Which tribe does Nahrsin belong to?" Endric asked.

Nessa huffed again. "You ask that now, outlander? You come north, in search of the Antrilii, claiming to fight the groeliin, and don't know which tribe Nahrsin belongs to?"

Endric shook his head.

"He belongs to the oathbreaker tribe."

Nessa continued forward, leaving Endric staring after, watching her back.

What had happened with his father?

Endric had come north, thinking that he would be welcomed here, thinking that the Antrilii would embrace him. His time with Dentoun and with Nahrsin had given him no other impression, had not made him believe that there would be anything other than a welcome here. But there was much more taking place than he knew.

They rounded a curve in the path, and the top of the turret came into view. Endric stared, mouth agape. It was more than a turret. It was a tower made of stone, a replica of the Tower of the Gods in Thealon.

There were many such replicas found in the south, though all were temples built by the Urmahne priests, designed to celebrate and worship the gods. Endric was surprised to see one here.

He had known the Antrilii to be devout. All of the Antrilii he had encountered when traveling with Dentoun had believed in their purpose and had believed in the way that they served the gods. In that respect, it should not surprise him that he would find a tower, a reflection of the power of the gods. Yet it surprised him that the Antrilii would create a replica of the tower.

"Why here?" he asked.

Nessa pressed her lips together in a frown before answering. "I told you that we came to meet with the Yahinv. They will help me determine what should happen to you."

Endric frowned, watching her. "I thought you had already decided."

Nessa nodded. "I did. But if you are the son of the oath-breaker, the Yahinv must determine what happens to you." She turned toward the tower and motioned Endric to follow. "Come. And hope that the Yahinv is forgiving."

7

The inside of the tower was lit with nearly a dozen lanterns. Elaborate tapestries hung next to each lantern, the light shining brightly enough for Endric to make out what was depicted on each tapestry, and he marveled at the reflection of the gods depicted there.

This was not artwork of a simple people. They were far more developed than he had known. How could no one else have known about the Antrilii?

There were shelves arranged around the room with hundreds of books. The scholars in Vasha might even be impressed with their collection.

He turned his attention back to Nessa, a question on his lips that went unasked as she motioned him toward a stair near the back of the room.

They climbed the stairs, moving swiftly up the curving steps. Endric felt a slight burn in his calves as he went. As much as he felt as if he were recovered from the wounds sustained fighting the groeliin, moments like this made it clear that he had not yet fully recovered. He still didn't know how long ago it had been that he had fought the groeliin or even how long he had been out after being brought to Farsea.

He didn't recall the travel to the village, and if he passed through the mountains, that meant that it would've taken several days, possibly a week or more. All that time, he had been unaware. Perhaps it was a blessing that he had not been.

As they made their way along the stairs, Endric noted additional tapestries hung here. They were just as ornate as those in the entryway and depicted what he suspected were scenes of the gods. On one, he saw what appeared to be the gods standing atop a mountain peak, snow swirling around them, and what appeared to be streamers of heaven opening to them. Endric might not be devout, but he recognized the Ascension of the gods.

On another, Endric saw depicted a vast forest. Within it was a strange, softly glowing light that reminded him of the charged teralin. Another tapestry clearly showed the mountains to the north, and even beyond them, an image of men fighting what appeared to be clouds of black. The men were painted, faces marked with black and red and orange and some with blue and purple, and he realized that this was a depiction of the Antrilii and suspected they were fighting the groeliin.

At the top of the stair, she paused, bringing him out onto another stone floor. It opened up into a wide space much like the one below. Lanterns were set into sconces along the wall. Unlike below, no tapestries hung along the walls. No shelves were filled with books. Instead, he noted sculptures. Some that had the long, exotic features of the gods, features that were surprisingly consistent across all depictions of them.

Six women sat around a circular table, each with black hair, some braided while others left theirs hanging loose, all woven with colorful strands of fabric much like Nessa's hair. All looked up when he entered.

They were all older, each with wrinkled eyes and faces that carried the wisdom only years could bring. They walked in, sharing the same distrust Nessa had exhibited.

Nessa took her seat, occupying the seventh—and final—chair. She left Endric standing, facing the women at the table. The women ignored him, looking at each other, having evidently decided that Endric was not someone of consequence. He felt dismissed in a way that he had not felt before.

"You are late," one of the women said to Nessa.

Nessa tipped her head, the slightest of nods. "There were things that needed to be accounted for before I could make my way here."

"Such as bringing an outlander to the Yahinv?" one of the other women asked. She had a sharp voice and full cheeks, with dark freckles upon them. Her hair was different than the others, tinted with a hint of red.

"Such as understanding why an outlander would be found near seven dead groeliin," Nessa said.

"And the hunters who slaughtered the beasts?" one of the other women asked. She turned her head and bells tingled softly, having been woven into her hair.

Nessa tipped her head toward Endric. "He claims there were no hunters."

"Then how were the beasts slaughtered?" the woman with the bells in her hair asked. "Only the Antrilii can—"

"Not only Antrilii," one of the others said. She was older than the others, streaks of dark gray mixed into her hair, which was braided into a single braid and hung down to the middle of her back. The bands of silk woven into her hair were only orange, a single color rather than multicolored like many of the other women. Endric wondered whether the color meant rank, or whether it meant something else.

The others all looked at her and then turned away.

"And you believe him?" the freckled woman asked.

Nessa shrugged. "I don't know what to believe. He claims that he can see the groeliin, along with something else, and that is the reason for my delay. "

The older woman sat upright, her back straightening, and she turned, considering Endric with eyes that shone with a great intensity. For some reason, her gaze reminded him of the merahl studying him. She made him feel much the same way. What did she see when she considered him? What were they concerned with?

"We need to find the Elbow Tribe hunters and direct them to the Chisln," the woman with the bells in her hair said. "Anything else is secondary."

"Even secondary to the son of the oathbreaker returning to the Antrilii?" Nessa asked.

The women all stared at her, all but the oldest. And then, one by one, they gradually turned their attention to Endric, looking at him with heat in their eyes.

Endric was taken aback by the intensity of it, taken aback by what seemed almost anger in their expressions. More and more, he began to wonder what exactly his father had done to upset the Antrilii as much as he appeared to have. Why would these women—those who Endric was beginning to think were the leaders of the Antrilii tribes—resent his father, and by extent him, so much?

"My father is no oathbreaker," Endric said.

The woman with the freckles looked at him, her judgmental gaze dismissing him. "You would bring the son of Dendril before the Yahinv?"

The older woman finally pulled her attention away from Endric and sent her gaze across each of the others, weighing them, practically judging them. "The son of Dendril has every right to come before the Yahinv."

"The oathbreaker—" the woman with the bells in her hair started.

"Enough!" The older woman raised her hand, silencing the others. "You know so little about oaths if you accuse Dendril of breaking his."

Nessa studied her, watching for a long moment before turning her gaze upon Endric and staring at him. She seemed to consider him, as if seeing something about him that Endric couldn't see. He wondered what it was that she knew.

"The oathbreaker has not returned to Antrilii lands since he abandoned his oaths. What else are we supposed to think of him?"

The other woman stared, meeting Nessa's gaze. "As I said, you know nothing about the oath you claim has been broken. If you did, you would not accuse Dendril of what you do."

Endric watched her carefully. Was she from the tribe his father had come from? Was that why she seemed more accepting than the others? Or was there another reason?

"We have more to be concerned about than the oathbreaker. We need to find the Elbow Tribe hunters and see what happened to them. They were lost, and we've heard nothing from them in days."

"Weeks," the woman with the bells in her hair said.

"Perhaps they found the Chisln. And the merahl. If we don't find it soon..."

All eyes turned back to the older woman, and she shook her head.

"There has been nothing to indicate the Chisln nearby, Melinda. The beasts would not risk it so close to our lands."

Melinda shrugged. "The Elbow tribe disappearing is a sign."

"Which is why we all have our hunters searching. We will not lose any more hunters the way we lost yours. We *need* the help of the merahl."

Melinda frowned. One hand touched the back of her neck, fingering her braid, and Endric noticed how she ran her fingers over the silk within it. "Dentoun served the Antrilii well."

"Outside of our lands," Nessa said.

Melinda glared at her. "Are you so confident that Dentoun did not lead the hunt that you would risk disbelieving them?"

The others stared at her.

"We have been over this, Melinda," the woman with the freckles said. "Even you have agreed that it was unlikely there was any real movement. Certainly, nothing that would require a great hunt. Dentoun went south to answer Dendril's request. And because of it, we lost more hunters. We have lost far too many."

"Dentoun faced the groeliin in the south," Endric said. All eyes turned to him, and he went on, hurriedly. "I was there. I saw the attacks."

"You couldn't see the attacks, not if the groeliin were involved," the woman with the bells in her hair said.

"He could if he was Dendril's son," Melinda said.

Endric nodded. "At the time, I don't think that I could see the groeliin. I knew the Antrilii faced something and knew that they were dealing with some horror that I couldn't understand, but I could only see the groeliin after they were dead. Dentoun kept me from the fighting."

"And how did you learn to face these beasts?" the freckled-face woman asked.

"How could you learn to face any creature?" Endric asked. "My father taught me how to fight with the sword. I continued my education since then. And I barely survived the groeliin." He tipped his head toward Nessa. "Nessa can attest to that. I don't know how badly I was hurt, but I barely survived. Were it not for—" Endric didn't know what it had been for. Were it not for his boot knives, would he have survived? Had the howl of the merahl scared off the groeliin attacking him? Was it something else? "All I know is that I nearly died. So if you're attributing some sort of prowess to me, keep that in mind. I nearly died."

The women all stared at him before turning back and resuming their hushed conversation.

Only Melinda watched him. At length, she rose to take Endric by the arm, leading him to a corner of the room. "You are Dendril's son?" she asked.

Endric nodded. "I am Dendril's son. The brother of Andril, and en'raen of the Denraen soldiers. I came here to understand my heritage. I wanted to know more about where I came from."

"Did Dendril not warn you?" Melinda asked.

Endric shook his head. "Dendril understood that I needed to know more about my family. I think he hoped that I would find Nahrsin and that from there I would learn."

Melinda frowned, tipping her head as she watched Endric. "Didn't he warn you?" she asked again.

"Warn me?"

Melinda nodded. "Yes. Did Dendril not instruct you to search for Nahrsin and the Scroll Tribe?"

It was Endric's turn to frown. "He didn't tell me to find any tribes. He let me travel north, letting me go with Brohmin —"

Melinda sucked in a breath. "The Hunter was with you?"

Endric nodded.

"What happened? Where is the Hunter?" Melinda asked.

"I don't know. When the groeliin attacked, Brohmin saw them and helped me face them."

"Of course, he did. He is the Hunter."

Endric wondered what that meant, but also wondered how Melinda knew about Brohmin's Conclave title. "He fell. I defended him as well as I could. There was only so much I could do when the groeliin attacked. They were more than I could withstand."

"Yet you live."

Endric nodded. "I live. And I don't know what happened to Brohmin."

Melinda considered him for a long moment, her eyes seeming to weigh him. Behind her, Endric noted the other women of the Yahinv all speaking softly, their hushed voices occasionally growing louder as they seemed to debate some issue that Endric suspected had to do with him, or with his father.

"Why do they dislike Dendril so much?" Endric asked Melinda. Of the members of the Yahinv, he thought she was the most likely to answer.

Melinda glanced over her shoulder. "Each Antrilii made an oath long ago. It was one given to the gods themselves, a promise made."

"Promise? Is this about defending the north from the groeliin?"

Melinda turned back to him, nodding once. "This is about defending more than the north. The Antrilii made an oath to the gods that they would protect the land, that they would prevent the groeliin from spreading, from descending upon the rest of the world as they once did. It is an oath that the Antrilii have taken seriously for the entirety of our existence. All men serve as hunters, searching for signs of the groeliin, keeping them from reaching beyond the Ailenii mountains."

Endric thought he was beginning to understand. If his father had been expected to serve as a hunter, then he would have abandoned his oath by going to the Denraen.

"And Dendril left the Antrilii, which upsets everyone else?" Endric asked.

Melinda shook her head. "Dendril abandoned his rule, passing it on to his brother."

"My father was to lead the Scroll Tribe?"

Melinda smiled. "Dendril was to lead the hunters of the Scroll tribe. I lead the Scroll Tribe."

Endric met her gaze. "I am sorry about the loss of Dentoun. His sacrifice allowed many others to survive."

"I know. Nahrsin shared with me what happened. I have no reason to doubt him, even if these others do. And my son has always been vigilant in his task, and ever faithful to his family."

Endric's heart quickened. "Your son?"

Melinda nodded. "Dentoun was my son."

Which meant Dendril was her son as well. Which meant…

"Grandmother?"

Melinda frowned at him and said nothing.

8

Melinda returned to the table with the rest of the Yahinv. She left Endric standing there, his mind racing. For years, all he had known was his father and his brother. He had no other family. His father never spoke of his time before coming to Vasha, and never spoke of his mother, despite Endric's curiosity about his father's family.

Was it possible that Melinda knew more about his mother? Was it possible that his mother had been Antrilii as well?

Endric suspected that it was. It would have to be, for Dendril to have passed on the same gifts to him.

He turned his attention back to the women debating.

Why had Nessa brought him here? She had known that he was related to Dendril, but as soon as she had, she had begun referring to him as oathbreaker. Would they allow him to go with Melinda? If they did, he could reach Nahrsin, and he could begin to discover what he needed to know about his people and where he had come from.

But the longer that he was here, the more Endric began to worry that perhaps they wouldn't allow him to leave. Perhaps they would hold him and question him more.

Endric had no additional answers. He didn't understand the politics of the Antrilii, and he wasn't certain exactly what they would want to hear other than that they accused Dendril of breaking his oaths. Endric had the sense that Melinda—Dendril's mother—hadn't completely forgiven him either.

"We have sent the Shin tribe searching for the Elbow hunters. We have found nothing. Either they are absent, or perhaps they found the Chisln."

"The movement of the beasts might indicate the timing of the Chisln, but they wouldn't have one so near our lands," Nessa said. She seemed exasperated by repeating herself. "Why would they risk it here? Our hunters—"

"Will find them, and we will bring great glory to the Antrilii," the pale-faced woman said.

"Glory? That's not what any Antrilii seeks," Melinda chastised.

They fell silent for a moment until Nessa interrupted. "We all want the same, Melinda."

"Yes, but some are more willing to pursue it than others."

"You blame my hunters now?"

"The hunters will take no blame," Melinda said. "They fight the beasts, especially when they move in numbers such as they do now."

"Is that why I was attacked near Farsea?" Endric asked, approaching the table.

The women ignored him. The woman with the bells in her hair said, "The beasts have been confined to their nests."

"There are more hordes now than there have been in years."

"What is a Chisln?" Endric asked.

They glanced his way but dismissed him quickly.

"There has been movement in the Aspen chain," the woman with freckles said.

"I've been patrolling through the north," Endric said. "If you tell me what sort of word you would expect, maybe I've heard something."

Melinda turned to him. She had an expression that appeared to be either irritation or frustration. It was a sour look that reminded Endric of his father.

The women turned their attention back to him, glancing at him one by one. Finally, it was Nessa who spoke. "What is the plan for the oathbreaker's son?" she asked.

"There must be punishment for him. If his father will not serve the penance, the son of the oathbreaker must."

Melinda shook her head. "As I said, you don't understand what you are doing. You don't understand the task Dendril has put upon himself."

Nessa shot her a hard glare, surprising Endric with the intensity of it. "It's not surprising that you would defend the oathbreaker, but you must remain silent in this, Melinda."

"It is agreed, then?" the woman with the bells in her hair asked. "That he will be subjected to the punishment that was meant to be for Dendril?"

The others each nodded.

"What punishment? Endric asked.

"It is only fitting that he should face the consequences. We can send word to Dendril, and if he feels that he would rather take the place of his son, we would welcome the oathbreaker back to face the consequences of his actions."

Melinda shook her head. "This is a mistake. You are risking what you do not understand."

"No," one of the other women said. "Tradition must be followed. Oathbreakers must be punished. If they are not, then others who choose not to hunt, others who think they need not serve the way the Antrilii have served for countless generations may begin to choose the same path."

Melinda shot the woman a withering glare. "Do you really believe that others would choose to serve and subsequently lead the Denraen? Do you not understand how Dendril serves? Do you not understand how he helps protect our people in his position? There is value in having my son in Vasha watching the Magi, observing them, preventing interference with what we must do."

"Serving in Vasha is an easier life. Even you must recognize that," Nessa said.

"I recognize that the Antrilii made a vow to the gods, one that we have honored for a thousand years. I recognize that we serve as protectors of the north, defending the rest of the world from a threat they do not even know exists."

"My father serves more than the Antrilii. He serves a council you cannot understand. Ask—"

Nessa frowned at him. "You would claim that Dendril serves some other council?"

"I would claim more than just that. He is not the only one. The—" Endric started but was cut off by Melinda.

"This is a mistake. Send him back to his father. He does not deserve even the chance at penance. At least there, he can still serve the gods."

"If you believe that, then you are a fool," the woman with the bells in her hair stated. "There are the groeliin, and there are the Antrilii who oppose them."

"And there once were others," Melinda said.

"Until they abandoned their vows," the woman with the freckles said, more venom in her voice than Endric thought necessary.

What did they mean that others had abandoned their vows? Who else had once faced the groeliin?

"They had a different responsibility thrust upon them," Melinda said softly. "They became the force for peace. Surely you cannot deny that they serve in that way, Isabel," Melinda said, casting a condemning look at the woman with the bells in her hair. "Or you, Shannah." She eyed the woman with the freckles. "Bethal? Jasphen? Rebecca?" She eyed each of them in turn, and the women all stared back at her defiantly. "You call him an oathbreaker, and you have demanded punishment of him, and now you would take it from his son, a man who does not know the ways of the Antrilii, who does not know what you would subject him to, and a man who—"

"Who came to us willingly," Shannah said. "Let him choose."

The women turned to Endric, who didn't know what to say or do. What did they expect of him? He had come wanting to know of his family and to understand where he came from, but with their feelings about his father, that would prove difficult— unless he made a sacrifice. Was he willing to make a sacrifice to know?

Melinda watched him and seemed to know the difficulty he had because she shook her head in a warning.

All eyes turned to Endric. He had an unsettled feeling, one that made him think that perhaps he hadn't thought things through well enough. These women, members of this council of

Antrilii, looked upon him as if he were some sort of dangerous animal. They stared at him almost like he were one of the groeliin. He almost shivered but feared that doing so would be seen as a marker of weakness.

Instead, he looked back at them, trying to find a hint of both defiance and reassurance, needing to work with them so that he could understand what it meant that he was descended of the Antrilii. It might be that there was nothing he could say and nothing that he could do to reassure them, especially considering what he knew of their feelings toward his father.

"Do you accept the punishment of the oathbreaker?" Nessa asked.

Melinda shook her head. "No. You will not put that upon him. He does not deserve that punishment."

Shannah glanced at Melinda. "It is not for you to decide this, Melinda."

"If he claims my tribe, it would be for me to decide."

Nessa shook her head, this time with more vigor. "No. This one belongs to no tribe, which means that you cannot claim him. He is not of the Antrilii, as the oathbreaker abandoned our people. He abandoned his vows. Do not think that you can claim him. Do not think that you can redeem him."

Melinda stood. She crossed her arms over her chest and anger flashed across her eyes. "None of this is according to custom. None of this serves the gods the way we have been instructed to do. So do not think to use your weak arguments on me that your choices are made on behalf of our people. The choices you make are out of ignorance and out of fear."

"If out of ignorance, as you say, then tell us what we need to know. Tell us what it is that you think your wisdom has given you over the years." This time, it was Nessa who stared defiantly, turning her gaze upon Melinda.

Endric could not be a part of any argument where the Antrilii fought as they did right now. They had a greater purpose.

"I accept."

They ignored him, forcing Endric to take another step forward.

The women continued to argue, and Endric took a third step forward, trying to draw attention to himself.

"I will accept the punishment."

Gradually, they turned to him. Melinda stared at him, a mixture of emotions in her eyes that he didn't fully understand and couldn't completely place. There was disappointment there, but it was mixed with sadness as well. There was a hint of acceptance there also.

Nessa stood. "You accept the punishment of the oathbreaker?"

Endric looked around the table. It was difficult to know what they intended of him and what his acceptance would mean, but how could he not? If there was a way to settle this disagreement, how could Endric not take it?

He nodded.

Nessa took a step toward him. "Endric, son of Dendril, oathbreaker of the Antrilii. You will accept the just and proper punishments of the Yahinv?"

Endric avoided Melinda's gaze. He thought that if he were to meet her gaze, he might hesitate, that he might second-guess what he needed to do. He needed to do this. For him to have the answers that he wanted, answers that he thought that he needed, this was something he would have to agree to.

It was possible that if he didn't agree to this, they would send him from the north, force him back to the south, and possibly without weapons to protect himself. It was possible that he wouldn't get the answers that he wanted, regardless of Melinda helping him. He needed to complete whatever punishment they asked of him so that he could understand what it meant for him to be Antrilii.

"I accept the just and proper punishment of my father, Dendril, general of the Denraen, descendant of the Antrilii, son of Melinda."

Melinda tilted her head as she considered him.

Isabel smiled widely, though Endric wasn't certain why that would be. There seemed almost a hint of satisfaction in the way she looked at him, as if whatever he had said had not only met her needs but would somehow injure Melinda.

"Then it has begun."

9

"**W**here are we going?" Endric asked, led by Nessa away from the makeshift tower. It was late, and darkness had spread across the sky, leaving only a hint of the fading sunlight. There were wispy clouds in the sky, and the gentle breeze of a cool wind gusted down out of the mountains. It carried with it some of the chill that he had experienced when riding with Brohmin, though this chill felt unexpected. Since coming to the Antrilii lands, Endric had been comfortable as lightly dressed as he often was.

Nessa paused at a massive tree along the path. She stared at the trunk, studying it, before turning her gaze toward the top of the tree. Full leaves unfurled from the branches, some of which had begun to change colors with the season. "It would have been easier for you to have accepted your return to the south."

"I came here with a purpose," Endric said.

"You might have come with purpose, but you came ignorant

as well. If Dendril allowed you to come with ignorance, then he was even more of a fool than I would've expected."

"I don't think he expected me to encounter such hostility from the Antrilii," Endric answered honestly. For Endric's part, *he* hadn't expected to encounter such hostility. He had thought that he would be welcomed among them. He had thought that from his brief experience with Dentoun, and then Nahrsin, they would allow him an understanding of the Antrilii lands so that he could understand the people he had descended from. He had not expected such outright hatred.

"Many things have changed in the time since Dendril spent among the Antrilii."

"What does that mean?"

Nessa shook her head. Endric couldn't determine whether she was trying to be helpful and failed or whether she honestly did not care for him, hating him for the sins of his father. He wasn't sure what to make of her. While in the Yahinv, with the others there, he believed that she shared all but Melinda's opinion of him and his father. Apart from them, Endric could almost believe that she would be interested in working with him and trying to help him understand the Antrilii.

"The seven tribes are no longer unified as they once were. When Dendril departed, there were some rumblings of this, but it has grown worse in the years following. Many thought Dentoun would be the one to unify us once more, but he was not."

"And if he had survived in the south?" Endric asked.

Nessa turned her attention away from the massive tree and looked at him with haunted eyes. "Perhaps he would have been able to unify the tribes. If it was as you say, if he was on a great hunt, then he might have been able to convince the remaining tribes and their leaders that we needed to come back together."

"Why fight? Why not work together to fend off the groeliin threat? I see how those of the Yahinv work together. The rest of the Antrilii could do the same."

Nessa grunted. "You saw seven women bickering. Even we cannot get past old disagreements. We who are supposed to be the wise ones of the Antrilii. We who are supposed to know how to lead our people, to bring us forward, to continue protecting the north and defending our vows. Even we are unable to get past such petty differences."

She started down the narrow path, and Endric followed. How much of this disagreement had Dendril known about? How much *could* he have known about? He wondered if Nahrsin might have been able to help, if his cousin would've been able to provide him insight as to the disagreements among the Antrilii. Would that have changed anything for Endric? Would he have chosen not to come?

"What is this punishment the Yahinv was speaking of?"

Nessa shook her head. "You should have not have accepted. You are not Antrilii."

"But I'm descended from the Antrilii."

She turned to him, her eyes still with that haunted expression. Endric thought he recognized it now but didn't understand why she would wear regret so deeply etched on her face.

"You may be descended from the Antrilii, but you are not of the Antrilii."

Endric tipped his head. "What is it that you're not telling me? What is this punishment?"

Nessa smiled sadly. "Were you of the Antrilii, you would not be asking such a question. All know what is asked of an oath-breaker."

"Then tell me."

"You have claimed victory over the groeliin," she started. The tone of her voice indicated to Endric that she still didn't believe. He wasn't certain what she believed, and whether she thought that he had the help of some hidden Antrilii. Did she think a tribe of hunters had come through, slaughtering the groeliin before Endric had come upon them, or did she think that the Antrilii had killed the groeliin and then been taken?

"Now that you have accepted punishment, it will be carried out in the morning. You will rest here," she said, motioning to the massive tree. "Here, surrounded by all the gods have made," she waved to the distant mountains, just barely visible with the snow-capped peaks reflected in the moonlight, and then to the land all around her, and then, lastly to the trees, "and in our place that calls upon the ancient gods, you will reflect. Rest well, Endric, son of Dendril, oathbreaker."

She started away, leaving Endric standing, staring after her. This was his punishment? He was to remain in the open and simply reflect? That didn't seem harsh enough, not for an oath-breaker. Endric thought of what the Denraen would do to someone who had violated their vows and didn't think it would be something as simple as reflection. They would be tasked with a harsher punishment—possibly exile, much as he had when he disappointed his father. They would require that the Denraen attempt to regain their trust, though it rarely would be possible. It would take an act of great sacrifice to do so.

In Endric's case, that act of sacrifice had been his willingness to risk himself and his life to do what he knew was necessary and right so that he could protect Vasha.

What would such a requirement be for the Antrilii? Did they have something similar?

"Nessa?"

The woman paused and glanced back, barely meeting his gaze.

"This is the penance? This is what you would've asked of my father?"

She shook her head. "This is your preparation. You will take tonight, you will do as I said, and you will reflect. You will think about what the gods would ask of you, Endric, son of Dendril, oathbreaker. And in the morning, your penance begins."

Endric shook his head. He felt more confused than ever. They were going to leave him here in the open and then expect him to know what to do in the morning?

"How will I know when the penance has been served?" he asked.

This time when Nessa smiled, there was no doubting the sadness on her face. "There will be no question. The penance and punishment will be served if you survive."

With that, she turned away, leaving him once more, leaving him alone, wondering what exactly the Antrilii would ask of him, and wondering if he had made a mistake, accepting the punishment of his father.

10

The night stretched on slowly. Endric leaned against the trunk of the tree, finding the bark rough and carrying with it an almost rank aroma. Occasionally, he heard what he thought was a howl that made him think he might not be alone. If the merahl were out there, he hoped they would protect him and keep him safe rather than attack as the one had done to Brohmin.

He drifted into a slumber, leaving him with flashes of dreams. Some were memories of his life, and most came from the last few years. It had been a tumultuous time; he had been tasked with more responsibility, which he had wanted.

He would wake at times, and as he did, he heard the distant howl of a wolf and stirring of small insects. Endric was not afraid of the night, and he was not afraid of the dark. Years spent with the Denraen had quashed any fears he might have possessed. Even if they hadn't, the last few months made it so that he could sleep on the road like this.

Yet, he found that his sleep was difficult. At least difficult to maintain.

He would fall asleep and jerk awake, convinced that he heard or saw something before realizing that most of those sensations came from his dreams. He had been told to reflect, but he wasn't certain that he was reflecting the way Nessa intended.

The night continued to pass, minutes stretching to hours. Endric lost track of time and lost track of how much he actually slept. The moon and stars shifted overhead, their lights a bright glow in the night. As he watched, he imagined the greater powers watching over him, almost enough to help him believe in the gods, to feel their presence.

Was that what Nessa had wanted of him? Was that the kind of reflection she had asked of him?

Endric watched the horizon as the sun began to appear. It came first as colors that drifted over the eastern mountains, reflecting off the snow, sending glittering patterns into the sky. The appearance was quite striking, and Endric found himself simply staring. There was nothing else for him to do.

As the morning progressed, he shook the sleep from his eyes, finding even that a struggle. He must have rested some, though did not feel well rested. He had a slight nausea in the pit of his stomach, the kind that came from too many sleepless nights, though it had only been this one. Maybe it was apprehension or the fact that Endric didn't know what to expect as the morning came on, not knowing what the punishment would require of him. He found it hard to believe that he might not survive it.

By the time the sun crested the mountain tops, Endric had stood, trying to clear the sleep from his mind. He continued to stare at the sky. He'd never *really* watched a sunrise and was amazed by the steady change, the gradual way light spread across the sky and felt a hint of what he had to believe was faith. Perhaps this was the reflection that Nessa had wanted from him.

Shapes moved in the distance. It didn't take long for him to see that they were women of the Antrilii, and it didn't take long for him to recognize Nessa, Melinda, and Isabel. They wore cloaks slung over their shoulders, and strips of fabric were woven within their braided hair.

When they approached, Melinda stepped forward. "Endric, son of Dendril, general of the Denraen, descended of the Antrilii," she began, and Endric noted how she used his phrasing rather than adding the term *oathbreaker* as the rest of the women of the Yahinv were so insistent upon doing. "You have accepted the penance on behalf of your father. You will face the penance of one who has abandoned their vows. I ask you again, do you accept?"

Endric looked at the three women. Melinda shot him a warning glance that seemed insistent upon telling him not to accept this punishment. Even Nessa stared at him with an expression of regret. Only Isabel watched him with any sort of gratification on her face. As she had the night before, she had small bells woven into her hair.

"I accept the required penance on behalf of my father," Endric said.

Melinda pulled a horse forward and motioned for Endric to climb into the saddle. He did and, without saying anything else, they started west, riding quickly, leaving Endric to follow them. Now that he was mounted, he suspected that he could ride off. He might be able to return to the south if he could discover a way through the pass, but now that he was here, he was more curious about what was expected of him. What would this penance entail?

He had reflected as they had required, though he still wasn't certain what that reflection was intended to accomplish. He had spent the night having flashes of dreams, but not much else. He had stared at the rising sun and had thought somewhat of the gods, but not with the same devotion he knew the Antrilii to possess.

None of the women spoke as they led him.

The horses were swift. They were Antrilii mounts, and Endric had some experience with them from his travels with Dentoun and Nahrsin, noting even then how impressive their horses were. They chewed up ground as they rode, passing across rolling hillsides and heading toward the distant mountains. Every time he attempted to ride closer, the women created more separation.

They did not intend to provide additional answers. He might have agreed to whatever punishment they intended to inflict upon him, but that did not mean that they would share with him all that entailed.

By midday, they had reached the mountains, and the women barely paused as they guided him into them. They quickly ascended, the horses having no difficulty climbing here, not as the Denraen horses would have struggled. They still had not explained what they expected of him, though Endric started to wonder if they intended for him to leave the Antrilii lands altogether. Perhaps that was the punishment of an oathbreaker.

They reached a shelf partway up the mountains, where they paused. The women arranged their horses, blocking him from going any further.

"From here, you will go alone."

"What do you expect from me?" Endric asked.

Melinda met his gaze, Endric thought for a moment that she would be the one to answer, but it was Isabel.

"We ask only that you answer the penance and fulfill your obligation." She reached for the reins of his horse. "Now, you will dismount."

Endric climbed from his saddle, moving hesitantly. When he was down, Isabel guided his horse away.

"If you were born of the Antrilii, you would not need an explanation as to what was asked of you. As you are not," she said, her voice dripping with accusation, "we will tell you what is expected." Isabel looked at Nessa, then Melinda.

Melinda took a deep breath and let out a deep sigh. "From here, you must travel alone," Melinda started. "You will go unclothed, the way the gods brought you into the world, and you will go with no weapon. You will be given only what the gods provided you."

Endric looked from each of the women, beginning to feel uncertain. "Where am I to go?" He was in the mountains and worried what they intended of him. What had they planned?

"You must fulfill the vows given to the Antrilii by the gods themselves," Melinda said. "You will go to the through the mountain pass, and you will confront the groeliin."

Endric's heart began to quicken. They couldn't really expect him to face the groeliin naked and unarmed. "How long must I do this?"

"The penance for Dendril the oathbreaker was to kill an entire brood."

"A brood? I don't know what that is. I don't know how many that is."

Isabel glared at him. "Were you Antrilii, as you would claim, you would have no need to ask questions. Were you Antrilii as you so claim, you would know that a brood is a clan of groeliin. You would know what you are expected to do. You would know exactly how difficult this penance is."

"How many?" he asked once more.

"A brood varies in size," Melinda said. "Most average fifty, though some are more."

Endric shook his head. "How am I supposed to kill that many groeliin without a weapon?"

Isabel was the one who stared at him the longest, a hot glare in her eyes. "You accepted the penance. Do you now refuse to comply?"

Endric looked to Melinda for answers. She met his gaze but said nothing. "How many have survived such a penance?" he asked.

The others all stared at him, a blank expression on their face.

"How many?" he asked again.

"Few have returned from their penance. Most sacrifice themselves returning to their vows," Melinda said.

Endric felt a shiver of fear work through him. "And if I don't do this? If I refuse to take myself into the mountains, expose myself to the groeliin, and attempt such a sacrifice? What then?"

Isabel stared at him, something of a triumph in her eyes. "Then you would also be an oathbreaker to the Antrilii. You would have double the debt. The penance for that is different."

Endric didn't like the sound of that.

Melinda shot Isabella a hard-eyed stare. "If you refuse this penance, you will have then violated a second vow," Melinda said. "The Antrilii do not offer a third opportunity."

Endric shook his head. "So you would send me from the north, and I would return to the Denraen?"

Melinda met his gaze. "It is not as simple as that."

Isabel spurred her horse forward. She offered a dark smile to Endric. "If you refuse this, you will be tied by each limb to one of these horses. We will then ride in separate directions and leave your remains here for the groeliin to feast on."

Endric licked his lips. They had gone suddenly dry, and he didn't know what to say. He had little reason to doubt that they would tie him to the horses and quarter him, and little reason to doubt that they had the strength to do so. They were Antrilii, and though they were women, they were all armed, and he didn't doubt that they would be skilled enough to stop him.

The other option was a slower death. He could venture into the mountains as they suggested and attempt to escape to the south, but he suspected that they had chosen this location for a reason and that by coming here, they had brought him where the groeliin would be found and where there would be no chance for him to escape.

No good options.

He'd wanted to know about the people he descended from. This told him about their brutality. They had allowed his father to leave and had not forced him back, though they considered him an oathbreaker. Endric would have been given the same option. He could have simply left, but he had made the mistake of thinking that he could suffer this penance, that he could take on his father's punishment, and in doing so, he could find a way to understand the Antrilii.

It was now clear to him that had been a horrible mistake. It was now clear that Melinda had been trying to protect him by encouraging him to refuse. He had let his eagerness drive him.

Not only eagerness but his desire to understand. He had wanted to know about the Antrilii. Now that he learned what they did to people they felt violated their sacred vows, he had learned something more about them. He had learned how hard they could be, and how unforgiving. Endric swallowed and stepped forward.

Isabel tracked him with her eyes, her gaze practically daring him to attempt to run. He suspected she would take sadistic joy in chasing him down and, in the hunt, do whatever it took to return him so that she could quarter him.

He looked at Melinda. "I, Endric, son of Dendril, general of the Denraen, descendant of the Antrilii, accept this penance."

He removed his jacket first.

He turned to Isabel. "I will assume the vows you claim my father broke. I will follow the customs of the Antrilii and will head into the mountains as the gods made me, naked and unarmed. When I slaughter my brood, I will return."

While holding her gaze, Endric pulled his breeches free. He stood there in small clothes, and a shiver worked over his skin.

"When I return, I expect to be welcomed among the Antrilii. I expect my father's debt to be forgiven."

With that, he pulled off his small clothes and stood there naked in front of them. He felt exposed in a way that he never had before. There was nothing more he could do.

Melinda nodded. "It will be what the gods choose."

With that, Endric started into the mountains, naked and unarmed.

E ndric headed into the mountains. A chill worked through him as he did. He wondered whether the cold would kill him before he even reached the groeliin. It seemed a cruel fate to send someone out into the mountains this way. Even crueler was that if he survived the cold of the mountains, they expected him to slaughter an entire brood of groeliin.

Only, they didn't expect that. They expected him to fail, and they expected him to die.

A narrow trail worked its way through the mountains, so Endric followed it, snaking his way along. Without his boots, the rock ripped at his feet. He felt pain where the stone tore at him, scraping away flesh. Traveling for too long this way would leave him shredded, a bloodied mess, and an easy target for the groeliin to track. Perhaps, he wondered, that was entirely the point.

The wind began to whip around him, growing increasingly

colder. He was forced up, given no choice but to continue to climb, the road through here so narrow that he either had to follow it or he would have to take the time to scramble up the face of the rock, a much harder route.

What was he thinking agreeing to this? What was he doing risking himself? It felt incredibly foolish to him, as if he were sacrificing himself to a cruelty that he should not need to subject himself to.

Yet, what alternative did he have? He had drawn himself in so deep, had forced his way into this. He had no one to blame but himself for his predicament. In some ways, that was even worse.

He continued climbing, moving steadily upward.

As he did, the wind and the cool air became more brutal. Before long, he would need to find protection from the wind, only he wasn't certain what he would discover. There was a nothing but more rock around him.

He paused, standing exposed to the elements, forcing his mind to work through what he needed to do and how to get himself to safety.

If he were to face the groeliin, he needed protection, which meant both clothing as well as a weapon. A weapon would be almost easier. There were plenty of rocks around, but that wasn't going to be enough to keep him safe if the groeliin attacked. With their clubs, what good would a rock do? The damned creatures moved too quickly for him to defend himself with only a rock. He could find a tree, break off a branch, turn that into a club, and use that, similar to how he would have used a sword to defend himself. That seemed the easiest solution. First, he had to find a tree, then he had to find a way to break something off.

More than that, he would need to discover some way to get himself clothed. That would be the most difficult. If he didn't protect himself from the elements, he wouldn't last long in the mountains. Even if he managed to find a place to hide, someplace where he could remain protected from the wind and likelihood of snow, and even from the groeliin were they to attack, he needed to focus on that first.

His mind went through lessons that he'd had over the years, each of them from the Denraen. Most came from lessons his father had taught, or lessons that his brother had taught. From them, he had no answers. How did he intend to protect himself? How would he dress himself without fabric?

Endric surveyed the land around him. It was mostly barren, although there were patches of long, dried grasses that cropped up in places. To the south and to the east, he noted a few twisted trees. He began to think through the possibilities. He could use the trees. He might need them anyway for firewood as well as the club he had already determined he would need to create.

Endric grabbed the grasses, carefully plucking them from the base, and bundled them together as much as he could. With these, he could at least weave some sort of covering.

Endric hurried from one clump of grass to another, taking what he could. Most of it was not long enough to do much with, but he was willing to try, and when he had several fistfuls of grasses collected, he made his way toward the distant tree. He didn't want to remain out in the open, though here he was exposed everywhere he went. If he could find a cave or a rock overhang, at least he would be protected. Endric didn't like his chances if even something as simple as a mountain wolf came at him in the middle of the night.

And he thought his night of reflection had been not very restful.

When he reached the place where he saw the trees, he realized they were off the narrow path leading through the mountains. That forced Endric to climb, but he hoped that the soil was better there, that maybe he could find more of the grasses. When he reached the trees, he saw that wasn't the case at all. They somehow grew through the rock, sending roots deep below. He didn't recognize the type of tree this was, but it had a rough bark, a sharp contrast to the smooth bark of the tree he had rested next to the night before. The branches were twisted, all of them warped in such a way that he doubted he could make an effective club. He would worry about that once he managed to find a way to clothe himself. Already the wind was growing chilly, and his feet throbbed where they had scraped along the rock.

He sat and began weaving strands of grasses together. It was slow work, but what did he have other than time?

As he worked, his stomach rumbled. A new concern came to him, one that he hadn't considered before. What would he eat? The mountains weren't plentiful with food. There wouldn't be much he could forage for here. Had he even a slingshot, he thought he could hunt, but he would have to do so by spear, or by using the blunt force of throwing a rock.

His gaze drifted to the tree, but he saw no branch straight enough to be an effective spear. That meant that he would have to throw a rock.

He continued weaving the grasses together, his stomach rumbling, and he forced himself to ignore it, much like he forced himself to ignore the increasingly oppressive chill that surrounded him.

Night had come on. Endric had managed to weave together something of a wrap that he had wound around himself, providing some protection from the wind. The grasses scratched and itched, but he had forced himself to ignore it. At least he buffered some of the cold. Much more than that, he would need cloth or for. His fingers throbbed from weaving the grasses together. And he felt the steady burning where the grass rubbed along his flesh. It was an unpleasant experience, but one that he knew he would have to get used to.

He leaned against the tree, holding onto the irregularly shaped branch that he had dragged free. The tree was tough; at least he had that going for him. Had it not been, he wasn't sure that he would've been able to use the branch for defense.

He'd been shivering for the last hour. There was not much else that he could do. After a while, he suspected he would grow numb to the cold and suspected that he would no longer be able to withstand it. He needed more protection than what he had now.

Even sitting as he was, leaning against the tree, he needed to keep himself moving. He had to survive this somehow.

After only a day in the mountains, already Endric had begun thinking of simply surviving. It was a strange transition from wanting to prove himself and agreeing to accept his father's punishment to now wanting only to survive. Doing so meant one of two things. Either he managed to cross the mountains and return to the south, or he would somehow manage to slaughter an entire brood of groeliin armed with only his twisted and stunted club and whatever rocks could find. Endric liked the odds crossing the mountains much better than surviving an attack on a brood of groeliin.

Another gust of wind blew through, and he shivered.

He couldn't stay here. Doing so would leave him too exposed and in danger of the elements killing him before anything else had a chance to do so.

No, he needed to keep moving.

Endric stood and carefully made his way along the rocks. As he did, he focused carefully on moving slowly. A single misplaced foot would cause him to tumble down the rocks. Endric was not willing to perish that way. There were plenty of other ways for him to go, and that would not be one.

When he reached the trail through the rock, he had some protection from the wind, though it wasn't much. And certainly not enough to keep him safe. There was a bite to the wind that blew through his grass wrap and overwhelmed even that thin ability to protect himself. Without it, Endric didn't know if he already would have been frozen.

Endric ran his hand along the rock as he made his way, forcing him up the slope of the mountain. As he did, the contour of the rock changed, leaving him more and more exposed. Perhaps it was a mistake coming this way and leaving himself exposed like this. He wondered again what he had been thinking.

In his tired and cold state, he decided that he really wasn't thinking. His mind wasn't working as it should, and as much as he might want to, he couldn't generate the drive to keep his mind clear.

He kept his eyes open, searching for an opening in the rock, something that would offer protection, that would shield him from the wind.

He stumbled onward. After a while, he began to lean on the makeshift club for support, using it almost like a cane. His feet were numb. His face and mouth felt frozen shut. Each breath labored. He had become slightly delirious. The hunger he'd been feeling earlier, pulling at his stomach, reminding him of his last meal in Farsea, had settled to a muted ache. It was still there, but not with the same intensity. At least that much suffering was no longer there.

He stumbled, tripping over a rock, scraping his foot painfully. Endric almost cried out but clamped his mouth shut, fearful of what might live in the mountains. He was less concerned about things like the merahl, creatures that he had come to know as almost benevolent hunters, and more concerned about wolves or foxes or, the gods knew, groeliin.

Would he even notice the groeliin when they attacked?

When he had survived them before, there had been only the help of Brohmin that had helped him recognize that they were coming. Without him, and without one of the merahl hunting, braying as they did and raising attention to the groeliin, Endric doubted that he would have enough notice, that he would even be aware that they were there. If that happened, all he could hope for was a quick death. He doubted it would be painless, though he had that hope as well.

Staggering forward, he found himself leaning on the branch more and more, and it became a crutch. After a while, he was dragging it, no longer even aware of the noise that it made. His breathing was more like a wheeze. The air still had the same cold chill to it, but he was becoming numb to it as well. His mind drifted from thought to thought, flashing through memories, similar to what it had done the night before when he had been instructed to reflect. In his current state, he knew the danger of that and knew that he risked himself by not thinking clearly.

Endric shook his head, trying to clear it. It did so slowly.

The pathway twisted, taking him through rocks sloping down on either side of him. He fell forward and remained lying there for a moment. His eyes struggled to stay open, and he blinked, seeing flashes of color that he knew weren't there.

As that flashing of color faded, what was left was streaks of darkness.

Endric reached a hand toward it.

His heart skipped. An opening.

Could he have found a shelter in the rock? Could he have found someplace where he could get safety?

It seemed almost too much to hope for.

But what else did he have but hope? He was hopeful that he had found safety. Hopeful that he could sleep for a time, maybe protected from the wind, and perhaps even use his grass-woven wrap to warm up.

Endric squeezed the wooden club and crawled toward the opening. It was a tight fit, but he squeezed through. He was forced to let out his breath as he did, forced to expel everything on the way in. He had a fleeting thought that he might get stuck here and that this would be a worse way to die than either the groeliin finding him or being quartered.

Then he was through. The inside of the cave was fairly low, but it was enough for him to sit up. And it was deep enough. Endric crawled in, still dragging the club as he did, before finally settling along the far wall. His eyes drifted closed. Even as they did, Endric knew they shouldn't, knew that he should try to warm himself, but doing so was beyond him.

A scratching sound in the cave woke him. Endric rose, his body tensed from the sound. He squeezed the stick and rested it on his thighs, holding it ready. It would be his club, and it would protect him, but he could see nothing. There was nothing but darkness around him.

The scratching persisted, this time closer.

His heart hammered. What if this was a groeliin?

No. That seemed unlikely. They would've struggled to get in through the mouth of the cave. Endric had done so through desperation. The groeliin would need to do so because they knew he was here, and he didn't want to attribute that much intelligence to those creatures.

"Hello?"

He felt ridiculous calling out, but a part of him was hopeful that perhaps the Antrilii had come after him. What if Melinda had a change of heart and had either come herself or sent someone else up the mountain and into the cave after him?

There was no answer. Only more scraping.

This time, it was clear that it was the sound of claws on stone. There was breathing, the steady sound of it, a rhythmic, halting sort of breathing.

Endric squeezed the club. His muscles tensed, stiff and achy from the day spent climbing the rocks and the night spent practically frozen.

Likely this was nothing more than a mouse, possibly a squirrel. Either creature would be in the mountains and just as likely to use this cave as anything else. In the darkness, his mind created images of massive rats, or of squirrels with sharp fangs chewing on his exposed flesh. In the dark, it was easy to imagine any sort of horror coming for him. None of them were reasonable, and Endric knew that. It didn't change the fact that those thoughts came.

The sound came closer.

Endric could wait no longer. He swung with his wooden club, batting at whatever was nearby.

He missed, sailing through the empty air. He landed sprawled across the stone of the cave, his face scraped as he did.

There came the clatter of claws across the stone again.

It wasn't his imagination. There was something here, and close. He rolled, swinging the club overhead. Once more, there was no resistance.

Endric shuffled backward, pushing with his heels along the rough rock of the cave floor, tearing them up even more. Pain shot through his heels as he did, but he ignored it, his heart now hammering in his chest.

He swung the club in front of him, praying that it would connect, but it never did.

Was it only his imagination? Was there nothing here with him?

No, he didn't think that was possible.

There *was* something here.

He wasn't able to reach it. The creature, whatever it was, managed to sneak away. Unless it was nothing more than his mind. Maybe this was nothing more than some small animal, that he was swinging too high to reach it.

He wanted to return to sleep. To rest. A distant part of his mind, the part that wanted to survive, knew that if he managed to connect, if he managed to somehow crush this creature, he might have food to eat.

Endric focused, listening. The breathing seemed to come from everywhere. It was quiet and steady, but it filled the cavern. The soft clatter of claws on the stone was there to his right.

Endric lunged forward.

This time, he swung up with the club, swinging with all of his might.

When it connected, he felt a jarring sense through his arms. There was a strange whine.

Endric didn't allow himself to think about it and swung the club back down once more. As he did, he heard another soft whine. Then there was nothing. No movement. The breathing stopped. The sound of the claws on the stone stopped as well.

Moving back along the rock, he finally allowed himself to let out a relaxed sigh. He rested there, listening, but no other sounds came. There was nothing.

Finally, he managed to drift off into a semi-restful sleep. The sounds of the cave around him were no longer terrifying. Even if there were anything here for him to worry about, Endric had decided that it couldn't change anything. There would be nothing that he could do.

As he drifted into his slumber, he wondered how many more days he could survive like this. Would he be able to last long enough to even reach the groeliin? And if he did, he doubted that he would be any in any shape to fight them, and doubted that he would be in any shape to survive if he did face them.

Perhaps that was the cruelest thing of all that the Yahinv had done. They had offered him ways to pay penance for his father breaking his oaths and had given him the hint of a hope that he could survive, and that he only had to destroy a brood before he could return, but he might not even reach the brood to face them. Surviving the mountains naked, unarmed, and alone might be more than what he could do.

Those thoughts haunted him as he drifted to sleep.

12

W hen Endric came awake, a hint of light drifted through the mouth of the cave. The air stunk, and it took him a moment to realize why. The animal that he'd killed the night before still rested near him. Some of the stink might actually be him, from his scraped and opened wounds, or it might come from the filth that he had dragged himself through during the last day. If some of the stench came from a wound that he might have sustained, it was one that might already be infected and already festering. If that were the case, Endric didn't like the odds of surviving for long.

He backed away from the creature, moving closer to the mouth of the cave. He felt better than he did the night before. At least he wasn't as tired. His body ached, throbbing from what he'd been through, but not so much as he thought it should.

He glanced at the fallen creature but couldn't make it out in the faint light streaming in through the opening of the cave. A momentary fear surged through him. What if he'd attacked a merahl?

That wasn't possible. If he had, Endric wouldn't be able to return to the Antrilii, even if he managed to survive. If he had attacked and killed one—even unknowingly in the darkness— he doubted they would welcome him back.

Endric paused near the mouth of the cave. He needed to know, didn't he?

Scooting forward, Endric reached for the shadowed shape of the creature, praying that maybe he was mistaken. Maybe he it had been something smaller than what he first thought.

Using the broken off branch that had been his makeshift club, he pushed on the creature but found it too heavy to move.

Endric felt his heart fluttering.

He scooted around the animal, and used the club and shoved.

As he did, there was a soft scraping along the cave floor. It reminded him of when the animal had prowled around him the night before when it had been attempting to attack him. He listened, making certain that the damned creature wasn't still alive.

There was no movement and no other sound.

Endric started pushing again, this time with as much strength as he could muster. The animal flipped over, and he saw a flash of dark fur.

As they neared the mouth of the cave, relief swept through him. It wasn't a merahl all. It was a laca.

This seemed too far north for them to prowl. And they hunted in packs. This one had been alone—hadn't it?

He nudged it with the club a few more times, but it didn't move.

His stomach rumbled, and he swallowed. He was thirsty and hungry. Now that he had an animal here, could he bring himself to eat laca? He'd never had laca, but there was no reason he couldn't eat the creature.

Better yet, now that he had the laca, he had an alternative to the woven grass wrap that he had created. All he had to do was bring himself to hack through the creature's hide, and if he could, he would able to clothe himself. Laca fur *was* used for warmth, so Endric had little reason to doubt that he would be able to use it to wrap around himself. He might even be able to cut sections free to make coverings for his feet. He wouldn't have thread, so he would have to find some other way to wrap the hide around his body. The options weren't necessarily appealing, but he could use the bone from the laca, sharpen it against the stone ground, and perhaps thread tendons through it, using those to weave coverings for himself.

Doing so would take the better part of the day, but he needed to find a way to protect himself first, then he could continue onward.

With growing certainty, he knew that he couldn't complete what had been asked of him for the penance, but he allowed himself a hint of hope that he might be able to survive long enough to move beyond the mountains and reach the south-lands once more so that he could rejoin the Denraen.

By evening, Endric had managed to clean most of the hide. He had cut narrow strips to wrap around his feet and used tendons to weave through them, tying them around his feet. He kept the fur side toward his skin, the soft fur providing welcome relief from the pain of the rock that had scraped him. They weren't much, but it was better than what he had.

Cutting the rest of the hide was more difficult. He hadn't decided the best way to do so, but he didn't want to waste any of the fur. All of it would be necessary to keep him warm. He had been careful, using a sharpened stone, jabbing through the creature's hide as much as he could. It was slow work, and he did the best that he could.

Now that he was done, he set the animal hide outside in the sun to dry. He anticipated spending another night in the cave. It was safe here. Protected. More than that, he had taken some time to examine the location and was comfortable that there was no other way into it. The only way in and out was the way he had come in, and the way he suspected the laca had entered as well.

Now that he had the animal skin, he had to think about what he would do with his hunger. The idea of eating raw—and possibly already rotting—laca flesh didn't appeal to him. He considered starting a fire, but would there be an easy way to do that?

He didn't have much that he could burn. There was the grass that he had plucked and then woven. There was the club. Other than that, even were he to have a fire, there wasn't much else he could use for fuel. Endric didn't want to venture out of the cave and didn't want to risk getting stuck trying to squeeze back in, and possibly risk another animal making its way in here. That left either going hungry or eating raw flesh.

Endric decided to go hungry.

Even more than his hunger, he would need to find something to drink. Experience had shown him that dozens of small streams work through the mountains, steadily dripping down from snow melt high above. All he had to do was find one and he would have something from which he could drink. Even if he weren't able to find a stream, he had the hope that could he climb high enough, he could reach some of the snow and could melt and drink that were it necessary.

He was tired already from the day spent working at the laca. Removing the creature's hide had been incredibly wearing. Could he rest already? Doing so felt as if he were giving up but he didn't think he had the strength to venture out of the cave and risk himself once more.

Endric sank to the cave floor and pulled his knees up to his chest. He still wore the grass skirt wrap. It had provided more warmth than he had expected and he was thankful that he had taken the time to do so.

As he sat there, it felt as if time slowly crept by.

Endric stared outside, watching the sun, feeling the wind as it whistled into the open cave mouth. He remained silent, the sound of the wind his only company. After a while, even that began to change, shifting so that it no longer gusted so loudly into the cave.

Endric awoke to even louder whistling. He sat there, his mind struggling to adjust. In the darkness, he heard something smacking, a steady, rhythmic sound that seemed to come from outside the cave. It took Endric a moment to realize what it was that he heard.

The hide that he had spent most of the day cutting and trimming now flapped violently against the mouth of the cave. If he did nothing, he suspected it would blow away, and all of the work that he had done, all of the time that he had invested in trimming it away, would be wasted.

Endric crawled toward the mouth of the cave and reached up, into the darkness, and grabbed the hide. He dragged it back into the mouth of the cave and tossed it off to the side. It still needed time to dry, but it was better than it had been before.

He heard a soft growl, and Endric tensed.

What was that?

It was close. Much closer than he was comfortable with.

Was it within the cave or did the sound come from outside?

Endric clutched the club, ready to strike. He'd felt the nervous anxiety of fear when he thought that he might have attacked one of the merahl and it made him pause as he listened for the growl. When the sound came again, Endric crawled toward the back of the cave, waiting.

Shadows drifted across the cave.

This time, Endric wasn't about to wait and wasn't about to risk getting attacked. When the clattering of claws came upon the rock again, Endric lunged forward, swinging his club with the same ferocity as he had the night before. He connected on his first blow. There was a satisfying— if sickening—*thunk* as the club struck.

He heard a soft whimper, and he struck again.

Was that another whimper?

If it was another laca, he could use the fur. Maybe even the meat.

Out of necessity, Endric struck again and again, until he was certain the creature was not moving.

He sat back, leaning against the wall of the cave. He didn't know how long he was there when he heard another soft growl.

This time, he recognized the sound. There was no mistaking

that it was a laca. They were pack animals. The one he had killed the night before had been the first of the pack, perhaps coming to investigate either their home or a new place to use as a den, and now the others were coming. How many more would attempt entry into the cave?

He wasn't sure that it mattered. He had to prevent them from reaching him.

As the creature snuck through the cavern, Endric clubbed it, much like he had clubbed the others. He was met with a satisfying whimper of pain. When this one stopped moving, he sat back, the wooden club resting on his knees, waiting.

More howls came from outside of the mouth of the cave. Endric began to wonder how large of a pack waited outside. At least this time, unlike the other time he'd encountered a pack of laca when he'd been near death, lying on the plains outside Vasha, he had some way of fighting back. This time, he was not caught completely unprepared. Only, he didn't know how many he would need to fight off.

There would be no rest tonight.

Endric would remain awake as long as needed. In the morning—if he survived—he might have enough fur to completely cover himself.

Maybe the gods hadn't completely abandoned him here.

13

E ndric now had enough furs to keep him completely covered. He'd cut all of the laca fur free, separating a total of five hides from the creatures. He had even used the bones to form needles and had effectively created a pair of tight-fitting shoes as well as a cloak and pants. It was enough that he might be able to survive out in the cold. The hides carried with them the stench of the creatures, but the fur was soft, and the leather was supple.

It had been three days in the cave, three days since he had been released by the Antrilii to wander. In that time, he hadn't eaten anything. He still hadn't drunk anything. He was growing dehydrated. Endric had to move to find a source of water, or he wouldn't survive any longer.

The sky was overcast, a change from the bright sunshine that he had experienced the last few days. There was a hint of rain in the air as well. With that, Endric considered remaining in the cave to stay covered, but doing so would only delay what he needed to do. It was time for him to return to the south and abandon his attempt to learn more from the Antrilii.

The air was cool, but Endric didn't feel it as the same cold as when he first ventured out. The furs were warm enough to keep him comfortable, at least for now. How much longer would that last?

Endric started up the mountainside. His mind was tired and almost heavy from his restless nights. He felt the growing discomfort from his rumbling stomach—he hadn't been able to bring himself to eat raw laca—and his mouth was dry, his lips already starting to crack. Findings a source of water had to be the first thing he did. Once he did that, then he could focus on filling his stomach.

He carried with him the woven grass wrap, as well as the wooden club that had saved him and allowed him to kill the lacas. The grass could be used for kindling if he could start a fire. The club would have to do as a weapon until he found something better.

Endric climbed, moving slowly. His feet no longer scraped along the stone. With the laca fur, he didn't have the same grip that he had otherwise, but it was worth the sacrifice. He made his way steadily, careful not to move too quickly, not wanting to exhaust himself before he found another safe place to stop for the night.

It was midday when he came upon a stream. Endric fell upon it and thirstily scooped water to his mouth. The water was cold, almost painfully so, and he drank it until he no longer felt his stomach grumbling. Endric paused, letting the water settle, wishing he had a waterskin to carry more with him. He had to hope that he could come across another stream, and if he couldn't, he would simply have to keep going until he reached snow he could melt.

Endric continued onward, strength gradually returning, his mind clearing somewhat. As he went, he started to question. All he had was time, and with that, all his mind did was race, rolling through curious thoughts. Had his father known what he would encounter? Had his father sent him, intentionally planning for him to be cast aside?

Endric shook that thought away. Dendril had welcomed him back into the Denraen. There had been no plan for him to disappear like this. At this point, his father needed him, especially now that he had lost Andril and Listain.

No, his father didn't know, and that meant that he hadn't expected this much resistance. Perhaps his father didn't know that the Antrilii were divided.

Maybe that should trouble him. Shouldn't his father, as leader of the Denraen, have known what was taking place with the Antrilii? The Denraen didn't patrol this far north. They didn't have any sort of influence, which was reason enough to question why his father wouldn't have known.

Endric understood that his father avoided the north, but maybe that had been a mistake. They needed to understand what had unsettled the Antrilii and why they no longer worked together as they once had.

He found a small cave late in the day. He considered continuing on, but doing so would leave him potentially exposed for the night. Near the mouth of the cave, he saw a few small shrub bushes, and he gathered a few branches, enough that he could get a fire going if he could manage. He'd made the mistake of not cutting off hunks of laca meat, which left him with nothing to eat. He was given a reprieve as he entered the cave and found a nest of mice. Endric clubbed them, knowing they wouldn't taste very good, but there was something more palatable about eating the mice than the laca.

It took many tries, and many swears under his breath, but he managed to get a fire going. He roasted the five mice that he'd killed and had a quiet meal. At that moment, he thought he might be able to survive his way through the mountains.

Endric awoke to the sound of howling.

It came outside his cave. This one had a larger opening than the previous one, and he didn't like the odds of being able to defend it well if creatures managed to crawl inside. With the other cave, the laca had to come one by one. They were small creatures, but the entrance to the cave was small, limiting how many would have been able to make it inside.

This time, Endric had been able to come in on his hands and knees, enough that two or three animals could enter at once. If three laca came at him, Endric didn't like his odds in his weakened state. If something larger — such as one of the wolves that he suspected prowled these mountains — he doubted very much that he would be able to survive.

As he startled awake, he listened. The howling sounded distant, not near the mouth of the cave as he had first feared.

There was a note to it that was familiar, one that...

Could it be a merahl's howl?

Endric scrambled forward, reaching the cave entrance. He stood there, listening into the night. The moon was a half sliver and didn't provide much light. What light it did provide came through the thick bank of clouds overhead.

The howl came again, bouncing off the rocks, and this time, Endric could tell that it seemed to come from up the mountainside.

Yes. It was definitely off the mountain rather than back the way he had come.

If he found merahl, did that mean he would find Antrilii?

If he came across hunters, what would they think about him? Would they recognize that he had been sent to serve a penance? He doubted they would recognize him as Antrilii, but what would Nahrsin think of him appearing dressed in makeshift laca fur, his body filthy, the stink of the dead laca hanging on him?

It didn't matter. Nothing mattered so long as Endric survived.

He sagged back into the cave, listening. The howls didn't come again.

Did that mean that the merahl had been silenced? Or did that mean that the hunt had finished? Either way, Endric suspected it meant groeliin.

He shivered. The women of the Yahinv might want him to slaughter an entire brood, but armed with only his club, he didn't think he was able—or capable—of doing so much as stopping a single groeliin.

He sat awake, listening to the sounds of the night, hearing the wind as it whistled around him. Every so often, there came another sound, that of movement along the rock, enough that it made him feel as if an animal might attack, jostling him awake as he drifted toward an unpleasant and uncomfortable sleep. Then it faded, disappearing into nothing, carried off by the wind.

He began to wonder whether he imagined those sounds,

whether they were his tired and hungry mind latching onto imagined sensations, but he had no choice but to pay attention to them. If he didn't, if they were real, if there were some creatures making their way toward him in the night, Endric wanted to be ready.

He was not ready to die.

He still wanted to serve as Denraen, and he wanted to return to Senda.

He slept poorly throughout the night, jerking awake every so often at a new sound. Each time he did, he was convinced that it was nothing more than the wind, but each time the sounds came, it took a long time before his heart stopped hammering, and it took a long time for his body to settle. On a night in which he had finally had food and water for the first time in days, and one in which he was fully dressed, no longer cold and miserable as he had been, it was the worst he had spent since he was sent from the Antrilii.

He crested a peak, snow now commonplace as he walked. There was a path through the mountains, and he took it, knowing there was no other choice. As he did, he worried that perhaps that since this was the only path through the mountains, other creatures took this same path. Did it mean the groeliin would have to come this way as well?

He had no other choice but to press onward. The higher he climbed, the more he saw snatches of life. The grass that he'd seen lower down the mountain became more plentiful. Trees were a little bit more frequent here, giving him a chance to use branches for firewood. He paused at one of them and cut a length of unusually straight branch, then lashed a sharpened rock to the end, fashioning something of a spear. It would be only partially effective, but better than only having his club. Endric strapped the spear to his back and continued climbing.

The days passed. He managed to find water frequently. He surprised a squirrel one day, clubbing it with a rock and feasting on its meat that afternoon. Other times, he forced himself to choose the insects he came across. They would provide some nourishment—possibly enough to keep him alive —and that was all he cared about. The higher he climbed, the more it seemed the mountain stretched indefinitely. He had a moment of fear that he had been traveling along the east-west direction that would take him along the length of the mountains but realized as he watched the sun's movement that he continued south, a path that should take him beyond the mountains and back to lands that he had once patrolled. They should take him back to safety.

He began to focus on the next step, and then the next, and then the next. When he stopped, he began to think about water or food. He rarely thought about what he would do when he reached the south, and he rarely thought about the reason he had come north in the first place. If he ever managed to make it free and back to his father, then he could address those issues. Perhaps he could attempt another journey north, travel with his father, and see if there was anything they could do to bring peace to the Antrilii. They would need to unify them, find a way to bring those people together as they faced the groeliin, and might be the only people who could.

He lost track of days, simply trekking through the mountains, following the pass.

As he went, he searched for any sign of movement. For the

most part, he saw small mice, the kind he had feasted on the first night he had eaten. Other times, he saw insects scrabbling along the rocks. His awareness of these movements allowed him to keep eating, and he subsisted on food he never would have before.

It was in this way that he caught sight of movement late in the day.

Endric no longer knew how many days it had been. The thick laca hide leathers he wore had long since dried, formed to his side. He had turned the fur side out, keeping the now-dried leather against his flesh. This provided more protection for him and more warmth. He had been forced to adjust the tendons that lashed his makeshift boots together, and they were beginning to wear. In time, he suspected that he would need to fashion another pair. He doubted he would be as lucky to encounter a cave where laca thought to make a den. And he hadn't seen any creatures larger than squirrels in the time that he had been climbing.

When he caught sight of the movement, he froze, pushing himself against the rocks. One advantage of the laca fur leathers was that they blended somewhat into the rocks, having swirls of brown and gray along with darker stripes. Endric doubted he would need such camouflage, but now, that additional advantage became clear.

As he stood there, hunkered against the stone, his eyes began to make out the shape that he had seen, and he realized that it was a dark swirl moving along one of the upper slopes.

His breath caught, and his heart hammered suddenly.

Endric recognized that dark swirl and the hideous gray flash.

Groeliin.

He stayed in place, not moving for long moments, not certain what he should even do, as he debated.

Did he follow it and risk himself, or did he continue climbing up the side of the mountain and hopefully on to safety?

Movement down the slope caught his attention as well, and Endric turned to stare.

As he did, it became clear what he saw. More groeliin. Too many for him to face.

He had no choice but to continue up the slope.

Endric started forward, away from the groeliin down the slope, but it forced him toward the groeliin up the slope of the mountain. As he walked, he carefully shifted the spear, removing it from where he had strapped it to his back, and prepared for whatever attack he might have to face.

14

E ndric crept carefully, his spear in hand, his heart fluttering in his chest. After the days he'd spent hiking through the mountains, days where he had begun to feel a sense of relaxation, where all he had to worry about was survival, now he was faced with the real possibility of his death. If these groeliin attacked—if they turned and noticed him—he didn't like his odds armed only with a spear and club.

He paused as the path through the mountain began to angle backward.

Heading in that direction would take him away from the groeliin, but it also would prevent him from knowing if they followed him.

Going downslope risked facing the groeliin, but could he do it on his terms?

A memory flashed into his mind, something that his brother had once said to him. It was strange that Andril would come to him at this time, strange that his brother would be the one he would think of as he struggled with what he was doing, but Andril often had good advice, often times gleaned from their father. Endric hadn't nearly as much time in Dendril's good graces to have learned what Andril had.

His brother had said that sometimes the Denraen had to move backward before they could go forward. At the time, Endric thought it made no sense, but it seemed particularly apt at this time.

He tested his spear, shifting his grip on it so that he could ensure that he was comfortable with it.

The spear had a solid weight, and he had been lucky enough to find a branch that was straight enough. He hoped that were he to need to throw it, he could chuck it with enough force to stop the groeliin. After the days spent in the mountains had left him weakened, he no longer knew if he would be able to, but it was better to be on the attacking side than to be attacked.

He waited near the bend in the path. As he did, he listened, focused on whether there was additional movement along the slope. He heard nothing.

Had he made a mistake? Had they changed direction?

The groeliin were difficult to see, and Endric stared, keeping his focus where he thought they should be. He remained on edge, his heart hammering, but knew that if he moved, he would draw their attention. He didn't know how many of the creatures were there and doubted he would be able to fight off more than a few, but as he weighed the risks and benefits of his strategy, he decided that staying here, planning for the possibility of an attack, was worth that risk.

As he stood there, he saw finally saw movement.

It came slowly as shifting—almost shimmering—of shadows. Endric could almost believe that it was nothing more than shadows across the stone. He prepared to attack but hesitated as the shadows shifted again.

There were more than one.

As he waited, he saw that there were at least three groeliin.

Had he his sword, perhaps he would be able to withstand an attack from three of the creatures, but armed only with a spear and club, he didn't like the odds. He might be able to kill one with the spear and might be able to surprise another, but three?

He was foolish to even think about it.

But as he thought through it, he started working out how it might work. He had the element of surprise. He would be able to remain hidden, stay behind the barrier of the rock here, and he could use that to surprise them. He could be upon the first before they even knew they were getting attacked. With the second, there would still be the element of surprise. That left the third he might struggle with.

The groeliin moved closer, the shadows swirling around them.

It was too late to change his mind now. They were too close, and he was too exposed. The time to have made a different decision would have been when he first observed them. He might've been able to find a place to hide, and might've been able to see whether he could have ducked between the rocks, perhaps remain hidden that way. He had to attack.

Endric remained low, ducking as he clutched the spear.

He stretched his neck around, looking beyond the rock, and saw movement.

The groeliin were there. Three, much as he thought on the first inspection. It was possible there were more, that he would be surprised, but he didn't think there were any more than that.

Taking a deep breath to steady his nerves, he swung around

the bend in the rock and jabbed at the first groeliin with the makeshift spear.

The creature staggered forward, startled but still powerful.

Endric swung up with his club, catching it in the skull, and pulled out his spear at the same time. He spun, moving in a pattern that flowed from those that Senda had taught him with the staff, and clubbed the next groeliin, stabbing with his spear into the third one at the same time.

One of the groeliin attempted to climb over the middle one, and Endric used the longer length of his spear and stabbed at it again, catching it in the chest. The groeliin was pushed down, and Endric smashed it on the head with his club.

He darted back, holding both spear and club ready, but they no longer moved.

His heart hammered.

He had survived. He had taken out three groeliin, and he had survived.

Even that much had been more than he had thought he could achieve.

He remained crouching, holding spear and club ready, watching for signs of movement from the creatures, but none came.

Their blood spilled onto the rocks, and a foul odor drifted to him. He hadn't noticed it when they were alive, but the beasts had a repulsive stink.

Once his heart steadied and his breathing had slowed, he approached them. He needed to understand more about them so that he could know what he might need to do were he to face them again.

They were hideous, grotesque creatures with grayish skin. They had vaguely manlike features. Sharp teeth fit into their jaws. Their noses appeared shaved off, leaving odd-looking spaces. They had nothing in the way of ears other than small holes on the sides of their head. None of the creatures had any hair. There were clothed in strange drab-looking wraps. All three carried long, spiked clubs.

Endric looked at his club and debated. Did he keep his, or did he take the risk and switch, use one of the groeliin clubs?

Holding on to his club might the best; it had saved him and served him well. With this, he had defeated the laca and had managed to bring down three groeliin, but having one of their clubs with spikes on the end might give him an advantage.

Endric decided to hold onto his along with grabbing one of the groeliin weapons. There would be no harm in having multiple weapons, certainly not as he attempted to traverse the mountains, exposed to ever greater dangers.

Endric didn't want to remain here any longer than necessary. He started forward, heading up the mountainside, moving quickly. In the distance, he noticed that the trail shifted, turning back toward the east. This would bring him in the direction of the groeliin he had seen before.

As he made his way forward, he began to wonder if this had been part of the penance. Perhaps there was no choice but to face the groeliin if he were to head through the mountains.

Then again, why wouldn't it have been? What purpose would there have been in penance if he had been able to avoid the punishments they had for him?

He would need to be careful now.

Endric crept forward, focused on what he might face, and he listened intently. He kept his head constantly swiveling, looking for signs of movement. The fact that his awareness of movement had increased over the last few days during the time that he'd been wandering the mountains seemed to help. He could use that focus as he sought to remain safe. He had already observed while traveling with Brohmin that the groeliin could move along the face of the rock, so he had to watch in all directions.

Endric surveyed the rocks as he went. He climbed a small rise, one with two twisted trees growing up on either side of him. As he did, he saw movement. Groeliin movement again.

Endric remained motionless near a tree. He hoped the laca fur allowed him to blend into the trunk, and he hoped that he could use that to remain shielded from the groeliin.

He listened.

Much like with the laca, he heard their claws as they clattered across the stone. He could see something of a smoke that surrounded them, and this approached first as they came from up the side of the mountain slope, heading toward his trail.

How many were here? Would there be as many as the last? Now that he had defeated three, he thought he had a chance if he were to encounter that many again. More than that would overwhelm him.

He took a steadying breath, forcing his heart to slow, readying his mind as he had been trained by his father, and stepped around the tree.

This time, there were five groeliin.

As they noticed him, Endric jabbed with the spear toward one of them.

He aimed for the belly, wanting to disembowel the foul creature. As he withdrew his spear, he spun, swinging the groeliin club at the nearest creature's head. The spikes connected with a sickening thud. The creature fell.

Endric spun, jabbing with his spear, and this time he

connected with the shoulder, pinning the creature back. He swung the club, connecting with the side of its face.

Something caught him from behind.

Endric staggered, swinging his arms around as he did, and managed to connect with a groeliin there. The club pierced its chest and blood splattered.

How many remained?

Endric swung around, using the club and the spear to give himself some distance.

How badly was he injured? If they had spiked clubs much like the one he had taken, he worried that he had already been injured too much.

He would have to think about that after he survived. *If* he survived.

Two groeliin remained.

One of the creatures had an injury to its shoulder. This was the one he had stabbed with the spear. It came at him, its arm dangling uselessly.

Endric couldn't focus too much on this one.

He stabbed at the other groeliin with the spear.

The creature twisted and the spear missed. As the creature shifted its stance, Endric swung the club, catching the side of its face and sending it spinning.

Endric continued his motion and connected with the other groeliin, knocking it backward. With both on the ground, he jabbed at them with the spear, piercing their hide.

Finally, there was no more movement. The groeliin had been stopped, at least for now.

He waited, worried that they might move again, but they did not.

As he stared at them, he noticed something surprising.

There was a brand upon each of them on both shoulders. The brand was the same, a strange twisting sort of triangle with a line through the center.

Endric frowned. He hurried back down the slope, returning to the first three groeliin. He looked at them and noticed the same brand on their arms.

Had he found a brood?

If he had, and if Nessa had told him the truth, that meant there were upwards of fifty groeliin. And he had killed eight.

Could he finish off more? Could he finish the brood?

He would have to have some way of proving to the Antrilii that he had.

If he were to return, he would need some form of proof.

Endric used the sharpened stone tip of the spear that he had created and carved into the flesh of the nearest groeliin. The stench coming from the creature intensified as he did, and he managed to cut free the brand. He hoped the stench would decrease the longer he was around it.

Endric started back up the slope of the mountain, his mind churning. Something else troubled him as he did. He had been gone from the Antrilii for a few days. Perhaps a week and a half, maybe longer. But that meant these groeliin were only a week and a half or so away from Farsea. Did the Antrilii know? Were they aware of how close the groeliin were to them?

If they didn't, that troubled him. What if they weren't prepared for an attack? From what he'd seen, their hunters had been sent away on a different hunt. He remembered Nessa telling him that they had gone east, and had gone in search of a different brood.

More than that, he had seen these groeliin heading down the slope. Were they readying an attack?

Endric shook his head. He wasn't Antrilii, and he didn't understand the nature of these creatures. Perhaps he was reading it wrong.

But he didn't think so.

As much as he wanted to cross the mountains and return to the south, he worried that if he did nothing, the Antrilii would be in danger.

Even with the thought, he realized that was his arrogance speaking. The Antrilii had fought the groeliin for generations. They knew better than he how to protect themselves.

He would continue south, continue across the mountains, but as he did, as he encountered groeliin and was forced to attack, maybe he would come to a better understanding about what the Antrilii faced.

Wasn't that understanding the reason he had come north in the first place?

15

It was nearly night when Endric encountered another group of groeliin. He'd not seen any more sign of them as he had wandered up the mountain. He moved quickly, trying to keep ahead of additional groeliin, pausing long enough to take drinks from a stream. His stomach grumbled at times, and he realized that he hadn't eaten in the last day or so. With the groeliin around, he wondered whether he would even see signs of any wildlife around him. If the squirrels and mice were smart enough, they would hide.

He was tired and ached, and he smelled nothing more than the stench of the chunk of the groeliin skin that he had cut free. That, combined with the stink from the laca fur, though fading, left him with an undercurrent of nausea as he made his way south, continuously forced to climb up the slope.

As the darkness began to set, and as shadows began to creep from the fading sun, smears of darkness meandered around the jagged end of the otherwise stark rock.

Endric scanned the landscape around him.

He saw nothing that would provide him any sort of shelter, nothing that would provide him the same protection that either the tree or the bend in the trail had provided for the first two attacks. This time, he would be out in the open, completely exposed. This time, Endric would not have the advantage of knowing how many groeliin he would face before the attack came.

He wished that his eyesight were better, thinking of the rumors of the Magi eyesight, and thinking of how beneficial that would be to possess. He was only a man, though one who was descended from the Antrilii, which meant that he had to suffer with the darkness.

The twisting shadows began to coalesce into the form of the creatures.

In the muted light, Endric strained against the darkness, struggling to see how many he would face. He had survived three and had struggled against five, lucky enough that the club that he'd taken to the back had struck in the thick laca hide, which had deflected most of the blow. He couldn't even tell if one of the spikes from the groeliin club had pierced his skin. Endric had been lucky, almost as if the gods were watching over him.

As the groeliin appeared, he counted five.

He readied his spear, remaining frozen in place, hoping they didn't notice him. Perhaps he could get the advantage, and they would not see him before they came close enough for him to attack. He had to pray that perhaps the laca fur might provide some concealment. Maybe they wouldn't notice him if he didn't move. Some predators required movement to be recognized.

As they neared, Endric realized they weren't aware of his presence.

They were moving up the slope and angling in a direction that meant they had come from below him but off the trail.

The groeliin found it easy to cross the rock, and he wondered if they used their claws to dig into it, to give them purchase where it would take him more time, and, with his makeshift boots, be practically impossible.

When they passed him, Endric decided to spring forward.

He jabbed with his spear, catching the first creature in the back, feeling no remorse for an attack in this way. There was nothing cowardly about destroying one of the groeliin from behind.

The others spun toward him, and this time they weren't limited by the trail.

The groeliin had always seemed mindless in their attacks, nothing more than an animalistic style of attack. This time they came around him, circling him, almost as if they coordinated it.

Endric kept track of where they stood, mentally following them as they surrounded him. Would he be able to withstand four converging on him at once?

Perhaps he should have allowed them to pass by. He could have followed them to their brood, or—maybe the better option —found a way to avoid them altogether.

He jabbed at the nearest groeliin with his spear. The creature shifted and grabbed the spear, pulling him forward, toward the creature.

That was new.

Endric swung the spiked club, catching the creature in the face.

His spear was released. Endric spun toward the nearest groeliin and smacked the next with the stolen club.

He ducked an attack and was forced to drop to the ground, rolling to the side as he brought his club up, using that to block one of the attacks.

He spun the spear, using it something like a staff and thinking briefly that Senda would be proud of the fact that he was using it in this way. He managed to connect with one of the groeliin, but two came toward him, one from each side. Endric could only attack one at a time. He spun, swinging the club, and hurled the spear.

It was a gamble, but one that he had to take, especially if he intended to survive this attack.

The spear connected with one and his club pierced the side of the next groeliin's flank, and the creature pinned it with his arm.

Endric grabbed the club he had lashed to his side, the one that had saved him in the beginning. He swung this, connecting with the groeliin's arm, and it freed the other club. Endric was able to swing around and cracked the creature on the head.

None of them moved.

His breathing came out slowly. In the remaining light, Endric looked for the brands on the arms. They were the same as the others. At least he knew he still faced a single brood. He kept track in his mind, counting how many he had encountered. The longer he went, the greater the likelihood that he might actually survive attacking a single brood became.

Would Nessa and Isabel even allow him to return? When they believe him if he came back to the Antrilii, demanding answers about his people and claiming that he had destroyed an entire brood?

First, he would have to do it.

Then he would worry about the proof.

Endric continued forward. It was time for him to sleep, but he would need to find a safe place to do so. He did not intend to rest near the groeliin, not wanting to sleep where the stench of their bodies remained.

It was now nearly completely dark, which would make finding a safe place to sleep difficult at best. Only a thin trail of light remained, a soft glow that seemed to come from the stars overhead, mixing with the moonlight that bled through overhead clouds.

How would he know if groeliin appeared? He realized that he wouldn't.

He debated heading back down the slope. He knew there was a cave, but it would take half the night or more to return to. No, he needed to continue onward. He needed to climb.

Endric offered a quick prayer to the nameless gods, hoping that they would listen and that they would grant him safety.

It had to be near midnight when Endric finally found a shelf of rock that he could use to protect himself. He ducked underneath it to remain hidden. He hoped that if he did and remained motionless, if the groeliin were to come upon him, they would simply pass him by.

He rested, but like most nights since traveling into the mountains, it was a practically restless sleep. Now that he was beginning to have some success against the groeliin, he had allowed himself to think that he might survive this, and he began to think that perhaps—if he were lucky—he might be able to make it to the south. All he would need to do was move beyond the brood of groeliin.

In his mind, that continued to be the goal. Not destroying an entire brood, as was the penance, but simply survival. If he survived, if he could reach the southlands, he would take that as a victory. He wouldn't hesitate to return to his father and to the Denraen. He would have considered that he had learned enough of the Antrilii and that he had learned enough of the groeliin. He would remain ever thankful for their presence here, and thankful for their role—and their vows—but wanted nothing more to do with the people.

When morning came, Endric blinked against the rising daylight. He wasted no time getting himself up and continuing along the path as it wound through the mountain. As he did, he realized he should be surprised by the fact that there was such a pathway here, but it was less that there was a distinctive trail and more that there was simply an easier way to climb.

The higher he went, the more he was forced to climb up and over rocks. The trail became less obvious, forcing him to climb more often. At times, patches of snow slowed him. He paused at every stream, drinking thirstily, and never came across any additional creatures, nothing that would give him hope that he wouldn't see the groeliin.

As the day passed, he began to relax. There had been no further evidence of the groeliin. No further evidence of their passing and nothing that placed him in danger.

As night fell, he found a small cluster of rocks and crouched behind it, using them as a way to protect himself. He hid there, tucked among them, thinking that he could pass the night quietly.

He started to settle in and didn't fight sleep as he had before, drifting into darkness when a sound startled him.

Endric jerked awake and cracked his head on the nearest rock.

As he rubbed his head, feeling foolish, the sound came again.

It was a soft sort of whine, not a howl, and not the sound that one of the laca would make. He'd seen no evidence of them the higher he climbed, anyway. They preferred the plains, though Endric wondered why they had wandered into the mountains when he'd come across them.

Endric sat motionless, listening.

The sound came again.

This time, Endric was aware that it was not that far from him. Close enough that he felt compelled to investigate. If he remained here by the rocks, he doubted he would sleep much with that sound occurring. More than that, he wanted to know what it was. It was the first evidence of other life besides himself that he'd see in the last few days, ever since he had begun seeing the groeliin.

He moved slowly, gripping the spear, keeping the club in his other hand.

He paused, listening. The sound came again.

It was up the slope, but off the trail he had been following.

Endric frowned. Did he risk himself in the night and brave climbing the rocks?

It was dark, but not nearly as brutally dark as the night before. It was more of a cloudless night, and starlight created a soft glow he could follow. It glinted off the snow and made him fear that sections would be slick, possibly too slick to navigate safely.

The whine came again.

Endric felt his heart race. A strange sort of energy worked through him, almost a thrill. He felt compelled, drawn forward.

He started up the rock. The steepness of the slope forced him to tie his spear to his back and forced him to trap the club to his side as well. Endric didn't like that he was forced to, but each time he heard the soft whining, he felt a renewed sense of urgency and felt that he needed to keep climbing.

The rock was steep here. He found handholds in it, enough that he could continue to climb. Places that he thought were slick with ice turned out only to be wet. Surprisingly, the laca skin boots gave him more traction than he expected. Thankfully, he didn't scrape his feet, and he managed to continue making his way up the rock.

The whining he heard came every so often, punctuating the night. And each time he heard the sound, he felt even more compelled to hurry forward.

Why would he feel that way? Was it simply curiosity? Was it the fact that he didn't recognize the sound? Was it a concern for a possibly wounded animal?

No, not concerned. If there was some animal wounded, he could end its suffering, and he could use the meat. It had been two days since he'd last eaten.

He reached a flat shelf, the rock sloping back down at the far side. When the whine came again, he recognized that it came from below him.

Endric began to descend. He moved carefully, but the nature of the slope gave him a little easier time. He pulled the club free from the straps along his side. A few trees grew along the rock here, and he grabbed branches, using those to help him down.

On the side of the slope, there was a wider path. It seemed

to head in the same direction he had been going. The whining came from further along that path.

Endric made his way carefully, padding along on soft, silent feet.

Then in the distance, he saw the source.

Endric froze.

There was a creature with a collar of some sort bound around its neck, trapping it to a nearby boulder. From where he stood, he didn't recognize the creature, though it wasn't large, probably no older than a cub. The collar told him *someone* had been here, but who?

As he remained hidden, the creature barked a few times in his direction.

Endric frowned. There was something in that sound that was familiar.

A sharper howl rang out. This time from down the slope of the mountain.

Endric recognized the sound: merahl.

He swiveled his head back, looking at the cub. Could this be a merahl cub?

Why would it be bound and trapped to the rock? Who would do such a thing?

Not the Antrilii. They revered the merahl.

He hadn't seen signs of anyone else, but someone—*something* —must have tied it here.

Endric remained motionless. He had to understand what it was that he had come upon. As he stood there, he saw a strange flicker of movement.

In the darkness, it was difficult to tell. It seemed as if it was barely more than a shifting shadow. Endric had learned to trust himself the last few days when he saw those signs of movement.

Groeliin.

Could those creatures be responsible for trapping the merahl here?

That involved a greater level of planning than he would have attributed to them. But if they collared a merahl, he had to wonder at the reason.

The howl of the other merahl—the adult—came closer. It was answered by another. There were several, and they were all around him—coming for the cub.

A trap. That had to be the reason for the groeliin using the merahl cub.

Could they really have enough insight to plan for an attack like that?

The thought sent chills through him. Was it possible that they were more intelligent than he realized?

Another merahl howl rang out. This one was distinct from the other two.

Could it be that there were three converging on him?

If so, it was possible that it meant Antrilii were with them.

If that were the case, why would the groeliin set a trap?

No, Endric didn't think that was the case at all. Something else was taking place.

Could the groeliin be trying to hunt the merahl? Did they attempt to draw them here?

The merahl cub whined again and barked in his direction.

Endric swore under his breath. He couldn't simply remain here, doing nothing.

How many groeliin could there be?

There would have to be enough to pose a threat to multiple merahl. Endric had seen the merahl hunting and realized that they were capable of withstanding several groeliin attacks.

Did that mean ten? A dozen? More?

Was there a way he could turn this against the groeliin?

The merahl cub whined again.

It was answered by the howl from the adult.

Endric waited, knowing that he would have to time anything just right. He had to help. The merahl hunted the groeliin, and Endric knew that was valuable. He couldn't allow the merahl to be destroyed, not if they were more capable than even he at defeating the groeliin.

As the distant sound of the merahl echoed again, Endric stepped forward.

Shadows started to turn toward him.

As they did, Endric made out several different shapes of groeliin. He counted them and shivered.

Not ten. Not a dozen. There had to be two dozen.

He would fight, and he would have to hope the merahl near him arrived in time to offer some assistance. If they didn't... he couldn't think like that.

Endric charged forward, spear and club in hand.

16

He was met by three groeliin immediately.

In the distance, he heard the steady call of the merahl as they came. He wondered if they would be fast enough to even help. Would he die trying to protect this cub?

Perhaps.

And, he surprised himself with the realization, it might even be worth it. There were many times in the last few months when he had risked himself, many times when he had very nearly died, that had come for less than good reason. This one, if he were to help the merahl, creatures that actively hunted the groeliin, would be valuable.

Endric let out a loud cry.

With it, he swung the club, smashing it into the skull of the nearest groeliin. It crumpled, dropping to the ground soundlessly. He spun, swinging his club around, sending it into the next groeliin. Like the first, it fell, creating something of a barrier to the other groeliin attacking.

One of the creatures approached, and he jabbed with his spear. It caught the groeliin in the gut. Endric allowed himself that moment of triumph, but it was only a moment. His movements were too slow. He could tell they were too slow. They felt jerky, as the last few days had worn on him.

Endric screamed again. He wouldn't last long with such stiffness to his movements. Somehow, he had to manage to make it long enough for the merahl to appear. Three merahl could assist him.

The groeliin were too much for him. They swarmed toward him.

Endric let his mind go blank, falling into movements he had long ago learned, patterns and forms he had been taught by his father and others. At some point, he dropped the club, using the spear as a staff. With its length, he could create something of a barrier between he and the groeliin.

Endric spun the staff, jabbing and spinning, attacking with renewed violence.

The fluidity returned to his movements.

Endric continued with the forms, remaining within them.

Something struck him on the back. Endric staggered forward, away from the pile of fallen groeliin. He continued spinning, the spear sweeping through movements.

Would it be enough? Could it be enough?

He knocked down two more groeliin, stabbing one as he did.

He was hit again, this one from the side, and staggered.

Catching himself, he spun around, colliding with the nearest groeliin.

The creature fell, but once more he was struck.

Endric staggered forward.

Now he was fighting near the cub. He stayed near it, protecting it, something he should have done from the very beginning.

Groeliin swarmed toward him.

The spear spun violently, and he wished for Senda's skill with it and wished that he would've taken the time to learn how to use it fully. Had he her gift, he might stand a chance.

He needed to last long enough to buy the merahl time. He needed to last long enough for them to reach the cub.

The thoughts remained at the forefront of his mind. Endric continued his attack, spinning, swinging, and connecting. His mind remained blank; the only thing that came to him was the sight of one groeliin after another.

As the next one appeared, he smacked it with the staff, spinning onto the next, coming back to where he'd been before, connecting with the creature again. It wasn't nearly as efficient as a sword would have been. With a sword, he could've cut through their hide. While the spear served as a staff, he was forced to hit the groeliin more than once each time, but it was all he had.

Endric danced around, always keeping his feet near the groeliin, always shifting himself back.

Then he heard a sharp, angry howl.

As he did, he almost hesitated. It was the sound of the merahl. It was repeated as another merahl appeared, then another. And finally, a fourth.

Endric hadn't realized there were four.

The merahl attacked with fangs and claws, a different sort of violence. The groeliin he was facing lost its attention long enough for Endric to crack it across the head and stab at the creature, driving the tip of his spear into it.

He continued to swing the spear, now stepping away from the merahl cub, pushing the groeliin that had brought their attack to him toward the merahl.

Endric was growing tired, but the presence of the merahl gave him renewed strength. He continued to fight, pressing forward. The attack became more intensified, the groeliin nearest him now fighting not only to destroy him but—he suspected—trying to escape.

Another howl came, this one distant.

Another merahl?

The merahl fought the groeliin, who responded with mindless violence. One of the merahl bounded past him, reaching the cub, before bounding back, jumping into the midst of the groeliin, attacking with sharp fangs and claws.

There was a violence bordering on hatred that came from the merahl.

Endric pushed forward, trying to reach the next groeliin. Even with the merahl, he felt as if they were outnumbered.

He continued to attack.

One after another, he hit the groeliin as he swung his spear.

Finally, there were no more.

Endric stopped, panting as he looked around, and noticed the one of the merahl remained near the cub, licking at the cub's fur. The other three converged on him. As they neared, Endric met each of the massive cat's eyes but wasn't sure which one was the leader. Part of him hoped they were hunting with the Antrilii, but the fact that no Antrilii had come made that less likely.

No, whatever hunting might have happened was driven by the merahl alone.

The nearest reached him and nudged him with its nose.

Endric stood, trying to remain both strong and not appear too defiant.

One of the merahl behind him caught him with its paws, spinning him around.

There was no hint of violence or malice to it. It was simply turning him.

Endric had a memory of how they had trapped Brohmin. If the creatures did the same to him, he didn't like his odds of getting back up.

He was turned again, the next merahl forcing him around, and it sniffed him.

All three had silvery black fur. All three had great eyes that watched him.

"I am Endric, son of Dendril, descendant of the Antrilii."

Endric didn't know whether the merahl could understand him and decided that it probably didn't matter. They had seemed to respond the time before when he had spoken. He had seen the way Dentoun had seemed to communicate with them as well. There was no harm in attempting to speak to the creature. Nothing other than the possibility that he might actually get through to it.

"I am serving the penance of my father, Dendril, who the Yahinv has claimed abandoned his vows as he went south, to lead the Denraen." Endric bowed his head, turning once more, this time meeting each of the four merahl's eyes.

Did they understand him? Did it matter if they did?

"I have been tasked with killing a brood. Only then will my penance have been served. Only then may I return to the Antrilii, so that I can learn about my ancestors."

Now Endric began to feel foolish. This had to be too much for the merahl to even comprehend. Even if they could understand what he said, now he was speaking of penance and return to the Antrilii?

To his surprise, the merahl nearest the club offered a soft howl.

It had a different note to it than the howl did when merahl were hunting. This carried with it something mournful. The sound tugged at his heart, one that he could almost understand before that feeling faded.

The merahl backed away from him, and one with darker fur around its eyes joined the fourth by the club. They both snapped at the tether that had been tied around the cub's neck, but Endric didn't think they'd be able to free the creature, not like that.

The other two remaining merahl watched him. Did they think he might attempt something? Did they think that he might harm them?

"I can help," he said. "Let me free your cub."

The dark-sided merahl tipped its head forward.

Was that a nod?

Endric hesitantly started forward. When he reached the cub, it licked at his hand, almost playfully. Endric smiled and scratched behind its ear.

One of the other merahl growled softly.

Endric looked over. "Fine. I'm not trying to harm the cub."

The rope that had been used to trap the cub had a strange texture to it. It was tacky and woven of threads of stringy fibers. As Endric pulled it free, drawing it over the merahl's neck, freeing the cub, he realized what it consisted of.

Flesh.

Not only flesh but tendons and flesh, much like the lace fur that covered his feet.

Had the groeliin used tendons and ligaments of some creature to create a rope that would bind the merahl?

Endric traced the end of the rope to the boulder. As he did, he noticed the stickiness more clearly.

Blood. Whatever they had woven the rope out of was still attached.

Endric looked at the boulder and pushed on it.

It was heavy, but it moved.

As it did, he held his breath, curious what he would find.

What creature had the groeliin woven these ropes out of? Could they have found a wolf? Endric had heard the wolves in the mountains but had never seen any. Could it be a laca, much like what he wore? There were other creatures in the mountains, but it would take something fairly large to cut strips wide enough to weave into the rope they had used around the merahl's neck.

When the boulder shifted enough, Endric's breath caught.

No creature at all.

A man.

The man's chest was caved in, crushed by the rock. Endric crouched in front, wondering how the groeliin would have come across a man when he saw streaks of paint across the face.

"Antrilii?"

He hadn't meant to speak aloud, but the merahl began to whine softly.

He looked over at them.

They watched him, intelligence gleaming in their bright eyes. Endric didn't understand what happened here, didn't understand why that would be one of the Antrilii, or even how the Antrilii had been captured.

He turned his attention back to the dead Antrilii warrior.

Strips of flesh had been flayed off the man's side, running all the way down his leg, reaching up to his chest. Those strips had been woven together, creating the rope that had held the merahl cub.

It was a horror the way the groeliin had done this.

Endric moved the man and heard the sound of metal scraping along the rock.

He rolled the man over and saw a sword.

Endric claimed the sword, feeling no remorse as he did. For him to survive, he would need more than a staff and a club.

Endric hesitated, frowning as he stared at the man. His face had been painted in streaks of orange and green.

Those colors struck a chord with him, a memory.

Nessa had worn similar colors woven into her hair.

Could there be could that be a coincidence?

He didn't know whether colors mattered, but when he had been before the women of the Yahinv, all had distinct colors. Perhaps those colors signified the tribe they came from. Perhaps that was how the Antrilii knew which tribe was which.

He remembered Nahrsin and Dentoun, both wearing deep red stripes with black on their face. They had a different color as well.

Could that be the key?

If that was the answer, then it meant this man was a member of Nessa's tribe.

Why would one of her tribe be here? They had been to the east.

Unless Endric had wandered too far east.

He had lost his sense of direction as he had tried heading south. Could he have headed southeasterly? Could he have come across the remaining Antrilii?

If that were the case, then where were the others?

They didn't hunt alone, did they?

Though, the more Endric thought of it, the more he realized that it was possible they did. Hadn't he seen an isolated Antrilii when he'd been on the plains with Brohmin?

He was tempted to claim the man's clothes, but that felt wrong for a different reason. Taking his sword was out of necessity. Taking the clothes felt more like he would be claiming the man's identity. He might be descended from the Antrilii, but he was not Antrilii, and the Yahinv had made that painfully clear.

Endric looked at the merahl. "What happened? Where are the others?"

The merahl nearest the cub let out a soft whimper.

"Where are the rest of the Antrilii warriors? If they're injured, I'll do what I must to help."

The merahl offered a soft howl. One of them barked. The two who had remained distant bowed their heads toward him. They started along the slope of the rock. Endric glanced over at them.

"You want me to follow?"

One of the merahl flared his mouth, a flash of teeth.

"Fine. First I need to see how many of these are part of the same brood."

Endric looked at the groeliin, forced to hold his breath as he came close to the creatures. They had a foul odor to them, one that practically took his breath away. He studied the fallen, noted that most bore the same irregular triangular shape branded on their arm with the single line through it.

Some did not. Some had a very different brand.

Endric stood, frowning. How many broods were here?

He didn't know how many groeliin he had stopped, and how many the merahl had killed. He had counted something near twenty, but was at all there were? Were there more?

One of the merahl offered an encouraging whine, and Endric looked over. They wanted him to follow.

Endric took a deep breath. Then he nodded.

17

E ndric climbed carefully up the side of the mountain, following the merahl. They moved on soft, padded feet, and though it was late, they seemed surefooted. The sky was a blanket of darkness overhead. He struggled to keep up, fearing that he might slip on the rocks, but every time he slowed, the merahl slowed as well, giving him a chance to catch up.

There was something reassuring about carrying a sword once again. It was not his sword, and it would take some practice to grow comfortable with carrying it, but having a blade with him again helped him feel almost... normal. What did that say about him that he required a weapon to feel complete?

He glanced back after a while and realized the other two merahl, as well as the cub, followed him as well. He suspected they made a strange procession were anyone to witness it, a single man walking with four merahl and one cub. He was thankful for the faint light from the stars and what illumination did manage to filter through from the moon, because without that he would not be able to know where he was going.

"Where are you leading me?" he asked the merahl.

It felt strange questioning them, but it was also strange to be walking among them. He had the sense that they understood his question. There was something of an understanding between them, and the lead merahl, the one with the dark eyes, swiveled its massive head and looked at him.

How had Dentoun ever known what these creatures were thinking? Endric knew that he had. There had been little question in his mind that his uncle could speak to the merahl, or that they could understand him. Stranger still was that it seemed that the merahl had some way of communicating back to him. Endric didn't share that with Dentoun. He had to simply wander without the same sense of understanding.

"Can you lead me through the mountains?" Endric asked

The lead merahl turned again, this time baring its teeth.

Endric shook his head. If it wouldn't take him through the mountains, that meant he was leading him somewhere else. Not back to the Antrilii city, but where? Where did they want to take him?

At times, he slipped, his laca-booted feet losing purchase, and one of the merahl following him nudged him, lifting him as he started to slip. The first time it happened, Endric had jerked around, startled. The second time had been less frightening. By the third time, Endric had practically expected the creature to be there.

The slope up the rock was steeper than what he had even attempted in the daylight. What was he thinking, trying this at night? What did the merahl intend for him to see by bringing him here?

He lost track of time. They continued for long enough that they got distance between themselves and the fallen groeliin. The part of him wished he would've had the opportunity to count and determine how many groeliin they had killed. It didn't matter how many; he had already seen that there was more than one brood present, which made keeping track of the total number difficult.

He wished for another Antrilii to question, to find out how often the groeliin traveled in combined broods. Was it common for them to do that? When Nessa had sent him on his penance, he had the sense he would only come upon a single brood, though when Nahrsin and Dentoun had come south, there had been hundreds of groeliin, hadn't there?

There had to have been. Otherwise, why would they have made the journey south? What would have drawn the Antrilii away if not for groeliin in numbers that could escape the Antrilii hunt?

By early morning, just as the sky began to lighten, the merahl sniffed and began pawing at the ground.

Endric took their cue and hesitated, waiting to see what the merahl might do, curious what had prompted them to stop. What had they detected here?

As he waited, he listened.

He heard the sound of his breathing. It was the loudest, and he forced himself to steady it so that he wasn't nearly so disruptive of the morning. There was the sound of the merahl. From them, he heard an occasional sniff, snorting that told him that they were smelling the air. Endric noted nothing on the air, nothing that hadn't been there before. There was the crisp bite to it, that of cold and snow and earth, the mixture that felt natural and right.

Though there was more to it.

As he focused on controlling his breathing, as he focused on listening to the merahl's breathing, he became aware of the scent of smoke in the air.

It was faint but other than himself, he'd smelled nothing else for days. The hint of it drifted toward him, and he wondered if they were near a camp.

Had the merahl led him to Antrilii? If they had, he might be able to get to safety. He might be able to continue south.

Mixed with it was another odor. This was something like the stink of rot like a carcass had been lying out too long. It was the scent that he had noticed from the laca after he slaughtered them. It was the scent that reminded him of what he had detected from the groeliin when they were dead. Strangely, he found he was never aware of their stench while they were alive. Only after he killed them did he note how foul they smelled.

Endric reached for his sword, fingering the hilt, allowing himself to be reassured by the feel of it, even if it wasn't familiar enough to be his own.

He had the spear and both of the clubs, but he wondered if he were in a battle if he would even bother reaching for them. Likely he would only reach for the sword.

He crouched down, crawling toward the dark-eyed merahl. In the time that he'd been traveling with them, he had the sense this creature led the others.

"What is it?" he asked.

The merahl's ears swiveled, twitching toward the west, upslope.

"Is it Antrilii?" Endric asked.

The merahl turned, shook his head.

With that single gesture, any question that the merahl understood him was gone.

How was that possible?

"Is it groeliin?" he asked.

The merahl turned toward him and flashed a mouthful of fangs at him.

"Does that mean yes?"

The merahl studied him, its ears twitching. Endric didn't know what to make of it and didn't know how to take that response. Did that mean he should worry about groeliin or was this something else?

The merahl started forward, hackles raised.

For the first time since Endric had begun traveling with them, the creatures moved cautiously.

They snuck forward slowly, their massive paws barely making a sound along the rock. Both of the lead merahl swiveled their heads as they went, their noses drawing in the air, their ears constantly twitching.

Endric found himself mimicking them, sniffing the air, turning his head so he could listen, scanning for signs of movement. He saw nothing.

The merahl paused and lowered itself.

Endric crouched, crawling forward.

He found a ledge of rock, and from that saw a drop-off. Far below was a shallow valley. A stream ran through it. On one edge of the stream was a narrow bank of land. A cluster of men camped there, a flame having burned out. Endric's breath caught, and he started forward, but both of the two lead merahl turned their heads and blocked him with their massive jaws.

The dark-eyed merahl flared a mouthful of fangs at him once more.

Something was amiss, but what?

The merahl seemed to know. That alone was enough to tell him he should move cautiously.

Endric studied the men below. He counted a little over a dozen men, all still resting soundly. Were they Denraen, there should be one or two on watch, but he saw none who appeared to be. Where would these men have come from?

He noted the dark streaks of paint along their faces and the leathers that declared them Antrilii. Had he come across a hunting party?

If that were the case, why were the merahl also hesitant to descend?

The merahl always seemed as if they willingly worked with the Antrilii, almost as if there was a bond between man and beast. This hesitancy left Endric curious, uncertain whether there was something going on that he might have missed.

He glanced behind him and saw the other two merahl shielding the cub with their bodies.

As he watched their behavior, he realized they were mother and father. The cub whined a quiet, soft sound that was deep in its throat. The hackles on its back stood tall, and he realized that the creature was more scared now than it had been when bound by the groeliin.

Endric crawled back and reached the merahl. He ignored the looks of the mother and father and reached between them, scratching at the cub's ears.

"It will be all right, little fella. I will make certain no harm comes to you."

He looked up to the cub's parents and met their eyes. He had the sense that there was something almost disappointed buried there. Did they fear that he might betray the cub? Or were they angry that he was not truly Antrilii?

He heard the sound of movement down below the rocks, and Endric patted the merahl on the cub on the head and crept forward once more.

At the edge of the rock, he paused, lowering himself to his belly, looking down. The other two merahl remained motionless, blending into the rock, and made no sound. They continued to sniff the air, and the fur on the back of their necks remained standing.

Something unsettled them. Endric knew enough to let it trouble him as well. These were proud and vicious creatures, and he'd seen them jump willingly into battle, facing superior numbers of groeliin.

Now they would display a sense of fear? What would cause it?

The men began to awaken. They worked in an orderly fashion, quickly breaking camp. They buried the fire, and each of them replaced their packs into bags.

Endric was tempted to hail them and, had he come across them without the merahl accompanying him, he would have. Having the merahl gave him additional reason to pause.

Where would these Antrilii go? Were they returning to another of the Antrilii cities? Were they going to continue on a hunt, tracking groeliin? Or was there something else taking place, something that had the merahl unsettled? What did these massive cats know?

As they broke camp, they started away along the streambed.

Endric glanced at the two merahl that he laid between, waiting for them to do something. "I'm going to follow them."

The dark-eyed merahl flared its teeth, and Endric shook his

head. "I don't know what is bothering you about them, but I'll follow them, and I'll see what they plan to do."

Endric would have felt better if the merahl had come with him, and didn't know if they would turn away, but as he crept along the ridgeline, the merahl remained with him, tracking beside him.

He moved in silence and was thankful for the dark laca fur cloak and breeches he had made. With the furs, he was better able to blend in, and he thought that he could almost pass as nothing more than another animal trailing along the ridge here.

The Antrilii were relatively quiet, at least from where he was. If they spoke, Endric couldn't hear them. They moved quickly and seemed to know where they were traveling. They were making their way west, heading quickly along the rocks.

Endric began to note that the two lead Antrilii in the rear kept their eyes focused on the ridgeline and he made certain to keep himself low. He might want to reach the Antrilii, but he wanted to know what he was going to encounter first. Why were they here if not for the hunt? And why were the merahl unsettled by them?

The merahl remained behind him, though they were down the slope a little bit now, almost intentionally keeping themselves out of view. When he shot the dark-eyed merahl a questioning glance, the creature growled at him. It was a soft rumble, one that was almost imagined.

By midday, the Antrilii paused. They stopped along the stream, drinking and taking a moment to pull meats and breads from their packs. Endric felt his stomach rumble, wishing for something better than squirrel or mouse or the insects that he had been forced to consume.

He leaned down and shimmied toward the rock so that he

could get a better view.

As he did, he saw that these Antrilii had deep purple and blue striped paintings on their faces. Endric had seen those colors before, but which of the women of the Yahinv had he seen with them? He couldn't remember. Possibly Isabel.

That was even more reason to hesitate. She hadn't cared for him and had seemed almost eager to send him into the mountains.

He began to formulate in his head what he might say were they to see him. How could he explain his presence, and his appearance, to Antrilii on a hunt? Would they take him at his word if he admitted that he had agreed to his father's penance? Would they attempt to return with him to one of the Antrilii villages? Endric wasn't certain that he could go with them if they did. If he went along with them, he worried that he would come back into contact with someone like Nessa, someone determined to quarter him were he to ignore the demands of the Yahinv.

No, in this way, it might be better for him to trail along behind the Antrilii, see where they were going and if he couldn't find some way to get to safety. If he came under attack from groeliin again, he might be able to use these Antrilii for help, but until then, he would remain hidden.

He could hear the voices carried on the hint of the breeze. They were faint and stoic. There was none of the jovial mood that he'd remembered from traveling with Dentoun and Nahrsin. He tried to pick up the conversation and caught snippets.

"How much longer are we going to keep at this?"

"You know what Isabel instructed."

This came from the two men leading the procession along

the stream. They spoke in hushed tones and sat apart from the others. Was there something they didn't want the others to hear? Endric's vantage nearly above them gave him the opportunity to listen in. Otherwise, he wouldn't have known what they said.

At least he knew he had been right. This *was* Isabel's tribe.

"The others aren't certain we'll find the Chisln this way."

"She was confident we would. She said the Yahinv saw the evidence. That is why she has sent us here."

"If the Chisln is here, then it's a dangerous time for us to work independently."

"Not independently. We're working together, but must wait for the others, as she said."

As he listened, Endric realized that they were hunters, but there was something taking place, some plot that involved the Antrilii, something that he suspected placed others of the Antrilii into danger.

"But the others—"

"It's possible a sacrifice must be made, Alleyn. For us to unify the tribes, a sacrifice must be made."

The other Antrilii, Alleyn, seemed to be troubled by that statement, and he fell silent.

Endric remained crouched where he was, trying to listen for more information, but there was nothing more that they said. The Antrilii continued their meal, eating in silence, before heading back out.

As they moved, Endric crept back, looking at the merahl. He focused primarily on the dark-eyed merahl, meeting the creature's gaze. "What are they plotting? What is it that has caused you to abandon these Antrilii?"

He wasn't certain whether his guess was right, but something told him that it was. The merahl no longer trusted these Antrilii, which told him that they likely had at one point, which meant they likely had traveled with them before.

What would they have done to have upset the merahl?

The dark-eyed cat watched him.

Endric let out a frustrated sigh. "I can't help you unless you share with me what happened. I can tell that something did. They were your tribe, weren't they?"

The merahl tipped his head. He flashed his fangs, and the fur on the back of his neck stood once more.

"This sacrifice they were talking of, what is it?" Endric asked.

The merahl growled softly.

Endric raised his hands. Whatever it was, it bothered the merahl.

"Can you show me? Can you help me see what it is that has troubled you?"

The smaller merahl with the streaks of black along its fur, the one that he suspected was a female, began to nudge him. Endric looked and realized that she was nudging him away from the ledge, away from the Antrilii.

With a dawning realization, he recognized she was sending him toward the south.

The message was clear: Away.

Endric shook his head. "I want to help. That is why I came."

That wasn't entirely true. He had come because he thought he needed to know the Antrilii. He thought he needed to understand them. Now that he'd been here, now that he faced the groeliin, he thought he did understand the Antrilii, if only in a certain way. Their vows demanded that they face the groeliin. Those vows demanded that they become hard. Those vows required that they be cruel at times. With what they were forced to face, Endric couldn't blame them.

It was much the same with his father. Now that he had seen the way the Antrilii acted and seen what had driven them, he better understood his father. He was a hard man, and could be cruel, and had shown a willingness to do not only what might be easy but what might be necessary. His father took his vows as seriously as the Antrilii took theirs. Only, Dendril's vows were to the Denraen.

Endric finally thought he understood why his father had reacted the way he had to Andril's death. He finally thought he understood why he had acted at the pace he had when it came to Urik. It wasn't a reluctance to fight, not the way Endric had thought. He was keeping focused on his purpose, on what he knew needed to happen. He remained focused on the ideals of the Denraen.

When had Endric ever had the same singular focus? Would he ever be able to maintain the same level of dedication his father had shown?

Somehow, he thought he would need to find a way.

Endric met the merahl's gaze. "I need to help. If the Antrilii have abandoned their vows, if they are somehow making a sacrifice that would be dangerous to the rest of the Antrilii, I need to help. Show me. Take me to where they're going. Help me understand what they're doing."

The smaller, black-streaked merahl looked at the dark-eyed merahl. She seemed to focus on him, waiting for him to choose what they would do.

The lead merahl howled softly. Endric thought he understood.

It was a summons to follow.

T he merahl led him east, but with a southerly direction as well. As they went, Endric could tell that the Antrilii that they had found and followed remained nearby. After the days that he'd spent alone, there was a certain reassurance in having someone else near him. The merahl remained silent as they tracked east, barely making a sound on the stone and never once growling or even howling, not as they had before.

At about the midpoint of the day after leaving the Antrilii, one of the merahl bounded off, powerful legs carrying the red-furred creature up the slope of the mountain until it disappeared altogether. Endric paused to watch, as always impressed by the creature and its grace. The smaller merahl with dark stripes through its fur nudged him, pushing him forward.

They began moving south, and the sky parted, giving a hint of warmth from the sun, the clouds that had been present finally clearing. Despite the heavy bank of clouds that he'd seen since entering the mountains, no rain had ever come.

The air was colder here, but with his laca fur coat, Endric barely felt the bite of the wind, able to ignore the way it gusted between the peaks and could push away the harshness of this land.

After a while, the merahl that had disappeared returned, carrying a pair of hares in its jaw. It set one of them down in front of Endric and then backed away, leaving him.

"Thank you," he said.

The merahl met his gaze, and he had the unsettling sensation that the creature could tell what he was thinking. Using the sword he'd taken from the Antrilii, he made quick work of skinning the hare. Then he collected a few branches for a small fire. While the hare roasted, he crouched, watching the merahl.

The cub made its way toward him and licked his hand. The cub's tongue was rough, and it felt almost like the cub was peeling the flesh from his hand, but Endric didn't pull his hand away. When it was finished, he scratched it under the chin and then moved to rub its ears. The cub watched him as he did, and Endric felt as if the creature could tell what he was thinking. Even in their youth, the merahl had a certain intelligence to them.

When the hare was done, Endric tore meat off it, chewing slowly and savoring the flavor. He tossed hunks to the cub, who caught them in the air with a sharp snap of his smaller jaws. The other four merahl all watched, and Endric wondered if they were going to share the remaining hare, or if they wanted to share with him. They waited almost expectantly, and he decided that he should throw them pieces of the meat. When the hare was gone, the red-furred merahl that had gone hunting pushed the other hare toward him.

"Do you want this one roasted as well?" Endric asked softly.

The merahl sniffed, a sound that Endric took as agreement.

He quickly skinned it and roasted it the way that he had the other. With a full stomach for the first time in days, he didn't feel an urge to rush it and took his time. When finished, he tore off chunks of meat and handed them to the merahl.

"It would be better with salt, but I imagine you can't find that for me out here," he said, smiling. Sitting by a fire with his stomach full and the four merahl around him made him feel like he could almost stay here and could relax and could almost believe that he was on patrol with the Denraen.

The dark-eyed merahl sat up suddenly.

The fur on his back stood on end.

Endric unsheathed his sword and stood next to the merahl, surveying the land around him. "What is it? What do you detect?"

The merahl sniffed and started forward.

Endric went with him, but the merahl swung his head toward him and blocked him from continuing. "I can help," he offered.

The smaller merahl, the one with the stripe of black, stalked forward, her hackles raised as well, and went with the other.

When Endric made like he might follow, they both turned back and flashed their fangs at him.

He let out a frustrated sigh. He could help the merahl, but they would have to let him.

He returned to the fire and decided that he should put it out, especially if there might be something here that had drawn the attention of the merahl.

With the fire extinguished, he kept the sword unsheathed and made a circuit of the small clearing, scanning all around him. The other two merahl sat motionlessly and seemed to be watching the rock around them. The cub patrolled differently, nipping at Endric's heels, tagging along behind him. Every so often, Endric smiled and returned the cub to what he thought was its parents. Each time he did, the cub returned to him, once more nipping at his feet. After a while, Endric stopped trying to avoid the cub and allowed him to keep pace.

One of the remaining merahl—the larger of the two, with silver through his fur—loped off suddenly, leaving Endric with the cub and what he suspected was the female. Then she bounded off as well.

That left Endric alone with the cub.

"Where do you think they went?" he asked.

The cub nipped at his heel in answer.

Endric shook his head. Did he attempt to go after the merahl, or did he stay where he was, knowing that the merahl seemed interested in protecting him?

He heard a sound on the other side of the rock that answered for him.

Endric started toward it, and the cub followed him. "No. You should stay here," he suggested.

The cub nipped at his hand.

"Fine. You can come with me, but I don't know what we're going to find."

Endric climbed along the rock, and the cub followed him. Where had the other merahl gone? Why would they have run off and left him with the cub? Had they detected groeliin? If they had, wouldn't they make some noise?

Maybe not. Not if it would draw the attention of the Antrilii, and not if there was some reason they didn't *want* to draw the attention of the Antrilii.

He crouched lower, not wanting to be noticed, not until he

knew what they were going to come across. As he did, the cub bit at his heel. Endric pulled the cub toward him and wrapped his arm around its neck. The cub tried to bite at his face, but he ignored it. Now wasn't the time for playfulness. Now was a time for... he wasn't entirely certain what it was time for. Caution. At least until he knew what they were dealing with.

As they reached the edge of the rock, Endric peered over the edge but saw nothing. He thought that maybe the Antrilii had returned, but that wasn't what had drawn the merahl away. Were there groeliin here? Something else?

He remained motionless.

He'd heard *something*, that much had been clear, but *what* had he heard?

Moments passed before he caught sight of movement.

It crept along the rock on the far side of the narrow valley.

Not groeliin. There was none of the dark smoke that he saw around the groeliin. It *was* a flash of darkness, but was that fur? Maybe a wolf. It was too high on the mountainside for a laca.

The cub squirmed in his arms, and he squeezed, trying to hold onto it. "Stop," he whispered.

Something grabbed his shoulder.

Endric spun, swinging the sword up, but another sword blocked it.

Antrilii.

He scrambled back but could only go so far because of the edge of the rock. The merahl cub remained lodged beneath his arm. Without the other merahl, he needed to be the one to protect the cub.

The face was painted in black. Endric didn't know which tribe that meant. Was it the same as the Antrilii he'd seen the day before?

"Who are you?" the Antrilii asked, his voice hoarse and with an accent that made it difficult to make out his words.

Endric looked around, but the Antrilii forced his attention back around with a swipe of his sword, forcing Endric to block.

"Not Antrilii. I would recognize another of the hunters."

Endric shook his head. "Not Antrilii."

As much as he had thought that he wanted to know about the Antrilii, and as much as he thought that he wanted to understand where he came from, that desire had changed, and he now wanted nothing more than to get back to the south—after he helped the merahl with whatever it was that made them nervous.

The man attacked a series of attacks, forcing Endric to block each one.

"Dressed in... laca fur?" the Antrilii asked.

Endric nodded.

The Antrilii took in his dress, then skimmed to his spear strapped to his back. His eyes widened slightly. "Penance?" he asked, bringing his sword back.

Endric nodded.

"Why? What offense did you offer to the Antrilii?"

The merahl cub wriggled in his arms. Endric feared dropping him, but he didn't know what would happen if the Antrilii reached him. Would he protect the cub the way that Endric intended? He was surprised that he had to question, especially since the Antrilii *should* be interested in keeping the merahl safe. They were partners in the hunt. But after the reaction the merahl had the night before, he wasn't certain.

"No offense."

The Antrilii prepared to attack. "No offense? The Yahinv wouldn't banish you to serve a penance if you did nothing."

"I accepted my father's penance," Endric said.

"Who is your father?"

Endric sighed. "My father is Dendril, general of the Denraen."

"Dendril. That would make you Andril?"

The Antrilii knew his brother's name. They would know his father. Endric needed to be careful here. "I am Endric."

The Antrilii narrowed his eyes. "Endric. Why have you come to the north? Why have you accepted your father's penance?"

Endric realized something that he should have noticed the first time the Antrilii had mentioned his father. He referred to him by his name, not *oathbreaker*, as the others had.

"Did you know him?" he asked.

"I knew Dendril many years ago," the Antrilii said. "You did not answer why you have come. Why are you here, Endric, son of Dendril?"

"I came looking for Nahrsin. I wanted to understand the people I am descended from."

The man studied him, watching with eyes that were as unreadable as his father's often were. "You search for Nahrsin?"

Endric nodded. "My father thought that I would be able to find him and that he might be able to help me understand the Antrilii. Instead, I found... others. And I think that I've learned all that I want to know about the Antrilii."

"Is that true? What do you think that you've learned, Endric, son of Dendril?"

"I've learned that the Antrilii take their vows seriously," he said. The other Antrilii arched a brow. "And that they have good reason, especially considering what the Antrilii face. The Yahinv is hard... and harsh."

"Because they must be, Endric, son of Dendril. If we

abandon our vows, more than only the Antrilii will suffer. Did you see that when you were wandering?"

Endric grunted. "I've killed..." He counted the groeliin that he had fought. How many had it been? Almost fifteen before the merahl had even appeared, and then how many more had he been a part of killing after that? Dozens. Not an entire brood —not enough to return to the Antrilii having served his penance. "Many," he finally answered.

"Many. There are few Antrilii who even make such a claim." The Antrilii took a step back, looking at Endric, considering him for a long moment. "Except you carry a spear you fashioned yourself. And you have a groeliin club. You have survived as long as any serving their penance."

"The other choice is dying."

"There is no shame in dying while serving the gods."

"I'm not ready to die."

"No? All men must make themselves ready. If you are not ready, Endric, son of Dendril, you need to find a way to become ready. Death comes to all."

"Maybe. But I'm not dead yet."

"No. You are not. You have found a sword?" Endric nodded. "And a cub. That is uncommon, especially for one not of the Antrilii."

"The groeliin used the cub to draw the merahl to them."

"That is not the behavior of the groeliin."

Endric shrugged. "I don't know what behavior is normal for the groeliin, only what I experienced. They used strips of flesh woven into a leash, holding the cub."

"He has chosen you?" the Antrilii asked.

"Chosen? No. He allows me to hold him."

The Antrilii laughed. In the starkness of the mountains, the sound was strange and caught Endric off-guard. "Hold him? Is that what you think you have done? The merahl has chosen you. It is a great honor, Endric, son of Dendril. The merahl are proud creatures, so for this one to choose you..."

"There were others. They kept me alive."

The Antrilii's laugh faded, and with it the smile that had been on his face. "There were other merahl with you?"

Endric had said too much. He didn't know what had happened with the Antrilii to make those merahl suspicious. Something had changed, something that made it so that they were unwilling to help the Antrilii. Without having a way to communicate with them as Dentoun had seemed to possess, he had nothing to go on other than the fact that they had been uncomfortable by the Antrilii.

"Were there merahl?" the Antrilii asked again.

"I saw another," Endric said. That was non-committal enough that he thought he could deflect other questions.

The Antrilii watched him, saying nothing for a moment. "You will come with me, Endric, son of Dendril."

Endric shook his head. "I'm heading south. I'm going to return to my lands."

"You do not want to satisfy the penance?"

Endric sighed. "I don't know that I could. I think the Yahinv knew that, and I think they intended for me to fail—especially Isabel. The Antrilii don't need for me to understand their vows, and I don't need the Antrilii to understand the vows that my father took that superseded those of the Antrilii. He is not an oathbreaker. He has taken a different oath, one that he continues to serve."

The Antrilii smiled slightly. "You think to lecture me on the vows?"

"I'm not lecturing you about anything. I intend to head south and return to my homeland so that I can continue to serve the Denraen so that I can abide by *my* vows."

"If you continue south, you will die," the Antrilii said.

Endric shot him a hard look. "I've lived this long. And that was without a sword. Now that I have a weapon, I have a better chance."

"Perhaps. Or you will die more easily. South, we think, you will find the breeding grounds. There will be more groeliin there, more than you will be able to withstand alone."

Breeding grounds. Hadn't he heard something from the other Antrilii relating to that? What had it been? What had he overheard?

He didn't remember. He'd been too tired, and still hungry, and exhausted from the time he'd spent in the mountains.

"Where would you have me go? Would you return me to the Antrilii and to the Yahinv?"

"Have you served your penance?"

Endric shook his head. He had killed many groeliin, but he had not taken out an entire brood. He wasn't certain that he would know if he did. "I don't know."

"Then I cannot return you to the Antrilii. You must serve your penance. But there is something I can do, and someplace that I can bring you."

"Where?"

"You sought Nahrsin. I can bring you to Nahrsin."

19

The Antrilii were camped near a stream much like the other Antrilii had been. They were all painted with red and black paint, though some were like the Antrilii he had met, with only black paint. Like the other group of hunters, none were mounted, which Endric found strange. When Dentoun had led men south, they had all been mounted, and they had all ridden well. Did the Antrilii not ride horses through the mountains usually? Then again, he didn't know how they would have been able to do that through the mountains here. The horses might actually have been a liability rather than an asset.

One of the Antrilii stood out, a man Endric recognized at once.

Nahrsin was large—muscular, much like Endric's friend Pendin—and seemed almost like he couldn't be related to Endric at all. He stood as the man led Endric into the camp and stared before a wide smile spread across his face.

"By the gods! Endric?" he asked, his voice booming. After

all the time trying to be careful about how much noise he made, hearing Nahrsin's thunderous voice startled Endric. His cousin hurried across the clearing and stopped a few paces away, pausing to study him for a long moment. "What are you doing this far in the north? I thought you had returned to the Denraen, and that your father welcomed you back."

"He did."

"And dressed like this? Did you lose your way as you journeyed through the north? Is that why you come to us dressed in this manner?"

The other Antrilii shook his head. "This is his penance, Nahrsin."

"Penance. Why would Endric be serving a penance?" He blinked and looked from Endric to the other Antrilii, shaking his head slightly.

Behind him, the other Antrilii were mostly silent, and the emptiness seemed to thunder around them. What would the Antrilii do about the fact that Endric was here? Learning that he was here for a penance, that he was supposed to serve by removing a brood of groeliin, but hadn't.

"Because I agreed to assume the penance asked of my father."

"Your father? Endric... that was a farce! You should not have needed to serve penance for him."

"The Yahinv asked it of me."

"And was Melinda there?"

Endric nodded.

Nahrsin frowned, looking at the other Antrilii. "Gron—why would Melinda agree to this? She knew the reason that Dendril left the Antrilii. She was there for those discussions, and she understood the sacrifice that he was willing to make, even if she didn't agree with why he left."

"I cannot speak on behalf of the Yahinv, but if Endric agreed to the penance, and accepted it willingly, then he needs to abide by the terms."

"Willingly? He is not of the Antrilii."

"Perhaps he is not, but his father had been. And if the Yahinv feels that Dendril needed to serve a penance for abandoning his vows, then I am not able to argue with that."

"Even knowing what we know?"

"Even then, Nahrsin. I am not above the Yahinv, and I am not above the vows. They are the keeper of the vows, and they have guided our people for centuries. We would do well to abide by their choices."

Nahrsin opened his mouth and seemed as if he were going to object before he clamped it closed once more. "He is here. That is the will of the gods."

"His penance is not fulfilled."

"What penance? He'd be lucky to kill even a single groeliin. That he survived this long is impressive, but were he to attempt anything more—"

"I've killed many groeliin," Endric said.

Nahrsin turned to him, watching him with a curious gleam in his eyes. "Many? How is that possible, Endric? You might be descended from the Antrilii, but even then, it requires a partic- ular awakening for a man to be able to see them and something more for them to survive facing them."

How *had* he managed to see them? What was his awakening? He remembered how difficult it had been to even see the groeliin when he had first heard of them when he first traveled with the Antrilii. Dentoun had kept him away from the fighting because he had doubted Endric's ability to see them—and must have doubted Endric's ability to do anything against them were he even able to see them. When had that changed for Endric... and *why* had it changed?

The only time that he could conceive that it might have changed was when he had begun using the teralin sword. Had the sword—or at least, something about the polarity of the sword—changed something within him? Maybe it hadn't even changed anything, but it had woken something that was already there. He *was* descended from the Antrilii, so there was no reason that he shouldn't be able to see the groeliin in the same way.

"The same way that you're able to see them, I suppose," Endric answered.

"I am Antrilii," Nahrsin answered simply.

"And I'm descended from one as well."

Nahrsin started to smile but caught himself. "How many did you kill?" He shifted his glance to Gron. "What is the record for the number of groeliin killed before a penance is served?"

"Typically, the Yahinv asks for five groeliin."

"Five. That is right. That is reasonable, and difficult enough when sent into the mountains with nothing but the grace of the gods to guide you. Were you asked to kill five?"

Endric shook his head. "If only it were. I've killed many more than five already." Had he only been assigned five groeliin, it wouldn't have felt quite so helpless. When he'd begun to fear death, he might have felt like there was a chance. Five would have been difficult—and probably more than he would have believed possible to face on his own with only a club and a spear.

"More than five?" Nahrsin looked at Gron. "Why would they

ask an outsider to kill more than five groeliin?" When Gron didn't answer, Nahrsin shifted his focus back to Endric. "Tell me, cousin. How many were you asked to kill? Ten? A dozen? If you've killed more than five, you must be nearing completion of what they asked of you for the penance. You can return, and you will have cleared Dendril's name to even the staunchest of the Yahinv."

"I'm not able to return, not yet," Endric said.

"How many?" Nahrsin pressed.

"I came looking for you," Endric explained. "I wanted to know about where I came from, my father's people. He sent me north, and likely thought that I would find you."

"Endric?"

He shook his head. "The Yahinv told me that I could not return until I fulfilled the penance. I want to know about the Antrilii—but I also want to live. The Denraen still need me."

"Some die fulfilling the penance," Nahrsin said, "but it is not so common. Most only need the reminder of their vow and they return."

That was a different sense than he had from the Yahinv. "I was told that I needed to slaughter a brood. Only then could I return."

Nahrsin barked out a laugh that began to die out slowly. "A brood?" He looked at Gron. "That would be a greater penance than any has served in... in longer than I live, Uncle."

"I don't know the will of the Yahinv," Gron said.

The merahl cub wiggled in his arms, and he shifted so that he didn't slip free.

Nahrsin stepped closer and lowered his voice. "They didn't really demand that you slaughter a brood, did they?"

"That was what they asked of me."

"And you attempted to do this?" He smiled and leaned closer. "Did your father demand that you die?"

"I don't intend to die," Endric answered.

"Facing the groeliin with no weapon and untrained? That is as sure a way to die as any that I know."

"I had a weapon."

"This?" Nahrsin grabbed the spear from his back. "You would be lucky to survive with such a thing. Better have nothing more than an axe."

"I would have preferred something with an edge, but I didn't even find a sword until I had to fight off dozens of groeliin."

"Dozens?" Nahrsin asked. He watched Endric, disbelief in his eyes. Endric met his gaze with a nod.

"That is what he told me when I encountered him as well," Gron said. "I don't know whether to believe him or send him searching for the breeding ground as punishment for lying to me."

"Can you show this?" Nahrsin asked.

"It's a day or more to the west," Endric answered.

Nahrsin waited.

Endric looked at the Antrilii arranged around him. There were probably thirty men, all with faces painted in a similar fashion, and all hardened Antrilii warriors. Once more, he noted that there were no merahl. What had changed for the Antrilii that the merahl wouldn't hunt with them? What had the Antrilii done to upset them? They were questions that he thought he could ask of Nahrsin, but not until he separated him from his uncle. Did he have a connection to Gron as well?

In order to reach the south, he would need help. And he'd come to the Antrilii hoping to reach his cousin. Now that he was here, he needed to trust that connection, trust that the man

who had helped defeat the Deshmahne would be able to aid
him. If Gron was right and the breeding grounds were to the
south, there would be more groeliin than Endric could face on
his own. He would *need* their help.

"I can show you, but only a few."

Nahrsin frowned and nodded.

They moved quickly, passing along the rock with a surer-footed
pace now that Endric wore better-fitting boots. The Antrilii
had outfitted him in spare gear, remnants of a lost warrior, and
Endric was thankful for them, even if the boots didn't fit his
feet as well as he would like. They were better than the laca fur
boots that he'd been wearing.

The cub came with him. Endric wasn't sure what to do with
him otherwise, not wanting to leave him with the rest of the
Antrilii tribe. There had been no sign of the other merahl, and
Endric wasn't certain where they had gone and whether they
would return.

Why had they gone with him as long as they had, only to
leave him again? And why would they leave the cub with him if
they weren't trusting of the Antrilii?

"You came through here?" Nahrsin asked as they made their
way along the rock. It was lighter now than when he'd come
through before, and there was something very different about
having others with him—at least others who would actually
answer him. The merahl had provided some company, but they
couldn't speak—not in his tongue.

Endric turned back to Nahrsin. They paused at one of the
many streams that flowed through here, and they each drank,

the Antrilii refilling their flasks. They hadn't provided one of those to Endric, though he was thankful that they hadn't taken away the sword. There had been questions when he had appeared, and they were the kind that he wasn't certain that he had good answers for. The other Antrilii had wanted to know about his penance, and Gron had deflected most of them, but he allowed some to remain. Since most of the Antrilii knew that he had been sent out on a penance—there was no good way to hide that fact, especially dressed as he was—Endric suspected he deserved that.

"We came through here before."

"We?" Nahrsin eyed the cub that had plopped itself down by his feet.

"There was a merahl traveling with me."

"That would be unusual." The way he said it made it almost like he meant it as an accusation, but Nahrsin seemed careful not to make it sound that way.

"When you see the groeliin, you will understand."

They didn't rest long, continuing on and making good time. The Antrilii let Endric lead, and the cub followed him, keeping pace easily. The larger merahl had bounded from rock to rock, jumping through the mountains with little difficulty. The cub didn't have the same easy gait, but he was agile enough that he managed to keep up with them.

It was late in the day when they reached the place where he'd faced the groeliin.

The bodies were as he had last seen them, though, in the fading light of the day, they appeared even more grotesque than they had at night. At least at night, they had the darkness to shroud them, and he had been able to imagine that they were something else.

Nahrsin stopped at the edge of the clearing, staring at the groeliin.

"You did this?"

Endric shook his head. "I don't know how much of this was me, and how much of this was the merahl. They fought with me."

"Nahrsin, you should look at this," one of the Antrilii said. He was an older man named Barden, one who had immediately volunteered when Nahrsin decided to return here with Endric and see the groeliin he'd attacked. Barden had a solid build, and he had deep-set eyes in a face narrower than most of the Antrilii. He wore stripes of red paint on his face, leaving patches clear, different than many of the Antrilii, who preferred to paint their entire faces.

Nahrsin joined Barden kneeling on the ground near the groeliin. The other man who'd come with them, Asgod, stood staring at the fallen bodies. "This is an impressive number of the cursed beasts."

"Cursed?" Endric glanced over to him. He would never have considered the groeliin cursed, but there was a simple sort of logic to it.

"They remain in the mountains, twisted and evil. I think they must be cursed for them to spend their days like that. What other creature spends its days in such a manner?"

"The Antrilii?" Endric asked.

Asgod smiled. "Perhaps you are right, Endric son of Dendril, though many would claim the Antrilii are blessed. We have been given the gift of the gods so that we can see the creatures we face. Many men—most men—are not able to make the same claim."

"Endric," Nahrsin said, looking up from where he was

crouched next to the groeliin on the farthest edge of the clearing.

Endric left Asgod and stood near Nahrsin. Barden was busy rolling one of the groeliin, staring at the creature as he did.

"What is it?"

"I can see the creatures you were involved with. You must have used the spear for most?" he asked.

Endric nodded. "It was spear and club."

"How many groeliin do you think you killed?"

Endric shrugged. "I don't know. There were thirteen before I ever encountered this collection. When I came here, it was because the cub's crying drew me. I think the merahl would have rescued it otherwise."

"Maybe. I do not know whether that is true or not. You said that you drew the groeliin's attention away?"

"I did what I had to do to get to the cub," Endric said.

The cub had returned to the site where he'd been tied up, and sat growling at the ground, flaring his teeth in a way that would be cute and amusing if not for the fact that Endric knew he would grow to be a dangerous hunter.

Nahrsin laughed. "I think I understand why it has chosen you."

"Why is that important to understand?" Gron had been the same way, seeking to understand why the cub had claimed him. Endric wasn't certain why it had, only that the cub had remained with him—and the merahl he thought were the cub's parents had allowed it.

"The merahl are known to bond with men," Nahrsin said.

"I remember."

"You remember what you saw of Dentoun and the way that the merahl reacted. They chose to hunt with us, but only one of

the merahl had chosen a person to bond. They are proud creatures, and they can be difficult to know their minds at times,
but when you do, you will see that they are incredibly intelligent and can be brutally efficient hunters."

"I remember," Endric said.

"Dentoun was the only one among us who had been
chosen by the merahl. That was how we could draw them
with us as far south as we did. They have a way of speaking
to each other, a way that lets them share what we plan.
Without that, we wouldn't have had the same hunters
with us."

"How many of the Antrilii have merahl that have chosen
them?"

"Not many," Nahrsin said. "Usually when we hunt groeliin,
there are merahl who have agreed to hunt with us, but that is a
choice that they make, not one that is made for them. "

Endric looked down at the cub. He didn't know if he'd been
chosen or not, though the Antrilii seemed to believe that he had
been. What he *did* know was that he hadn't been able to leave
the merahl to the groeliin.

"There are at least thirty groeliin here," Nahrsin said. This
time, his voice was edged with respect.

"I don't get credit for most of them," Endric said. "The
merahl took most of them out for me."

"I think you don't give yourself enough credit," Nahrsin said.
He began to make his way through the fallen groeliin, and
Barden came behind, pushing the groeliin into a pile in the
center of the clearing. Asgod began helping. They dragged the
bodies of the fallen creatures, seemingly unmindful of the
stench they still emitted. It was a foul odor, one that would be
worse if not for the fact that Endric had dealt with it for the last

few days, carrying with him the hunks of branded groeliin flesh.

Nahrsin pointed to groeliin clustered around the rock where the cub still crouched. Endric noted about a dozen groeliin there.

"These were not merahl kills," Nahrsin said. "These were something else. A man with a staff—or a spear." A look of respect crossed Nahrsin's face that hadn't been there before. "You should be proud of the fact that you were able to kill so many."

"Still not enough," Endric said.

"Perhaps not for the Yahinv, but I think you have killed enough for the merahl. Perhaps that is how you earned the respect of creatures that would normally not choose someone, and certainly would not do so with an outsider."

"Nahrsin," Endric began, making his way to the rock, "there was an Antrilii here. The groeliin had flayed him and had woven his flesh together to trap the merahl."

"That would be a foul thing."

"Are the groeliin considered intelligent?" Endric asked.

Nahrsin shrugged. "We haven't thought so, but we aren't entirely certain. We know that they have been found to plan attacks, and they coordinate less like wild beasts and more like creatures with real minds, like those with some intelligence, so it is possible that they are."

"This was planned like a trap. The groeliin wanted to bring the merahl here, and they wanted to capture them."

"The groeliin do not care for the merahl. They are even more efficient hunters than the Antrilii. But they would not have known how to trap them. This can't be what you say."

Endric looked at the stone. Beneath it would be the Antrilii that had been used. Why would the groeliin have captured an Antrilii—and where would he have come from?

He didn't know, but maybe Nahrsin would. He pushed on the stone, and it rolled away. Where the body had been, there was nothing.

Where had it gone?

The groeliin had been here, had remained where they had been when he'd killed them, but the Antrilii should have been with it.

"Endric?"

He looked up.

"You seem troubled."

"There was an Antrilii here. I don't know what happened to him."

Nahrsin looked around the clearing, but there was no sign of the fallen Antrilii.

"Are you certain?"

Endric nodded. "That was the man who had been flayed. I'm quite certain. Where would he have gone?"

Nahrsin turned his attention south, saying nothing. Endric felt a chill wash over him. He didn't know if that was the silence, or whether it came from something else.

20

After they had burned the bodies of the groeliin, the smoke a cloying cloud of darkness that Endric had made a point of standing upwind from, not wanting to be too close to the horrible burning stink the creatures emitted, they had started back toward the other Antrilii camp. None of them spoke, though Endric wasn't certain whether that was because there was something that had troubled the rest of the Antrilii, or whether it was because they didn't want to make much sound as they traveled.

It was late when they stopped to camp for the night.

Endric was happy that they hadn't camped near the dead bodies of the groeliin. Doing so would have left him unsettled. It wasn't the dead that bothered him; it was more about the fact that they were groeliin, and he wasn't entirely certain that they wouldn't find them again. Now that he and the cub had the Antrilii with him, he had the hope that he would be safer, especially since they had so much more experience hunting the groeliin, but Endric had managed for nearly two weeks alone. Wasn't his experience worth something as well?

The other two Antrilii collected firewood and quickly had a small flame burning, pushing back the darkness as well as the cool of the night. Barden handed out strips of jerky, giving one to each of them, including Endric. He chewed it slowly, savoring the heavily spiced meat, thankful that it was jerky rather than any of the strange things that he had been forced to eat during his time in the mountains.

"Why did you come north?" Nahrsin asked, ending the comfortable silence. They sat apart from the other two, and Endric wondered if that had been intentional. Had Nahrsin hoped to find something about Endric that troubled the other Antrilii?

"Understanding," Endric said.

"What kind of understanding?"

"When I met you, I had been exiled from Vasha. My father sent me out, thinking that I would learn something from your father. I don't think he expected me to find what I did, but it is fortunate that I did." He had never given much thought to the fact that it *had* been fortunate that he left Vasha when he had. Had he not, he might not have been able to learn what the Deshmahne had planned or understand the attack they intended on the city.

"The Antrilii understand the gods have a plan for all of us, Endric. It was in this way that they had a plan for even you, even if you do not believe it."

"I don't know what that plan might be. All I know is that I want to know what the Antrilii know. You are more skilled swordsmen than any other I've seen, excluding Brohmin."

"The Hunter," Nahrsin said.

Endric nodded. "He was with me. When we came north, we were attacked by groeliin in the mountains as we attempted to come through the pass. I was injured. Nessa nursed me back to health; otherwise, I would have died. I don't know what happened to Brohmin. They claim they didn't find him with me."

"It would be devastating if the Hunter is lost. He was impressive when I last saw him."

"I don't know how he could have survived. There would have been too many groeliin. And had he survived, he should have been found with me."

"You said this attack was in the pass as you made your way north?"

Endric nodded.

"And you awoke in Farsea if you were healed by Nessa."

Endric nodded again.

"That pass should have been protected. There should have been no reason for you to have been attacked. Nessa's tribe was responsible for patrolling there."

"I had the sense that they didn't know where the rest of her tribe was," Endric answered. "They had gone, and from what I had overheard, they weren't exactly sure where to find them."

"That is… troubling. At least as troubling as the fact that you were sent south the way you were and given a penance worse than any that would have been given to one of the Antrilii. They should have come this way to join in the attack."

Endric stared at the flames. There had been so few nights where he had been able to have a fire that having one now felt like a luxury. "I didn't know that the Antrilii had cities," he said.

"There are probably many things about the Antrilii that you

do not know. You weren't raised among the people, not as your father had been."

"My father doesn't speak of his time then. He doesn't speak of much beyond the present. He plans, and he worries about the safety of the Denraen—and the Magi—but he doesn't tell me about anything from his time before he came to Vasha. I know so little, not even about my mother."

"You thought that coming to the Antrilii would teach you about your mother?"

Endric shrugged. "I mostly wanted to know what the Antrilii know. I wanted to learn whether there was anything I could gain from studying with you. I would like to be able to fight like the Antrilii."

"It's not all about fighting," Nahrsin said. "The Antrilii serve a higher purpose."

"Your vow to the gods."

"Our vow to continue to fight and protect the north. That is why we serve. That is why the others do not care for Dendril leaving. They think he has abandoned his vows, though they do not know how he has gained vows they will never understand."

"Why does it bother them so much?"

"Because your father was to lead the Scroll tribe."

"Not Dentoun?"

"My father came to it after Dendril left. Dentoun was always capable, and he was always strong and devoted, but Dendril… there have been stories about Dendril. He was revered by the hunters of our tribe. When he came to his mother and announced that he needed to leave, she didn't understand at first."

"Melinda seemed to support his choice," Endric said.

"Perhaps now, but there was a time when she didn't. She

fought against it, and she was one of the most vocal about why Dendril needed to return, demanding that he serve a penance." He shook his head. "It's possible that the penance the Yahinv assigned to you was the same one that Melinda would have chosen for Dendril. I can't imagine that it had changed over the years, though her opinion about what Dendril did, and why he left has changed."

Endric wondered if Nahrsin understood anything about the Conclave. From Melinda's comments, he thought that she had, but maybe she didn't. They knew of Brohmin, but did they know anything else? Did they know that Tresten served in the Conclave? Did they know of his father's role? What of the historian? Dentoun had seemed to know the historian and Nahrsin had a certain familiarity with him as well.

He decided that it wasn't his place to share anything about the Conclave. If they didn't know about it, then he shouldn't be the one to reveal it, partly because he wasn't entirely certain what it meant or what the Conclave did.

"Melinda didn't want me to serve the penance," Endric said.

"Melinda would have wanted Dendril to return, and to serve it himself," Nahrsin said.

Endric sat back, staring at the fire. He was surprised to learn that Melinda had been unhappy with Dendril, almost as if when he had been with her, when she had been in the Yahinv, he had the sense that she sided with Dendril, but she seemed to understand some greater truth about the reason that he served.

Had he misread it? He didn't like the idea that he could have so easily misunderstood the situation. Then again, he had clearly misread the fact that the Antrilii weren't thrilled with his father's departure. He had assumed that they had allowed him to leave, that they had wanted him to go, but then again, he should've expected the fact that his father had not served as the rest of the Antrilii intended. Dentoun would've helped and would have been willing to help simply because he was Dendril's brother.

Endric began to wonder if perhaps Nahrsin felt the same way as the rest of the Antrilii.

"I don't think my father views himself as an oathbreaker," Endric said.

Nahrsin shook his head. "You do not need to fear that I view him as an oathbreaker. My uncle is a man of faith. My father recognized that. He claimed that your father was a brave man. A brave man would not abandon his vows."

"Dendril did not resist me coming north," Endric said. "I thought initially that perhaps he hadn't wanted me to come north, but now I wonder whether that was true or not. What if my father intended for me to come? What if he intended for me to learn what I have about the Antrilii? What if my father intended for me to know that he was viewed as an oathbreaker?"

"I can't say that I know what Dendril intended."

They sat silently for a while. As they did, Endric contemplated. The night grew long, and stars drifted out. Every so often, the merahl cub would lick at his hand, and he would rub behind its ears or scratch its chin. Nahrsin had wrangled a piece of jerky and had given it to Endric to give to the cub. The cub had taken it willingly and had eaten the jerky with a greedy sort of abandon. When he was finished, he went to the stream and lapped at the water until he'd had his fill, and then had come and laid down next to Endric once more.

It was hard to deny that the cub *did* seem to have some sort of connection to Endric. That much seemed true. But what

Nahrsin indicated was something greater than just a connection. Had the cub actually chosen him? That seemed to be more of an intelligent choice than he would've expected from an animal so young.

After a while, Endric shook his head. It was time to rest. He knew that he needed to get a full night's sleep. It had been a while since he had managed to get enough rest.

"What have the Antrilii done that has upset the merahl?" Endric asked.

It had been the question that had bothered him since joining up with the Antrilii. Something had happened, and Endric needed to know, especially because the merahl had now abandoned him and left the cub with him.

What happened with the four merahl that had been with him before? Would they return? Did they go and hunt elsewhere? Was there something more that he didn't understand?

Nahrsin looked over at him, a question on his face. "Nothing has happened between the Antrilii and the merahl."

"You don't have any hunting with you."

Nahrsin took a deep breath. "The merahl are proud creatures. They can choose for themselves who they hunt with, and when they hunt. We do not get to choose for them, though we often have asked for their assistance. It was that way when Dentoun went south. He had asked the merahl for their aid."

"You are in the middle of groeliin lands. I would have expected the merahl to have been with you, hunting with you. I remember what it was like when Dentoun led you south. They were critical to that battle, and an important part of the hunt."

Nahrsin stared at the fire. Endric had a sense that he intentionally avoided his gaze, but didn't know why he would. Had what Endric said offended him?

"The merahl have remained distant," Nahrsin said. "We have asked for them to hunt with us once more, but they have not answered the way they once did." Nahrsin spoke in a distant sort of way. Endric could tell that even admitting that much was troubling to him.

Did he share with Nahrsin what he had witnessed? Would it make a difference if he did?

Endric had to share something with Nahrsin. Maybe he would understand. He had to think that his cousin was not the kind of person that the merahl would grow angry with.

"I told you that there were merahl that helped."

Nahrsin turned away from the fire and nodded at Endric. "You said there had been one."

"I might have been underestimating how many there were," Endric said.

Nahrsin smiled. "You would've had to have been underestimating it. Considering the fact that I saw four different sets of prints at the groeliin attack site."

"They were cautious. I don't understand why, but there was something that made them nervous. They were willing to help me, and they led me and showed me another band of Antrilii hunters, but the merahl weren't willing to venture down to the hunters. They seemed almost worried about what the Antrilii were doing."

"Do you know what tribe you saw?"

Endric shook his head. "I assume the colors mean something." He watched Nahrsin expectantly, waiting for confirmation of his suspicions. Nahrsin nodded slowly.

"I thought as much. When I was in Farsea and encountered Nessa, it seemed as if she had a particular color woven into her hair, much like the others had a particular color in theirs."

"Nessa wouldn't have had a particular color," Nahrsin said.

"Why not?"

"Farsea sits centrally among the Antrilii lands. It is a place of study. A place where all members of the Yahinv come together. It is a place where the wisdom of their rule and guidance can bring us all together."

"The tower?"

Nahrsin considered him a moment before nodding slowly. "It is... surprising that you would have been aware of that."

"Why?"

"The tower is considered sacred."

"It's a replica of the tower in Thealon. There, it's even more impressive."

Nahrsin nodded slowly. "I have heard the stories of the Tower of the Gods. Those of my people who risk themselves to venture that far south all come back with the same story. Each of them comes back sharing that the tower is perhaps the most impressive thing they have ever seen."

Endric could see how that was the case. The tower *was* impressive. But, in some ways, other places were equally impressive. When he had been in Vasha, he found the palace of the Magi to be quite impressive. The Lashiin ruins were also impressive, but for different reasons. There were enough other places that Endric felt the influence of the gods, or at least the presence of those who came before him and recognized that he was part of something much greater.

"The Yahinv doesn't often allow anyone other than Antrilii to visit the tower," Nahrsin began. "Then again, there aren't many other than Antrilii who even visit our lands. The historian has come through a few times, and we have known the

Hunter in the days since we fought together. But there aren't many others than that."

"I would imagine your lands are difficult to reach?"

"You traveled to our lands. You know how hard they are to reach."

"I traveled into the mountain pass. I never made it much farther than that. We were attacked, and then I don't remember much else. I awoke in Farsea."

Endric still hadn't learned how he had been brought to Farsea or how long of a journey that was, and he hadn't learned how difficult it would've been for him to reach the city. Had it been a day's journey? Had it been another week? Perhaps that was a question he should have asked before.

"You still haven't answered what happened with the merahl."

Nahrsin sighed. "Mostly because I don't know. After my father's passing, after we celebrated his life, there was no sign of the merahl. We thought that it was only our hunters who had lost that connection. There were some among our tribe who felt that perhaps Dentoun's passing had separated us somehow. There were some who thought that we would have to re-earn the connection."

"What would it take to earn that connection once more?" Endric asked.

Nahrsin shook his head. "We have been connected to the merahl for hundreds of years. They have been as much a part of the Antrilii people as the people themselves. Always the merahl have been there with us, hunting with us, even when we didn't have those the merahl had chosen. The connection might have been more tenuous then, but it was still a solid connection. This... this is something of an absence. It's an emptiness, one that we have felt for the last few months."

"Do you think it has anything to do with your traveling south? Do you think it has anything to do with the Deshmahne?"

Nahrsin shook his head. "The merahl live to hunt groeliin. That is their purpose. They have long appreciated my people for that. They have no interest in hunting man."

"Would they have reason to be distrustful of man?" Endric asked.

Nahrsin shook his head. "I do not know. There are others who know the merahl better. Those who were chosen by them. What did you discover?" Nahrsin asked.

Endric considered his answer. The Antrilii needed the partnership with the merahl, one that he thought was likely beneficial for both parties, especially since both seemed eager to hunt the groeliin. Was there something more that he could understand?

"As I said, the merahl seemed upset with the Antrilii," Endric began. "They led me to a place where the Antrilii were camping below. I overheard snippets of conversation, but not enough for me to understand what they were referring to. After that, they nudged me away and guided me toward the east."

"They guided you?"

Endric nodded. "Guided. Hunted for me. Helped me. I was getting to the point where I wasn't certain what I would do. It was about the time when I came across the cub."

Nahrsin studied him for a long moment. "What would make you risk yourself for the cub?" he asked.

"I didn't intend to risk myself. I was trying to delay, buy enough time for the merahl to appear. When I saw the cub, I heard at least three different merahl heading in my direction. I thought that if I managed to buy enough time, that I might be able to allow the merahl to reach me. I thought that their hunting ability, at least from what I remembered seeing before, would be enough to overwhelm the groeliin. I thought that perhaps the groeliin would retreat."

"The groeliin do not retreat."

"Just like you said the groeliin do not plan," Endric said.

"Yes."

"Something has changed for the merahl. They fear something about the Antrilii." They sat in silence for a moment. "What sort of gesture would it take to appeal to the merahl?" Endric asked.

"I am not an expert with the merahl," Nahrsin said. "Those who know these things claim that we needed to make a profound demonstration for them."

"That's why you've come here, isn't it?" Endric asked. "That's why you are heading toward the breeding grounds."

He hadn't put that together before and thought that it was almost too much to believe. Why would Nahrsin's tribe risk themselves like this? The only answer that made sense was that they felt as if they needed to. They did it because they needed to make a statement to the merahl, that they needed to somehow convince their partners that they were still committed to the same purpose.

Had the merahl began to doubt them?

If that were the case, Endric wondered if this demonstration would be enough. Would they be able to convince the merahl that they were still committed to hunting the groeliin?

Was that why the merahl had been willing to assist him? Did they come with him because he had been willing to fight?

Endric didn't know. It was possible, and he had to believe that if that were the case, that taking the fight to groeliin, heading toward the breeding grounds, risking a sacrifice of themselves, might be enough to convince the merahl that the Antrilii still intended to fight with them.

But it didn't answer the question about what had changed.

Something *had* changed. There was no doubt in Endric's mind that there had been a change for the merahl. These were proud animals. And they had long been committed to the Antrilii. For that commitment to have changed, something had happened. It seemed odd that Nahrsin wouldn't know what that was, but it also seemed odd the way the merahl had behaved, staying away from the rest of the Antrilii.

"That is why we headed to the breeding grounds."

"Do you think that will bring you back into the merahl's favor?" Endric asked. He remembered what he'd overheard in the Yahinv. They had been concerned with finding the Chisln... and the merahl. Was this the reason?

Nahrsin shook his head and turned to stare into the fire. There was a hopelessness in his eyes that seemed almost despondent. It took Endric a moment to realize why. This was a man who realized he was heading to his death. And, more than that, he did so willingly.

"I don't know if it will make a difference. All I know is that we head south, that we intend to reach the breeding grounds, and Gron is hopeful that we will draw the notice of the merahl. He is hopeful that we will gain their favor once more. Otherwise, we will not survive."

21

They reached the rest of the Antrilii late in the day. Endric had spent the night sleeping fitfully. He had been roused from his sleep around the middle the night, awoken so that he could take his turn on patrol. He did so willingly, thankful for the opportunity to serve the same as the others. It was a relief to not fear for his own safety and to feel the reassurance of others watching over him.

Endric had tumbled into the rest of his sleep, curled up on his side. The merahl cub rested next to him, occasionally licking his hand. As he struggled to find sleep, he couldn't help but wonder what had changed for the merahl. And with whatever *had* changed, why was the merahl willing to help him but not the Antrilii? No answers came to him.

As they traveled back toward the rest of the Antrilii, Endric could only think about that question. Why had the merahl come to his aid? What had he done differently? And maybe it was nothing. The merahl hadn't really come to his aid so much as they had come to the aid of the cub—a cub he'd found tethered to a dead Antrilii. That seemed important, though Endric wasn't able to put a finger on the reason why.

"Where is home for the merahl?" Endric asked Nahrsin. The other Antrilii were a couple paces in front of them. Asgod perked his ears up while Barden made it seem as if he wasn't listening.

"The merahl roam throughout the mountains," Nahrsin asked.

"But where is home for them?"

"They prefer more forested lands," Nahrsin said. "Some merahl call the Great Forest their home, but most of the packs are found in the northern mountains, spread all across the chain of mountains here. They come into the mountains to hunt and breed."

"Breed?"

Nahrsin shrugged. "We find the merahl cubs here but nowhere else. This is where our hunters must come if they wish to claim a bond."

Endric had been surprised the first time he'd learned merahl were found in the Great Forest. When Brohmin had shared that with him, he hadn't asked how others hadn't observed them before now.

The merahl were smart. He suspected they would be able to hide, and that they could keep themselves shielded from others they didn't want to be noticed by. Likely they could simply detect the presence of anyone else.

"How many packs?" Endric asked.

Nahrsin shrugged. "We've never known with certainty. As I said, the merahl come to us when they choose. They remain as long as they feel they must before returning to their pack. Most believe the merahl continue to hunt the groeliin on their own, even when they don't hunt with the Antrilii."

"Have you ever heard of the groeliin using merahl to draw them out?" Endric asked.

Nahrsin shook his head.

"What if one of the other tribes found a cub and brought it with them?"

Nahrsin glanced over at him, his gaze flicking down to the cub. "That would be unusual."

"Unusual? As unusual as someone like me having a merahl cub follow it through the mountains?"

Nahrsin laughed. "That is also unusual."

They reached the summit of a small ridge. Patches of the ground were snow-covered, and others were icy. Small strands of grass peeked up through some of the snow. In the distance, Endric saw a small copse of trees, though their trunks were twisted and bent, much like the tree he'd come across that he'd made into his club. There were none of the pine he associated with the mountains.

The ground sloped away beneath them, the rock gradually dropping into another valley. From there, the mountain began to peak again, rising much higher.

"Doesn't get any easier, does it?" Endric muttered to himself.

Asgod chuckled. "The mountains are not for soft men," he said.

"I never thought I was soft before."

Asgod considered him for a moment. Endric was still dressed in the furs that he had stitched together himself. The only thing different was the Antrilii boots he now wore. He still felt like an outsider, dressed as he was in the laca fur.

"How far are the breeding grounds from here?" Endric

asked.

"The groeliin breed every few years and move their breeding location. We call it a Chisln, a time of danger for the Antrilii."

"Why?"

"They are protective of the breeding grounds. We have never discovered an active breeding ground."

"Never?"

"We have found the remains—and the remains of Antrilii who ventured too close—but never an active breeding ground. Until now."

"You found one?"

"The Yahinv think so. They are the ones who have sent us out on this task."

That surprised him, especially as they hadn't said anything about encountering a breeding ground while he was serving his penance. Maybe they hadn't expected him to reach any of the Antrilii in time to matter. "There is a single breeding ground?"

"The groeliin are comprised of something like tribes. During breeding season, the tribes set aside differences and come together."

"Like the different tribes that were found back where the cub was attacked?" Endric asked.

Nahrsin and Asgod met each other's gaze. Nahrsin nodded slowly. "It is unusual for broods to mingle. Even more unusual for them to do so without any bloodshed."

Endric chuckled darkly. "I would say they did more than mingle. They were working together, plotting against the merahl."

"As I said, unusual."

They started down the slope, and Endric touched Nahrsin's

arm. The two of them slowed, letting the other two continue ahead. "The coincidence between the timing of the merahl abandoning the Antrilii and breeding season troubles me," Endric said. He glanced down at the cub, who looked up at him, every so often nipping at his leg. The thick, laca fur protected his legs, but that didn't deter the cub.

"Yes. It has troubled Gron as well."

"Gron took the rule of the Antrilii after Dentoun's passing?" Endric asked.

"Graime was to have led, but he was lost during an incursion."

Endric shook his head. "I am so sorry to hear that, Nahrsin. I know how hard it is to lose your brother."

"Yes, I know you do."

"How did it happen?"

Nahrsin took a deep breath as he steadied himself. Endric could tell from the way he averted his gaze that this wasn't something Nahrsin was accustomed to talking about. He probably preferred to keep it to himself, much as Endric preferred keeping the difficulty he had with losing his brother to himself. It was easier when he didn't talk about it, easier to keep the pain inside, to know that Andril had died for the Denraen, but a death that could have been avoided.

Had Andril not died, Endric doubted that he would have become the man he had. He would have remained content to serve as a soldier within the Denraen and would have been content to continue causing his father—and his brother—difficulty. Were Andril still alive, would Endric ever have learned of his connection to the Antrilii? Would he have learned that there was another battle that took place, one that few south of the mountains understood? Would Endric ever have cared?

It was unlikely that he would have learned, much as it was unlikely that he ever would have learned who he was supposed to be. He would have been content remaining the malcontent, jumping from tavern to tavern—and woman to woman.

Nahrsin and the Antrilii believed in the will of the gods, but could his discovery of his origins really have been the gods' will? Could they really have wanted him to learn these things at the expense of his brother's life?

And how would Andril have felt knowing that it had taken his death for Endric to come to these realizations?

Endric knew the answer. Andril would have understood. His brother only wanted the best for Endric, even when Endric was not able to want those things for himself. Andril had always been the strong and devoted Denraen, which meant that losing his life for the betterment of the Denraen would have been worth it to him.

"We returned from the hunt with my father's body," Nahrsin started. "There were some who didn't think we should have risked heading south. They were those who didn't believe the groeliin had traveled south. The groeliin hadn't been seen south of the mountains… in a long time. For them to have made the journey like that without any sort of reason was unusual."

"It seems there have been many unusual things regarding the groeliin these days."

Nahrsin nodded slowly, scratching his chin. "There have been some things that are not easy to explain. I do not claim to understand, but then, I was never meant to lead our tribe. After Dentoun died, it was to have gone to Graime. He was nearly my father's equal."

They reached the small valley, and Barden started them along the valley and continuing to the east. Endric glanced up, staring at the steep grade up overhead, thinking back to the groeliin that had surprised Brohmin and himself on the way through the mountains. They had been in a place much like this. Then he had been surprised to come upon the groeliin. Now he expected it but was thankful that he hadn't faced them since the night he'd nearly died trying to keep the cub alive.

"The groeliin have been strange for some time," Nahrsin said. He had a halting pace to his words that made it seem as if he chose them carefully. "The brood moving beyond the mountains was rare enough, but something the Antrilii are prepared for. That is the reason for our vows. Stranger still is the way they have appeared in the months since them. They have traveled farther north than we've ever seen them, appearing in Antrilii lands, lands where they should fear appearing. We don't have any reluctance in killing the creatures. The Yahinv thinks this is tied to the Chisln."

"And this is the breeding season?" Endric asked.

"The Chisln is unusual as well. The merahl are often found wandering, but I can't believe that they would choose a place to breed this close to the rest of the Antrilii. We have never heard of such a thing before."

"What do you think changed?" Endric asked.

Nahrsin shook his head. "As I said, I'm not one who understands such things. I have not studied the groeliin the way some do."

"There are those who study the groeliin?" Endric knew he shouldn't be surprised. The Antrilii would need to study them, especially if they intended to prevent another attack. They would have to understand the movement of the groeliin and would have to understand where they bred.

In that way, Endric saw it as no different than his father

planning for different attacks. Wouldn't Dendril have taken the time to have gathered all of the information that he could to make an informed decision? The Antrilii would need to do the same thing.

"If you planned to travel to the breeding grounds, you can't have done that by yourself," Endric said.

Nahrsin shook his head. "No, we didn't plan this by ourselves. The other tribes also intended to meet, but we haven't encountered them yet."

"There was the tribe of Antrilii I came across. I wonder if they were heading toward the breeding grounds."

"It's possible, but we've been here now for the last two weeks, and there's been no sign of other hunters."

They fell silent as they continued east, and Endric didn't say anything more.

He wasn't exactly certain what was taking place, only that the merahl distrusted the Antrilii for some reason, and the Antrilii felt compelled to make some grand gesture to regain their trust. From what Endric had seen, he didn't think the merahl wanted to lose the connection to the Antrilii. They had come to help him. Maybe not at first, but they had. They might have come for the cub at first, thinking to rescue it, but they had remained with him, willing to stay as he continued his journey east. They had gone so far as to help provide him with food. That wasn't the mark of a creature that didn't want to have that connection with him or with the Antrilii. There was a hesitance, but it was one that Endric couldn't fully understand.

Those thoughts plagued him as they continued east, and he watched Nahrsin, feeling as if there was something his cousin wasn't sharing with him.

22

The path Nahrsin took them on was a difficult one, twisting up and over the rocks, forcing Endric to follow carefully, thankful for his boots. As they made their way, they came across no other groeliin. Endric found that odd, especially considering he had come across them three times during his journey to the mountains. Did the size of their hunting party scare away the groeliin? Or was there something else, something that he didn't recognize and something that Nahrsin didn't share with him?

He noted that Gron led with a confidence that reminded him of Dentoun. He hadn't known his uncle well, but the little glimpse he had gotten revealed a man who had known what he needed to do and was at peace with that. Gron was much the same way.

When they camped for the night, Endric found himself sitting away from the fire, once again thinking about their purpose and his own. He needed to do more than simply understand the Antrilii and definitely needed to grasp the entire situation with his father and what had brought Dendril away from the Antrilii. It had to do with the Denraen, but there might be more to it, even, if only he had the time to learn the whole story.

"Nahrsin tells me that the merahl assisted you," Gron said.

Endric glanced at Nahrsin, not surprised that he had shared that with his leader. "They came to the aid of the cub," Endric said.

"That's not all they did," Gron said.

Endric shook his head. "No, that's not all."

Gron worked a long-bladed knife along the surface of a length of stick, peeling away layers of wood. He worked with a casual sort of confidence. Without looking up, he said, "There once was a time when the merahl would hunt with others outside the Antrilii, but that has been a long time. I find it inter-esting that they would have hunted with you."

Endric looked down at his hands. The cub rested near his feet, not having moved in the time since they reached the camp. "I don't know that it's so much they hunted with me as it is that they hunted for me. I think they took pity on the fact that I was unprepared."

Gron nodded slowly. "There are some who claim the merahl are close to the gods. That they have a connection to them."

"Why do you say that?" Endric asked.

Gron met Endric's gaze. "I never said *I* said that. Only that there are those who study such things. They are the ones who wanted us to make this trip. They are the ones who recognized the need for us to regain the trust of the merahl. We have taken our vows seriously, hunting the groeliin for centuries, but it is not something that we could do without their assistance."

"How long have you hunted with the merahl?" Endric asked.

Gron returned his focus to whittling at the length of wood. "We have maintained our partnership with the merahl for more generations than I can count."

"Do you know what happened that it changed?" Endric asked.

"You mean do I know why the merahl have chosen to abandon us? No, I don't know what happened or what changed. We went from hunting with them to losing the connection."

Gron continued whittling at the stick, saying nothing as he did. Endric scratched the merahl cub's neck, ruffling his fur. The cub nipped at his fingers, and Endric jerked his hand back, always surprised by how sharp the cub's teeth were.

He laughed softly to himself. He'd never had a pet before and couldn't imagine having a merahl cub as his pet. What would happen when he headed back south? Would the cub follow him? Endric could only imagine the reaction his father and others would have with a merahl brought into Vasha.

Then again, taking the merahl out of the northern mountains seemed like it would be a betrayal. The cub belonged in these mountains and belonged here, hunting. The creature would become enormous over time and had a purpose that Endric wouldn't necessarily share.

"What happens if the merahl don't come to your aid at the breeding grounds?" Endric asked.

Gron didn't look up. "Then we will hunt and destroy as many groeliin as we can."

"At what price?"

Gron glanced up, frowning.

"If the groeliin destroy all of the Antrilii, what is the price you pay by bringing your men north? How many will be sacrificed in this?"

"We have fought the groeliin for centuries. The Antrilii know how to face them. We have never found their breeding ground, so if we do, and if only one of us survives, there is value in what we do."

Endric believed that there was, but he wondered at the strategy. Something about it felt wrong. He couldn't place his finger on it and didn't know enough about either the Antrilii or the groeliin to know why that should be the case, only that he felt it with certainty.

In the days following his return to the Antrilii, in the days since he had shown Nahrsin and the others the attack that he had faced with the groeliin, they made good time, continuing south through the mountains. Gron recognized the way through, and he moved quickly, leading them as they climbed around rock, gradually climbing higher. At the end of the second day since rejoining with Gron and the others, they had reached a peak and had begun descending once more.

"Are the mountains entirely like this?" Endric asked Nahrsin as they walked.

"The mountains are a continuous chain. There are a few passes that the Antrilii long ago learned."

"Where do the groeliin consider home?" Endric asked.

"They're found throughout the north. For the most part, they stay within the central portion of the mountains. It's harder for us to reach. That's part of the reason we've been unable to exterminate them."

"Would you if you could?"

Nahrsin turned toward him. "You've faced the groeliin. You should recognize the threat they pose. They are a blight upon the world. They twist the purpose of the gods and turn it into something else. This is something that cannot continue. This is the purpose of our vows. This is the reason the Antrilii exist."

"What happens when you succeed?"

Nahrsin met his gaze. He let out a long sigh. "When we succeed? There have been many who have dreamt of that day. There was a time when I dreamt of that day. But for us to reach that point, we must first remove the groeliin."

"What happens when you do? What happens when you're successful?"

"Then we get a chance to have peace. Then we can lay down our weapons, much like the Magi did long ago."

"Like the Magi?" he asked, staring at Nahrsin before looking around him at the other Antrilii. Was there something there that he had missed?

"The Antrilii and the Magi have always had a connection," Nahrsin said. "They may not understand it, but we have not forgotten."

"And what is that connection?" Endric asked.

Nahrsin shook his head. "It's a connection that you have to be willing to recognize. Even the Magi have preferred to keep that connection to themselves. Those of us who know, those of us who understand, recognize what price the Magi pay by having chosen to give up the connection we share."

Endric frowned. What connection could the Antrilii share with the Magi? What was there that would bind them together, other than a similar devotion to the gods? The Magi claimed the ability to speak to the gods, and they claimed the ability to reach them when no other could. Was there something similar in what the Antrilii could do?

Was it simpler than that? The Magi possessed magical abilities, those that were unlike anything any man could claim. Maybe it was something like that. Maybe there was power to the Antrilii. It would explain why only the Antrilii—and Endric —could even *see* the groeliin.

Was that why Tresten had wanted him to come north? The Mage had prompted him to search for his ancestors, had practically told him that he needed to make this journey, even though Endric wasn't certain why or what he would gain from it. Yet, he suspected Tresten had known. He *must* have known.

"Can you speak to the gods?" Endric asked Nahrsin.

Nahrsin shook his head, turning his gaze up to the sky. "There aren't any who still claim to speak to them. There was once a time when those among my people made such a claim, but it has been long enough ago that even that is no longer claimed. It is because of the gods that we have our vow. We remain committed to what they ask of us so that we continue to fight when none else will. That is how we maintain our connection."

Endric stared at his cousin. There was more to it than that. There had to be. "Do you have abilities like the Magi do?"

"You've seen us, Endric. You know the Antrilii do not." Nahrsin smiled. "We share a similar lineage, but we don't share the same power the Magi possess. They have focused on developing their connection to the gods, while we have focused on maintaining it differently. If we didn't, the groeliin would have overwhelmed everything in the north lands."

"Do the Magi even know about your sacrifice? Do they even know what you do?" Endric asked.

"It is doubtful that any know what we do. For the most part, that is how we would like to keep it. There is a certain protection in our anonymity. If others came to the north thinking that they could understand the Antrilii, they would likely encounter the groeliin, and they would die. It is the fact that they don't know us that keeps others alive."

They fell silent as they climbed, and Endric didn't push but felt a sense of unease at the fact that there *was* a connection between the Antrilii in the Magi, one that seemed crucial. If the Antrilii were stuck facing the groeliin, why weren't the Magi involved? Why did they not have a hand in this fight as well? Why must the Antrilii die while the Magi thrived? What penance did the Antrilii serve to be forced into such suffering?

23

The wind whipped around him. Endric was thankful for the laca fur, appreciative of the warmth it provided. The thickness of it prevented even the bitterest wind from reaching him, especially as he pulled his cloak around him. The rest of the Antrilii didn't seem quite as comfortable as they climbed higher into the mountains.

The merahl cub continued to trail him. Endric had begun to wonder whether the cub would leave at some point during their climb, especially as they got closer to the location Gron expected to find the breeding grounds.

Why was *he* risking himself to go along with them? What was he thinking? Coming north to learn about the Antrilii didn't mean sacrificing himself so that he could satisfy that curiosity. But he couldn't leave, not when he still didn't have the answers he wanted.

Snow covered everything around them at this point. It crunched beneath his boots, and cold seeped through despite thick Antrilii leathers. He wondered whether the laca fur would have been warmer, much as his cloak was warmer. Perhaps he had made a mistake accepting the boots. Yet his had been poorly stitched, and he suspected wind and snow would have seeped into them, making him uncomfortable.

They paused, taking a break around midday to eat and refill their water flasks. The Antrilii used snow, heating it quickly so that it would melt. As they waited by the rocks, snow under his feet, the wind whipping around him, a vague sense of unease came to him. The cub whined softly.

It was the first sound that Endric had heard from the cub in quite some time. For the most part, the cub was silent. It would nip at him playfully and occasionally would growl, usually done in a playful fashion. Most of the Antrilii regarded the merahl cub with acceptance, and all offered the cub food as they traveled. Now, more than a few of the Antrilii glanced over, frowning.

Endric crouched next to the cub. "What is it?" he asked the cub, scratching behind his ears.

The cub continued to whine, making a soft, low sound that barely carried. It was almost like the cub made a point of not vocalizing too loudly. The hackles on the back of the cub's fur stood on end. The merahl sniffed the air, lowering his body flat to the ground, and his tail stopped moving. Another soft whine escaped his lips.

Endric looked up, searching for Nahrsin.

Endric couldn't see Nahrsin, but as the merahl continued to whine, the sound adding to his sense of disquiet, he remembered the last time he'd heard the merahl making this sound—and that had been during the groeliin attack.

"Where is Nahrsin?" he asked Barden, who was sitting nearby.

The other man shook his head. "Went off scouting."

"Damn," Endric said under his breath.

Barden glanced at the merahl cub, seemingly only now aware the cub was whining. Endric realized that not all of the Antrilii seemed to hear it. Why would that be? "What is it?" Barden asked. "You think he's hungry? I have extra jerky I can offer."

Endric shook his head. "It's not hunger. I think he senses groeliin."

Barden started to grin. "The merahl don't recognize groeliin at this age. When we've encountered cubs, they always relied on the adults to help them understand that scent."

"Even a merahl who had been captured by groeliin?" Endric asked.

Barden shrugged.

Endric couldn't shake the unsettled feeling and turned his attention to the cub. "Can you show me what you sense?"

He wasn't certain whether the cub would understand him, but there was no question the adults seem to understand when he spoke to them. It was possible the cub did as well. If this *was* groeliin, Endric could use that connection to try to find where they were. It would be better finding them than to be surprised and have the groeliin come upon them unaware.

The cup began wiggling in his arms, and Endric set him down. The low whine continued as he started across the snow, his feet barely making a sound, not piercing the snow or making a print, and moving quickly. Endric unsheathed and started after the cub.

"Endric?"

He didn't glance back to see who called after him. The cub had disappeared over the peak, and he hurried forward, not wanting to lose sight of him.

On the other side, he found the cub and trailed him as he hurried down the slope. Endric followed carefully, climbing more slowly than the cub until they reached a narrow path that allowed easier movement.

The cub glanced up at him and whined softly.

"I'm here," Endric said, wanting to reassure him.

The cub seemed to nod, sniffing the air as he started forward again.

Endric trailed him, feeling the increased anxiety working through him. This was more than just an unsettled feeling now; this was true fear. He could protect himself, but would he be able to protect the cub were it to come to that?

Endric followed the merahl cub as it hurried along the path. Every so often, the merahl whined softly. As he did, Endric felt the nervous sort of energy continue to work its way through him. It filled him, leaving him on edge. He kept his sword unsheathed, afraid that he might need it, and he kept his awareness focused all around him as he searched for evidence of the groeliin.

He saw no sign of movement, but the ongoing whine made it clear that the groeliin had to be nearby. And then there was the concern Endric had for Nahrsin. His cousin had gone scouting. Endric didn't doubt his ability to protect himself; he had seen how capable Nahrsin could be, and knew that he was able to defend himself, but if there were more groeliin than he was prepared to face... Endric wanted to ensure there weren't more than he could manage on his own.

The cub scurried in front of him, blocking him. As he did,

he caught sight of movement high above in the rocks. There was no question that it came from groeliin.

With the groeliin that high over them, the creatures would reach the Antrilii.

Endric glanced at the cub. They couldn't climb the rock, not quickly enough to be of any use, but the groeliin was going to reach the Antrilii before they knew the creatures were there.

Was anything he could even do? He couldn't scale the rock as quickly as the groeliin, and without the merahl, he didn't know if they would be able to stop it.

Endric started up the slope. He had to move carefully here, afraid that if he didn't, he would slip and make noise. He needed to climb to the Antrilii, unwilling to do nothing, not when the groeliin were there, and the Antrilii were in danger.

Why had he come here by himself? He should have brought assistance rather than chasing after the merahl cub. The groeliin might overwhelm *him* if they reached him first.

As he remained there, he felt a rise in the strange, unsettled feeling that had washed through him when the cub had started out this way. He wasn't certain what that sense came from. Was it from the groeliin or was it something else?

Endric kept the sword gripped tightly, thankful that this time when he faced the groeliin, he would have a sword once more. He felt better prepared than simply having the spear with him.

Shadows shifted near him.

Endric embraced the emptiness in his mind and embraced the knowledge of his catahs drilled into his head, and slipped forward, slashing with the sword. It fell before him.

Endric spun, and the next groeliin fell, leaving a third. This one appeared different than the others, larger.

Endric didn't allow himself to think about what it meant. If he did, if he slowed down and considered what he might be facing, he would not act as he needed to. Fighting with the sword required a level of decisiveness. He had to push away all other thoughts and push away all hesitation. If he could manage that, he thought he might be able to survive.

As he attacked, the groeliin blocked his sword with his club.

Endric parried a few times, but each time, the groeliin stopped him.

A strange fog swirled around this creature.

Endric slashed again, attacking over and over, and each time, the creature met his sword, blocking him.

Could the groeliin be skilled enough to counter him?

The idea seemed impossible, but there was no questioning that was what the creature was doing.

The creature pushed him back.

Endric slipped, the snow catching his boot.

He swung his sword around, knowing that if he did nothing, he would be clubbed.

The creature batted away his sword, sending it out of his hand, clattering away.

A soft howl, one that carried a hint of menace, rang across the rocks. It was a weak cry, not the same sound the merahl would be capable of in the future, but the cub lunged forward, catching the groeliin at his ankle.

It was enough to send the groeliin spinning, lashing out with a sharp kick.

He almost caught the cub, and the cub jumped, managing to skitter away, just enough that the groeliin couldn't connect.

Endric needed to do something. If he didn't, the damned groeliin would stomp on the cub. He was responsible for keeping the cub safe, and so he was determined to do exactly that.

He didn't have his sword and didn't think the club would be useful. He managed to pull the spear out from behind him, and as the groeliin darted toward the merahl cub, he chucked it.

Endric didn't have much hope that it would connect, but then all he needed was to distract the groeliin.

Endric's spear connected with the groeliin, sliding through its back.

The creature staggered forward, grabbing at the spear, spinning as it did.

The cub lunged forward, nipping at the groeliin's heel once more.

The groeliin spun again.

As it did, Endric jumped forward, grabbing onto the spear, shoving it forward as hard as he could.

He clung to the groeliin's back. The creature had a foul odor this close, and his skin felt oily and thick. He had a coarse fur covering him that wasn't clear when looking at him.

The creature thrashed. Endric held onto the spear, keeping one arm wrapped around the creature's neck.

He feared that the groeliin might snap at his arm, might tear through his flesh, and he pulled, ripping back on the groeliin's neck. He could do nothing else.

Endric clung there, holding to the groeliin, a prayer racing through his mind.

All he could think about was dying like this, clinging to the groeliin's neck, one hand on the spear. The groeliin thrashed, and Endric held. The warmth of groeliin's blood seeped over his hand, and he held on with everything that he could.

Fear flashed through him. He had never really been afraid of dying before, but he didn't want to die holding onto a stinking groeliin. He didn't want to die in these northern mountains. He didn't want to die with Senda not knowing what happened to him.

Endric didn't want to die.

He pushed and heard a sharp crack.

Was that the spear? If it was, then he was essentially helpless to fend off the creature.

The groeliin sagged forward.

Endric splayed on top of him. The groeliin stopped moving.

Endric shook himself, managing to stand. As he did, he shivered. He went and reclaimed his sword, wishing for a stream to wipe his hands. The cub came over and rubbed up against his leg. Endric took a moment, finally able to see this groeliin that he'd been facing.

He had thought it larger than the others he'd faced. Now that it was dead, he could tell it was both taller and surprisingly stouter. Markings were burned into its flesh, some of them appearing to have a form of writing. They reminded him of other markings he'd seen on other groeliin.

This creature was covered with these markings. Endric studied it, trying to understand what they might mean, and realized they reminded him of the markings the broods had. Those had particular patterns, and he had seen several different markings that indicated several different broods. Did the fact that this creature had multiple markings mean that it represented multiple broods?

Endric wished he understood the groeliin better.

If he were honest with himself, he wished he didn't know anything about the groeliin. He couldn't imagine the Antrilii lifestyle, feeling like they had to constantly attack, praying they could eliminate these creatures.

Movement up the slope caught his attention. Endric jerked around and saw Nahrsin making his way toward him.

His cousin's eyes widened when he realized that Endric was there. He approached carefully and stopped before the body of the fallen groeliin. As he studied it, his breath caught.

"What is it?" Endric asked.

"We need to find Gron."

"Why?"

Nahrsin looked up at him but said nothing. It was enough for Endric's heart to race even more than it had been.

24

"What is this creature?" Endric asked.

Endric and Nahrsin had dragged the groeliin body back to the camp. Endric was surprised to see that there were no had been no groeliin attack there. He had thought that the group he'd seen up the slope would have reached them, but there hadn't been a sign of it.

When Nahrsin had come, he had helped Endric burn the other two groeliin, but the one with markings on its skin he had wanted to bring back to Gron.

"We haven't seen one like this before, Uncle."

Gron ran his fingers over one of the markings. "Most have brood marks."

Nahrsin nodded. "Brood marks, but this is something else. This is like multiple brood markings."

Gron looked up. "There are nearly twenty different markings on this creature. Are you claiming there are that many broods?"

Nahrsin shrugged. "We've never unable to get an accurate count of the broods. You know that."

"We haven't had an accurate count, but we've only seen fifteen or so brood marks."

"Have you ever completely eliminated a brood?" Endric asked.

Nahrsin glanced at Gron with a raised eyebrow. Then he shook his head. "We've attempted to eliminate entire broods, but we never were succeeded. Most of the time, a few remain, and they return to the breeding grounds and regroup. The broods return."

"You said you haven't made it to the breeding grounds."

"Because the breeding ground moves so it's not always easy to find," Nahrsin said. "This time is unusual in that we think we *can* find them."

"It is an unusual Chisln," Gron said.

There was something more that Endric didn't fully understand. Why did they think they knew how to find the breeding ground this time? What made it different?

Yet that wasn't the question he felt compelled to ask.

"And you've never seen a creature like this?" Endric asked.

Both Gron and Nahrsin shook their heads. "We've seen groeliin of different shapes. We've seen different brood marks," Gron said. "But we've never seen one this size and with these markings."

"There have been rumors of different groeliin," Nahrsin said.

"Different?"

"Groeliin with more power. We have never seen them."

Endric frowned. "What kind of more power?"

Gron shook his head. "We shouldn't be speaking of this. It is not wise."

"Look at this creature, Gron. What choice do we have but to speak of it?" Nahrsin asked.

"The Yahinv—"

"Are not here. They sent us out on this hunt, but they are not here, Uncle," Nahrsin said. He turned his attention back to Endric. "There have been suspicions that there are groeliin with a dark power. Perhaps even like the Magi you know in Vasha. It is not something that we fully understand."

Endric thought of the strange swirl of darkness around the groeliin. "Help me understand this power," he said.

"What is there to understand?" Nahrsin asked. "I have never seen one." He glanced at Gron as if seeking permission to speak. "There are many who don't believe they exist. There are others who do."

Endric thought he understood and looked at the older Antrilii. "You."

Gron avoided his gaze. "I do."

"What happens if there are some of these groeliin when you reach the breeding grounds?"

Neither Nahrsin nor Gron met his eyes.

"You think that you can find these creatures?" Endric asked.

"The merahl have abandoned the Antrilii," Gron said. "We have had a bond for centuries. For them to simply leave us, something has changed."

"And you think that the powered groeliin, whatever these creatures are, are the reason this has happened?"

"We don't have a good answer. The timing of the Chisln and the fact that the merahl have abandoned us is important. We know that."

Endric stared at Nahrsin and then turned his gaze to Gron. "So your plan to search for these groeliin... You didn't intend to come north simply to appeal to the merahl at all. You came north thinking that you might find and destroy creatures responsible for somehow influencing them."

Nahrsin stared at the body of the groeliin. "When we see creatures like this, something this different, I believe you, Uncle."

"Your father believed."

"Dentoun believed that the groeliin were guided by something. Their version of the gods."

"And if they are?" Gron asked. "If the groeliin have some version of the gods directing them? What then? Do we not bring all the force that we can against them? Do we not need to throw ourselves at them, risk everything and the possibility that we might finally end this centuries-old war? Would that not be valuable to our children, to give them a chance to live without war?"

Endric shivered. He couldn't imagine these men lived their entire lives, the way they suffered, all because of their vows. All they wanted was to end the violence and their suffering. They wanted peace.

Gron withdrew a long-bladed knife and began cutting along the groeliin's flesh.

"What are you doing?" Endric asked.

"We haven't seen a creature like this before. We need to bring these markings with us so that we understand just what it is."

He continued to slice through the flesh, peeling away a section of the groeliin's arm that was nearly the size of two hands. Gron worked with a neat and practiced precision that told Endric he'd done this sort of thing before. He sliced underneath the skin, leaving the creature's muscles exposed, dissecting the flesh away.

Gron worked quickly, peeling away the sections of flesh that were marked. Primarily this consisted of the groeliin's arms, though there was a fairly large sheet of skin on the groeliin's back that also had markings.

When he was complete, he went to one of his packs and pulled out a narrow strip of cloth and wiped the flesh clean. Nahrsin had gone to his pack and gathered a jar and removed a wax seal. A bitter scent emanated as he did that reminded Endric of the medicines Nessa had used, mixed with a hint of something else, something Endric couldn't place his finger on.

"You've done this before?" Endric asked.

Nahrsin looked up from smearing the liquid over the flesh. "We've done this before."

Gron took the oiled section of skin and rolled it tightly before wrapping it all in another section of cloth. The effect of oiling it and rolling it removed the stench from the flesh. Endric had become familiar with that stink when he had cut free the brood mark.

"Do you collect these?" He pulled the flesh he'd cut from the groeliin and offered it to Nahrsin.

"You cut this?" Nahrsin asked.

Endric nodded. "I thought that if I had proved to the Yahinv that I had done what they required of me that I would need some evidence they could account for."

He hadn't realized that there was no real way to eliminate a brood. There would've been no way to prove what he had done. And it might actually have been impossible to do. What kind of penance was there that would be impossible to accomplish?

Nahrsin took the chunk of flesh that Endric had obtained and motioned to Gron. The other man quickly unrolled the section of skin he had removed from the groeliin. Nahrsin set it down, looking at the skin, comparing them.

"Is it there?" Nahrsin asked.

Endric leaned over his shoulder, peering at the flesh. He scanned the markings, looking for the one for the brood that he had fought. As he did, it was clear that there were no signs of that irregular triangular shape. The brood mark was not found among the other markings on this groeliin.

"What does that mean?" Endric asked.

"It means nothing."

Endric didn't think that was true. The large groeliin he had faced had nearly twenty different brood marks. Already that was more markings than the Antrilii had ever seen. What did it mean that there was a pattern—a brood mark—that was not found on this creature's skin? Was there another groeliin like this one with similar markings?

The Antrilii had faced the groeliin for generations. They should be experts in how many broods there were. If they didn't know, then who would?

"What are you expecting to find when you get to the breeding grounds?" Endric asked.

"We expect to find groeliin," Gron said.

"And if there's another one of these groeliin there?" Endric asked.

Nahrsin grinned. "You've already shown how to kill one of these things," he said.

Endric shook his head. "I've shown that you have to be willing to jam a makeshift spear into the back of that massive groeliin, and then you have to be willing to jump on its back."

Nahrsin nodded. "Those are both excellent strategies. Neither are typical for the Antrilii, which I think is why an outsider was so successful."

Endric tapped the section of groeliin skin he had cut free. "I think we need to be prepared for the possibility that there is another one of these. I think we have to prepare that there are more broods than you realize."

"We've hunted the groeliin for hundreds of years," Gron said.

Endric looked at him, meeting his gaze. "I know."

"You think that you can tell us how to hunt the groeliin?" Gron watched him, the frown on his face difficult to interpret with the dark paint he wore.

"I don't claim to know more about the groeliin than the Antrilii. What I do know is what I've seen. I faced these creatures," Endric said, waving the section of flesh at Gron. "Nahrsin saw them. He was there when we burned the body. Bodies. I'm not sure what to make of the fact that there are these other groeliin, or what these markings on their skin mean, but I recognize that that there are probably more to the groeliin than even the Antrilii understand."

"Uncle, think about what we've seen. Think about—"

"I am thinking about what we've seen. And Dendril's son is right. There is more taking place than what we can understand."

"Should we still make this journey?" Nahrsin asked.

"What other choice is there? If these creatures are responsible for controlling the merahl, we have an obligation to help them. They are as much our vow as facing the groeliin are."

Nahrsin nodded, but Endric could tell that he had a distraught look on his face, one that told Endric that he wasn't certain whether continuing north was going to get them answers or get them killed.

Yet there was something that he agreed with that Nahrsin might not fully understand. With what Endric had seen, he thought that *he* understood. How could they not try to reach the breeding ground when the merahl might need their help?

25

It was around midday, and they had been traveling up a fairly rapid incline, the constant wind no longer something Endric could ignore. Now even the laca fur could no longer protect him. The Antrilii seemed to move easily, not struggling with either the steepness of the grade or the cool bite to the air.

The merahl cub didn't struggle either. He kept pace behind Endric, leaping from rock to rock, never tiring, never slowing. Endric worried for him, thinking that he wasn't getting enough to eat. He fed him jerky the Antrilii provided, but he didn't know how much a cub needed to eat.

He still hadn't seen other merahl. If they were out there, they were silent. Endric assumed they still trailed and followed him, but if they did, he would've expected to see them before now. That he hadn't made him question whether they were still there.

The sun was a haze through thick clouds. Endric continued to think they would eventually pass through the clouds, reaching a point where they would be above them, but that time never came. The mountains continued to stretch upward, and Gron led them on a meandering route through the mountains.

There had been no further sightings of the groeliin, so thankfully no additional skirmishes.

"Why haven't we seen any of the other tribes?" Endric asked.

"The other tribes were coming from different directions," Nahrsin said.

"But I saw one of the tribes moving," he said. "That was the tribe the merahl were reluctant to go to."

Nahrsin glanced over at him. "I think the merahl are reluctant to come to any of us right now. I don't think it mattered which tribe they brought you to."

Endric stumbled over a large rock as the ground start to slip. He jumped forward another step, avoiding a rockslide. He glanced back, but Nahrsin was bringing up the rear, so there were no other Antrilii following them. The merahl cub jumped to the side, avoiding the slide.

"If the merahl were avoiding all the Antrilii, why did they bring me to you?"

Endric hadn't been able to understand why that troubled him, but that seemed to be the key here. The merahl had brought him to Nahrsin and his tribe. They might have avoided the other Antrilii, and they might not have been willing to join with Nahrsin, but they hadn't abandoned Nahrsin—or his tribe —altogether.

Nahrsin shook his head. "I don't know."

They fell silent. As the day passed, Endric began to feel a sense of rising nausea. It came at the pit of his stomach, building slowly. He thought he was hungry at first, but the longer they traveled and chewed on jerky, the nausea didn't seem to abate. Pausing to drink from a water flask didn't make a difference either. The nausea didn't ease. Whatever it was didn't seem related to his hunger.

Was it the altitude?

Endric had known some Denraen recruits to struggle with the height of Vasha as they climbed the mountainside. Could it be that he simply didn't tolerate being this high in the mountains?

He doubted that was the case as he should have been affected before. It wasn't as if he climbed rapidly. He was on foot, and the men that he'd known getting sick had climbed up the road on horseback. There had to be another explanation, and the only one that made sense to him was that there was something else triggering it.

Could it be the groeliin?

Endric checked the cub to see if it was responding to nearby groeliin, but the cub gave no indication any were nearby. That left something else, though Endric didn't know what that something else was.

"Do you feel anything?" he asked Nahrsin.

Nahrsin glanced over at him. "Feel anything? Such as…"

Endric shook his head. What was it that troubled him? Maybe it was nothing. Maybe it was all in his imagination. Maybe it was only a sickness coming over him.

"I'm not sure how to describe it. It's just that… I've begun to feel something off."

Endric could just imagine what his friends back in Vasha would have said were he to make a report like that. How would they have reacted to him telling them that something was off? He could envision Pendin teasing him. Senda would press him, expecting a better report, Listain's servant in all things.

Thinking of them brought pain. He had lost track of how long he'd been gone, but it was long enough that they would have returned to Vasha. Pendin—who had been serving as his steward—would have been given another responsibility. He would have lost the privilege that working with Endric had given him. Senda would have been tasked with assuming control of Listain's network. It was possible that she would even be asked to question Urik, though Endric didn't know whether the others of the Conclave would have demanded their justice. Novan had wanted to exact his revenge for Urik's utilization of the historian guild knowledge. Maybe the Denraen no longer had Urik in their possession.

Endric shook those thoughts out of his head. It did no good thinking like that. He had to survive mountains here, and that was no sure thing. He might be descended from the Antrilii, but he didn't certainly feel like one of the Antrilii, especially as he struggled with what he had to face.

The unsettled sensation didn't leave as they continued their climb.

Endric looked at the cub. "Do you feel anything?" he asked it. The cub twitched its ears, looking back at him.

Endric felt like a fool. Why was he asking a cub what it felt? The merahl cub probably didn't detect anything.

The cub switched its tail and bounded off.

Endric swore under his breath. Had he said something to scare it away?

"Are you going after it?" Nahrsin asked.

Endric shrugged. "I don't know if I'm supposed to go after him. I asked if he sensed anything, and the next thing I know, he's running off."

"The merahl are intelligent. He probably understood you."

"It would be nice if I understood him."

Nahrsin chuckled. "That takes time and a measure of trust. My father had a way of communicating with the merahl who hunted with him."

"When I first met you, I thought the merahl you hunted with were all domesticated."

Nahrsin grunted. "After what you've seen of them, do you think the merahl can be domesticated?"

Endric thought of the creatures he'd experienced. Even those with Dentoun had a certain sort of pride to them. He didn't think they would allow themselves to be domesticated.

"Why is it that you're willing to make this journey with us?" Nahrsin asked.

"What do you mean?"

"This. This hunt. Why is it that you want to make it with us? You have no obligation to do this."

"You've always known your responsibility, but I came to your lands trying to understand mine."

"You would be Antrilii?" Nahrsin asked.

Endric shook his head. "I don't know that I can be both Denraen and Antrilii. My father discovered that when he left and became an oathbreaker to your people."

"You know as well as I did do that he never broke his vows. That penance was a farce."

"But Melinda—"

"Melinda was angry."

Endric shook his head. "Melinda was the one who tried to soften the punishment. It was because of her that I was offered the choice of avoiding the penance and simply leaving the Antrilii lands. I made the choice to stay."

Nahrsin shook his head. "You made the choice she wanted

you to make," he said. "It may not have felt like you were forced, but I can tell you that you were."

"You sound like you don't care for her."

Nahrsin tipped his head. "She might be your grandmother, but she's also the reason your father is subjected to the penance. Don't forget that."

Endric sighed. There was so much about the Antrilii that he didn't understand, so much that he wished that he had a chance to comprehend. Maybe now was the chance for him. He'd spent time with the Antrilii and hadn't taken the opportunity to ask questions. Hadn't he *wanted* to reach Nahrsin? He was the one he'd come north hoping to find.

"When the Antrilii aren't hunting, what is it that you do?"

"When we're not hunting, we are training our horses, or practicing the sword. We are becoming better soldiers. I suppose in that way, it's much like you when you're not on patrol."

Endric smiled wistfully. "Patrol is often the most boring part of the Denraen. Most of us prefer the training. At least when we're training—in Vasha—we're able to sleep in the barracks. We have a certain comfort there. On patrol..." Endric smiled to himself, thinking about how eager so many Denraen were to go on patrol, but the moment they were first out there, forced to sleep on the hard ground, beneath the sky, everything seemed to change.

"What happens when we reach the breeding grounds, and no others have come?" Endric asked.

"We will do what we need to. The plan is to find this place, and when we do, we will attack the groeliin breeders."

"Breeders?"

"We think that there are only a few of the groeliin capable of birthing their young. We call them the breeders. The Yahinv call them queens. There are others able to care for the young, but if we're able to eliminate the breeders..."

"That's why you've never been able to completely remove a brood?"

"We have come across a few breeders over the years. They are the most difficult to find. The groeliin fight to keep them protected, attacking with a frenzy when we get too close. If we can reach breeders, we might be able to finally slow the tide of groeliin."

"How did you learn about the breeding location this time?"

"We had word from patrols of groeliin movement. It's too much for anything other than a Chisln. The groeliin only move in numbers like this when it's breeding season. There is a particular behavior to them that we've seen over the years."

"But you've never come across an actual breeding ground."

Nahrsin shook his head. "We've never been able to get through. We've always been pushed back by the broods. There are limits to how much we can do, as there are only so many Antrilii. If we risk too many, others will be in danger."

The cub returned, barking once at Endric. He waved for the cub, motioning him over, but the cub ignored him.

"We need to keep the cub quiet," Nahrsin said. "We can't make too much noise so that we draw the attention of the groeliin. We are in their hunting range now, and it's possible there will be more than we could manage."

Endric went to scoop the cub up, but he started wriggling and scampered off.

Endric swore under his breath and chased after the cub. He didn't want anything to happen to him, not after all he had been through to keep him safe.

He was forced to climb along the slope of the mountain face. He slipped as he went, losing traction over the rock, and got caught in a patch of snow. Unlike the last time, he slid, unable to control his footing, and went slipping down the slope, around the side of the mountain, away from where they had been patrolling.

Endric scrambled for purchase, grabbing at the rock, trying to find some way to slow himself down.

He continued sliding and began picking up speed.

Endric grabbed at the snow, but there was nothing for him to hold onto. He continued sliding down the side of the mountain. He jabbed into the snow, punching at it, but each time he did, he wasn't able to grab onto it.

With another punch, his hand remained. He stuck in the ice.

Endric breathed out, hazarding a look up the slope.

He had fallen a long way. Long enough that he couldn't even see where he'd started the fall. Would Nahrsin even come looking for him? Would any of the other Antrilii?

Would it matter? He had slipped far enough that he wasn't sure how he would even get back to them.

Holding onto the face of the mountain, Endric jammed his boots to maintain purchase and turned around so that he could see where he had fallen. Far below was a wide valley. Along the sides of the nearby mountains, Endric noted dark openings—caves—scattered along the mountain face.

As he remained lodged where he was, trying not to slide any further, he noticed movement.

Not movement. Dark swirls of fog.

The fog appeared out of place, and it took a moment to realize why that was. He thought that he understood the nausea in his stomach as well. It was nausea that didn't leave, that stayed with him, that threatened him so that he almost wanted to retch.

All across the base of the valley were dozens and dozens of groeliin. There were probably several hundred of the creatures swarming through the valley.

Endric held his breath, afraid to so much as breathe.

How was he supposed to get out of here without getting noticed by them?

26

The rock held Endric in place, and he looked around, searching for some way to hide. The moment the groeliin noticed him, he would be in trouble. For now, it appeared they hadn't spotted him in spite of the noise he must have made sliding down the rock.

He contemplated how he could move. There was nothing he could do to get free, not without gaining the attention of the groeliin. The only thing that seemed to protect him so far was the camouflage of the laca fur.

Endric took a moment to examine the groeliin. There were dozens here, and they were all the twisted forms, with the strange gray hide, leaving him with a sense of bald flesh that he knew was not completely accurate. Those nearest to him had marks on their arms—brood marks. Given as many groeliin as he saw, had he come upon a single brood, or was this more than one, much like what he'd encountered when he'd found the merahl cub?

While watching, he saw a thicker band of dark fog appear near the mouth of one of the caves.

Endric's breath caught. He'd seen this before from the larger groeliin. The creature appeared, massive even from a distance, and the shapes on the creature's body were identifiable. They seemed like deep red welts.

That would make a second one of these creatures that he had now seen.

How many were there? If these were completely different markings than the last, that would mean nearly two dozen more broods. Nahrsin hadn't thought there were many more broods than that, but was it possible the Antrilii had completely underestimated the number of groeliin they faced?

And if that were the case, they were in more danger than they realized. If there were twenty broods marked on the flesh of the one large groeliin, and if this one had another twenty brood marks, how many more would there be?

If each brood had even fifty in it, the numbers were staggering. They were enough to pose a threat to not just the Antrilii, but to those outside of the Antrilii range. That was the reason the Antrilii patrolled, the reason they worked to defend and prevent the groeliin from reaching the south, but even while doing that, they hadn't known how many groeliin broods there were.

Endric continued to scan, running his eyes along the valley. It seemed as if the pathway swept around, but if that were the case, would the Antrilii eventually make their way here?

Would they have enough notice that they were heading toward this many creatures?

Endric had seen the Antrilii fight and seen how brutally

effective they were, but this would be too many for them to withstand.

If they still had the merahl hunting with them, they would have a better chance. Endric needed to somehow alert the Antrilii.

Anything he did would put him in danger. He would be forced to fight, and with the numbers of groeliin he saw, he doubted he would last very long. There were far too many for him to overcome.

And then there was the larger groeliin. That one posed a greater challenge than the others. Endric didn't think he'd be able to easily combat him; he'd only survived by chance the last time. He still had his spear, but there was no other defense.

What he needed was merahl help.

Two of the groeliin neared him. Endric remained pinned to the rock, the laca fur standing out from the snow. So far, they still hadn't noticed him.

He stared at the markings on their arms. This one had something like interlocking squares. Both were the same. They were raised, as if burned on. When the creatures moved past, Endric let out his breath. He had been afraid to move when they were so close, afraid to do anything other than watch.

Another small band approached to his right. As they neared, Endric noted a different marking on their arms. This was something like a zigzagging pattern that ended with a straight line.

Did the brood marks only identify them to each other, or did they have other meanings? Could the brood marks be some way of giving them power?

Endric turned toward the east. His gaze settled on the trail where the Antrilii would come through this mountain pass.

How much longer did they have before something happened here? How much longer before the Antrilii appeared? They wouldn't have the merahl cub to make noise, not like they had when he had discovered the other heavily marked creature.

There were shapes near the rock, and Endric hesitated, making his way toward them. When he did, he nearly froze.

Antrilii.

Dozens of Antrilii, all with the same blue coloring, and all lying dead.

Had the groeliin come across an entire tribe of hunters and slaughtered them?

As much as he wanted to investigate, he didn't dare. He noted movement near him. He looked over and saw one of the dark-skinned groeliin making its way gradually toward him.

Had he been seen?

The groeliin worked its way up the side of the mountain, moving more quickly, but in a direction that seemed as if it might move beyond him. Would it pass him altogether?

He rolled toward a large boulder that would block him from its view.

It was a gamble. All Endric wanted was to draw the attention of the single groeliin, not those down in the valley.

The gamble paid off. The groeliin paused and started toward him. As it came close, it hissed. Endric stabbed with the sword, driving it up to the hilt, and the hissing stopped suddenly. Endric withdrew his sword when the groeliin stopped twitching and shifted his attention back to the valley.

One of the nearest bands had paused and began making its way toward him.

Endric had made a mistake.

He rolled around the side of the boulder. On the other side, the ground sloped down, snow and ice creating a smooth sheet. If he took this, he would reach the floor of the valley and possibly not have a way out.

The band came closer.

Endric stepped over the edge and slid down it until he reached the valley.

The suddenness of his movement drew the attention of the band, and one of them hissed. Endric ran toward the opposite end. He knew the movement would draw the attention of the groeliin, but he had no choice.

The nearest groeliin hissed, and Endric avoided turning back, not wanting to see what it might do as it came toward him. The valley tapered at the end, and he thought he could escape that way.

He hazarded a glance back, looking over his shoulder. The groeliin moved quickly, the rock not slowing them as much as it did him, and gained on him. The nearest two had long, brutal-looking clubs. One of them was spiked much like the one Endric had claimed from one of the groeliin. The others were armed with long sticks that were like clubs, but Endric wondered if they would wield them more like a staff.

As he neared the what he thought was the end of the valley, where he had thought the ground tapered off, leaving him a place to escape, he realized there was no way for him to get free.

When he looked back, there were dozens of groeliin after him now.

With his heart racing, Endric did the only thing he could think of: he ran into one of the nearest caves.

He waited near the mouth of the cave, ready for an attack. All he needed was to combat the groeliin as they came in. At least here he could control the flow somewhat. He could avoid being overwhelmed by them. If he did this, he could take them on one by one, or even two on one if it came to that.

The first groeliin appeared at the entrance to the cave and Endric slashed at it, knocking the club from its grip and the creature cutting down.

The next one was the same. As they fell, another one replaced it, and Endric continued to attack, the movements of the sword growing more fluid the longer he worked. That had been lost to him in the time since he left the Denraen. He had missed the practice and had missed the art of using the sword. Now that he was here, he allowed himself to fall back into the empty mindset that he had to have to be an effective fighter. He flowed through the movements. Each one felt natural, each one led him to the next, and he cut down five more groeliin.

The entrance to the cave was littered with bodies.

The smell became nearly unbearable. The stench from the fallen groeliin drifted up to him, so much worse in death than in life. He would have held his breath, but the effort of fighting left him winded. He would've thought that the days spent hiking through the mountains would have kept him fit, but that didn't seem to be the case.

Two more groeliin appeared, and Endric sliced through them.

Then the attack ceased.

Endric waited, thinking that he needed to be ready for another onslaught. That he needed to be ready for something.

Nothing came.

He listened and heard movement outside the cave. He didn't dare risk going to the entrance, didn't dare risk looking out to see what the groeliin might be preparing. He might have killed ten of the horrible creatures, but hundreds more had to remain. An entire brood. Several broods.

He shook himself, staggering back into the cave. A hissing began outside the mouth of the cave, a horrible sort of sound that grated on his ears, leaving his head pounding.

Endric retreated into the cave. As he did, his eyes began to adjust.

There should be no light here, but he had a sense of warmth, something that he hadn't noticed before. There was a faint, dark glow to the walls that reminded him of the teralin that he'd seen when meeting with Pendin's mother.

His breath caught. Could there be teralin in these mountains?

The idea seemed almost too much to believe, but there was no mistaking the warmth that he felt. For there to be this sort of warmth around him, there had to be some explanation, and teralin made a certain sort of sense. The outside of the cavern was cold. The wind this high up in the mountains had been almost bitterly so. In here was practically pleasant.

The only thing that made it less so was the stench in the air.

Endric moved deeper into the cave. There was probably a dozen—possibly more—caves scattered around the base of the valley. Were all of them made of teralin ore?

As he thought about it, he began to have a different question. Was it possible that the caves were not natural caves? Could these be mines?

He continued along the cave, heading deeper into it. He knew he should stop, that he should wait and find a way to fight his way free. He'd already experienced the horror of remaining trapped in caves with no clear escape route, but he didn't want to risk staying too close to the mouth of the cave. At least in here, he could continue to hide, though he could do nothing more than that. He might be able to hide, to keep away from the groeliin at the entrance of the cave, but he didn't have any way of getting out. He would be trapped here.

At least in the mines beneath Vasha, there was a hope of escape. At least there, he knew that if he were to remain long enough, he would be able to find his way out. That wasn't the case here.

He noticed a shifting of the lights near the mouth of the cave and continued backward. If the groeliin chased him in, how long could he fight them off? How long would he be able to face them while in the cave?

How long until the Antrilii reached the valley?

The farther back he went, the more he began to feel another rising sense of nausea.

The last time he had felt it had been related to the groeliin.

Endric turned, taking a moment to survey the cave. If he had to fight, he wanted to have a sense of his surroundings.

The shifting darkness that he'd seen—the trail of lights along the walls—persisted, and he noticed it more strongly deeper into the cave. Now that he was here, now that his eyes adjusted, it was easier for him to see it. He wasn't certain exactly what it was, but the warmth of the tunnel made it likely that it was teralin. If it were dark like this, then Endric worried it was negatively charged.

What would it take to negatively charge an entire cavern of teralin?

More than he could fathom. When they had gone to Thealon, they had changed the polarity of the teralin there, but that had been with Tresten's assistance. This would be something much more, and Endric didn't think he would be able to do enough to counter it.

He continued back along the wall, keeping his hand trailing along the rock. It was smooth rather than jagged. Could it have been carved out by man?

The cavern continued much deeper than he thought. He continued into it, following the strange dark glowing, and realized that as he did, as his eyes continued to adjust to the darkness, he saw the shadowed outline of something in the distance.

Endric hesitated. What was it that he saw?

Sound from behind made him spin. The groeliin seemed to have started into the cave.

He hurried forward, toward the darkness he saw in the distance.

There, he froze. It took his eyes a moment to adjust and for him to realize what it was that he saw. He still wasn't certain that his mind was able to wrap around it.

An enormous groeliin sprawled along the wall. What appeared to be a dozen smaller creatures were there. A stench in the air seemed to emanate from that.

Endric recognized that was also the source of his nausea.

As his mind began to comprehend what he was seeing, he realized what it was.

He looked back, understanding why there had been so many groeliin here. It was the same reason there were so many in the mountains around here.

He had somehow come upon the groeliin breeding ground.

27

E ndric crept slowly forward. The only other option was to head back through the cave, back toward the groeliin waiting at the mouth of the cavern. He didn't want to risk that. This way, at least there was the possibility that he could find an alternative way out.

He expected to see other groeliin, but there didn't appear to be any. There was only the single breeding groeliin. It—she?—lay prone, slightly propped against the wall, her grotesque neck peering into the darkness. The small creatures around it—her—moved with a dark energy. Endric couldn't tell what they were doing, whether they were suckling on teats and feeding or something else was taking place.

Nahrsin had mentioned how difficult it was to find the breeding grounds, and how the groeliin had seemed to move undetected, and now Endric suspected he understood why. They occupied a series of mines.

All of the searching and he had somehow stumbled upon the breeding ground.

It didn't seem right that he should be the one to find it. The Antrilii had fought groeliin for generations, so for him to be the one to have discovered it felt unfair.

The creature seemed to watch him, though Endric couldn't tell. The dark glowing light, a faint blackness with a tinge of purple to it, surrounded him and surrounded her.

Was she watching him?

Endric moved forward with more speed.

He stared at the breeding groeliin, feeling waves of nausea come over him as he did. Endric licked his lips, swallowing, forcing down a rising bile.

Rarely had he felt so unsettled. Then again, rarely had he been so afraid. Standing here, alone amidst all of these foul creatures, he felt nothing but terror.

He continued forward, and the groeliin began hissing even more loudly.

Endric continued toward the groeliin, holding his sword clutched in hand, trying to decide what he should do. These were young groeliin, but were they born evil or did something that the groeliin do to them turn them that way over time? Was it possible that they could be saved?

He reached the offspring. They didn't pay him any attention, giving Endric the chance to examine them. They appeared to chew on something, though he couldn't tell what it was.

The nearest groeliin offspring had a mark already branded on its arm.

Whatever branding did was a part of the groeliin indoctrination and had already taken place. Did that mean that the groeliin were already twisted?

The infant looked up at him and hissed.

The sound was soft, like a painful scream, one that reminded him of a child screaming. It flashed its teeth, and Endric realized that blood dripped from them.

He looked down, studying what thing was feeding on.

An arm.

A memory of the fallen Antrilii came to him, and nausea rolled through him, this time separate from the groeliin.

He looked at each of the feeding creatures and realized they all appeared to feed off body parts. Were they fed this by the breeding groeliin?

Endric continued forward, and all the young began hissing.

The groeliin female watched him, her malevolent eyes trailing after him.

Endric noted that she wore three markings across her chest. Each was the same.

Did that matter?

He didn't know, but they were the same on the groeliin young.

He stabbed the female in the heart.

The young continued to feed on the body parts, and Endric backed away, not able to even look at the creatures.

Movement toward the end of the tunnel drew his attention, and he backed away even faster. There was the sound of scuffing along the rocks, and he spun and realized that another groeliin stood there. This one carried a long, slender rod that glowed a soft orange.

The branding rod.

Endric's eyes widened.

The groeliin hissed.

Endric darted forward, swinging his sword in a sharp arc.

The groeliin caught the sword with the rod, deflecting him down.

Endric spun, falling into his patterns. Had he not fought the groeliin at the mouth of the cavern, he might not have been able to do so as easily as he did now. But he had shaken free the rust from lack of practice. He attacked, but each time, the groeliin caught his sword, twisting him down.

Endric rolled, spinning in a movement that he'd learned from Senda while practicing the staff, and sliced up, severing the groeliin's arm. It dropped the rod, and Endric spun once more, taking off its head.

When the groeliin fell, he noted that its body was covered with brood marks.

Was this another creature like the one he'd killed before?

How many more would he find there? The Antrilii had not seen them before, and Gron believed them to be rare, but that didn't seem to be the case at all.

Other groeliin made their way down the cave, coming toward him. Endric didn't risk staying where he was any longer, afraid to remain.

What choice was there?

He turned and headed deeper into the cave.

The walls glowed and seemed to intensify the farther he went, almost like the power of the darkness itself began to increase in intensity. The warmth didn't change, a steady, constant sense that Endric felt deep within him. The hint of nausea persisted, and the deeper into the cave he went, the more he hoped that it would fade, but it never truly did.

He looked around and noticed something else along the wall. He approached it carefully and saw what appeared to be fur. It wasn't groeliin—what fur they had didn't look like this clump of bloodied fur—and not laca. Another clump was near it.

Merahl.

A cub.

It was too small to be the cub he'd traveled with, but had the groeliin been trapping cubs for other purposes? Why would they?

He heard sharp hissing beneath behind him, and he paused. The groeliin were there and must have reached the female.

Would they chase him into the cave or would they think that he'd been killed?

He watched the shadows, wondering if the groeliin would make it this way. At least here he had the darkness to conceal him. Thankfully, he saw no movement.

Endric continued backing deeper into the caves, trying to keep the sense of the groeliin in front of him. For some reason, they didn't continue toward him.

He reached a turning point in the cavern, pressing his back against the wall, and hesitated. Did the groeliin remain where they were?

He had come across the breeding grounds, which meant he had found something that none of the Antrilii had found before —at least not found and survived. If *he* survived—and with as many groeliin as were out in the valley, he didn't know whether he would—didn't the Antrilii need to know more about the breeding grounds?

So far, he knew that the breeding grounds were these caves. He knew that there was teralin in the walls. He knew that the young groeliin fed off bodies scavenged by the groeliin. He knew that the females were essentially immobile when they birthed their young. And he knew there was evidence of the merahl in the caves.

Other than that, what did he know? Was there something about the teralin mines that was necessary?

Endric took a deep breath while debating what he should do.

As he did, he heard movement.

He held his breath, making a point of not moving anything, daring not to do anything but listen. With the female dead, would the groeliin remain, or would they return to the rest of the groeliin outside?

What else could he do?

He felt as if he *should* do something more, find some way of gaining information that might help the groeliin in the future, but what could he do by himself?

An idea came to him that put him at risk, but it was one that might actually matter for the Antrilii, something that gave them the potential for peace that they had never had.

As he thought through his plan, he wondered—could he reach the other females? Could he destroy them so they couldn't breed anymore?

Could he survive long enough to make a difference?

D arkness completely concealed Endric as he crept
forward. The only sound in the cavern was that of his
steady breathing. He no longer heard the soft scuffling that he
attributed to the groeliin, and he no longer noticed the soft
hissing that he had heard when the groeliin—and the newborns
—were there.

He lost track of time, not sure how much had passed since
he had first come to the cavern or since he had killed the
female. Should he have attacked the groeliin offspring as well?
By leaving them alive, they would grow up to be creatures who
would assault the Antrilii. It might've been simpler simply to
remove that threat now.

Endric shook himself, his mind starting to drift. He was
exhausted but didn't dare allow himself to relax. He would have
to suffer another sleepless night—or longer—if he intended to
make it through this foolhardy plan.

The only thing that remained was the steady, dark light of

the cavern. The longer he was here, the less question there was that he was surrounded by negatively charged teralin. Endric had to push away the oppression and the sense that came from it and force himself to ignore the dark thoughts that came with it. Doing so was a constant struggle, but it became easier the longer that he was here.

Or was it?

Maybe the teralin began to influence him much like it had done so to Novan and Brohmin. Maybe he was starting to feel the influence of it.

He didn't think that was the case but tried to harden his mind, using his Denraen training to seal away those thoughts. Were he less tired, he thought it might be easier. As it was, he struggled to push away that darkness and managed only to leave himself with a hint of the sense of the dark teralin.

Endric paused where he'd left the dead female and her offspring. He stared into the darkness, looking for evidence that any groeliin remained, but nothing moved.

Endric crept forward and saw the female lying where he'd left her. Surprisingly, there were seven offspring lying next to her, unmoving.

Endric frowned. Why should the offspring have perished?

Unless she'd been feeding them.

That didn't make sense. They'd been feeding on the body parts. What would she have been feeding them that he would've taken away through his presence?

The body of the larger groeliin was missing. The head remained, which Endric thought strange, but the body—including the arm—was gone.

Why would the groeliin take the creature with them?

He made his way carefully through, heading back toward

the opening in the cave. Had the groeliin abandoned searching for him? Did they decide that he was either not going to be found or that it was not worth their time to search for him? Or was there something else?

When he reached the mouth of the cave, he saw that the bodies of the groeliin he'd killed remained.

Endric frowned. They had taken only the creature with the markings. They left both the dead female and the bodies of these others, those that he could only describe as soldiers.

Why did they value that one more than the rest?

And *did* they value it? Or was it the markings on the creature that they valued?

He crept forward, pausing at the mouth of the cave.

Darkness had fallen. He wasn't certain what to expect out in the clearing, not certain whether the groeliin would continue to patrol. That was the only description for what they had done before.

There was minimal movement. Endric was surprised to find the groeliin sleeping in clusters, similar to how they had patrolled. He wouldn't be shocked to learn that they remained clustered within their broods.

Would he be able to move quietly enough to the next cave?

That was his plan, but doing so would be dangerous. He should have asked Nahrsin how the groeliin hunted. He thought of other animals he'd faced, though the more he learned of the groeliin, the less he thought of them as simple animals. They were smarter than the Antrilii let on. Did they use sight or smell to hunt? Maybe it was movement that alerted them.

He hoped the laca fur had camouflaged him, but for what he planned, he needed something more than just the fur.

Endric turned to one of the bodies, holding down the rising bile that threatened him and cut into one of the bodies, smearing its blood on his arms and face. The odor was tremendous, but maybe it would be enough to help conceal him as he made his way toward the next cave.

Endric started out of the cave. The night swallowed him. He moved carefully, staying close to the rock. A hint of wind blew through the air, but not so much that it pulled on his laca covering. It forced the stench of the groeliin blood up into his nose, nearly making him retch again. He had to breathe through his mouth, but even that was not much better.

He kept his eyes on the patrol that ranged on the far side of the clearing.

In spite of the fact that the groeliin slept openly as they did, and the fact that they didn't seem to have any form of communication, this had the appearance of a coordinated camp. The patrols at least made it seem like they were coordinated.

If he managed to stay clear of the patrol, he was hopeful that he could make his way to the next cave entrance.

He stepped as lightly as possible, wishing again for the fur-lined boots he had made from the laca. At least with those, he had had an easier time with moving quietly. The Antrilii boots had supple soles, and they were comfortable and warm enough, but he didn't fit as well into them.

He noticed the next cavern about two dozen paces from him.

The patrol turned back toward him.

Endric froze. If they noticed him now, he would have to either make a run for it again, or he would have to retreat into the tunnel he'd come from. He doubted that they would abandon the chase quite as easily the next time.

The patrol moved toward him. It was a cluster of three groeliin. Like all of the creatures he'd seen in the valley, this one had the faint black fog surrounding them. It wasn't enough to obscure his ability to see them, though. The three groeliin carried long clubs. All three had scraps of drab black fabric tied around their waists. They headed straight toward him before swinging back around, looping toward the opposite side of the clearing.

Endric let out a breath.

They hadn't noticed him.

He still didn't know whether it was concealment from the groeliin blood or whether it was the furs. Either way, he had the reprieve.

He continued toward the next cavern. When he reached the mouth of the cave, he ducked inside and made his way carefully along it.

Much like the first one, this cave had smooth walls, and Endric suspected that teralin had been mined here previously. Had Antrilii mined it or had it happened long ago?

The heat pressed upon him and the walls glowed with a soft, dark energy, much like the last cavern did.

As he reached the back of the cavern, he saw what he suspected would be here.

Another female lay propped against the wall. Unlike the last, she had no offspring around her. Her belly was full and fat, and it writhed from the offspring inside her.

Endric move forward carefully, watching for signs of both her awareness of him as well as another of the strange, heavily marked, groeliin.

It took a moment, but he saw the massive groeliin first.

The creature stood, watching the female, his back toward

Endric. Endric crept forward, and—before the groeliin could realize he was there—he powered through a sharp arc, taking off the groeliin's head.

Endric raced forward and stabbed the female before she could hiss and make noise that would alert any of the others.

Endric's heart beat faster. Was he a murderer or was he doing necessary work now?

Either answer felt correct.

He headed toward the mouth of the tunnel, preparing to move on. He didn't know if he'd be able to make his way all the way around the breeding ground, but that was his intent.

Endric reached the mouth of the cavern. The patrol was on the far side of the clearing. Endric kept along the wall, moving slowly. He was determined not to make noise, determined to make it to the next cavern before the groeliin caught sight of him. This next one was closer.

Endric ducked inside, and two groeliin converged on him soon as he stepped inside.

Endric attacked, slicing through the first, managing to avoid a spiked club colliding with the side of his head as he spun away. He jabbed at the next, stabbing the groeliin in the gut. It caught the creature, and he sliced up, disemboweling him.

Only then did Endric realize that he'd been struck. The club had pierced his shoulder, having penetrated through the outer layer of the thick leathers.

He pried it free, and his arm throbbed where it had pierced him.

Endric made his way down the tunnel, cursing himself. He had been foolish. He had one experience where he thought he'd been safe and had let his guard down. Because of that, now he had an injury that made him fear he might be limited in his attacks.

Near the back of the cavern, Endric received another surprise.

Three groeliin waited.

It was almost like they expected him. As soon as he appeared, they converged. Endric stepped back, getting himself into his forms, following patterns that helped to settle his mind. He beheaded the first groeliin and was quickly moving on to the second when he was struck from behind.

Endric spun and nearly dropped his sword.

A man attacked him with a long length of staff.

Endric danced away, cutting down one of the groeliin as he did.

Another person appeared, this one a woman. Like the man, she carried with her what appeared to be nothing more than a tree branch, much like Endric had used a branch when he first had been released into the mountains.

As he adjusted to the fighting, he realized both the man and the woman were naked.

Had they been sent on a penance?

They stared at him, eyes seemingly glazed.

He noticed a flicker of movement and Endric spun, realizing that the third groeliin attacked from the side.

Endric danced around, spinning so that he put the groeliin between himself and the people. They seemed to be attacking on behalf of the groeliin, and he wanted to understand what was happening before he harmed them.

The groeliin fell, cut down quickly with the sword.

These weren't the massive groeliin, and these were not

anything particularly powerful, but they had nearly over-whelmed them simply because they had surprised him.

With the groeliin dispatched, the two people remained.

Endric hated the idea of attacking them, but they both came at him, swinging their makeshift clubs at him.

Endric didn't have to kill them.

He grabbed the spear that he had strapped to his back, and swung this, connecting with the woman. He hit her on the side of the head, not using all of his force. She crumpled. The man lunged toward him, and Endric spun the staff, striking the man. He fell as well.

The female groeliin sat at the back of the cavern. This was different than what he'd seen with the others. A dozen or so offspring crawled around, most of them clinging to the ground.

As he approached, he wondered what was it about the caverns that the females needed to breed here.

Endric stabbed the female, piercing her heart.

The offspring started hissing, much like they did when he had killed the first female.

Endric grabbed the spear and clubbed each of the infants until they stopped hissing.

He needed to know why they were here, why they chose this place for their breeding. He shifted them, sliding them away from the female. There was nothing clear, no obvious reason for their presence here that he could determine.

Was there something about the position of the female?

Endric sheathed his sword, strapped the spear to his back as he had before, and dragged her off to the side.

As he moved her, he noted a surge in the dark light of the cavern.

Teralin.

Not just teralin, but dark teralin. Negatively charged teralin. She'd been sitting on it.

Was she trying to protect it?

Was there something else here that he didn't fully understand?

As he watched, he realized there seemed to be a thready connection from the teralin to the female. It grew weaker rapidly.

Endric frowned. He took groeliin's arms and rolled her, and gasped.

Dozens upon dozens of markings had been made on her back. Unlike the heavily marked groeliin, these were blackened rather than raised in red. These appeared to be tattooed into her, as if the teralin had been infused under her skin.

His gaze drifted toward the teralin, and he had to wonder: Was she somehow drawing power from the teralin in the tunnels?

Was that what she was feeding to the groeliin offspring?

Maybe that was the reason the groeliin he'd seen all had the hazy clouds around them. Maybe that was why they were so difficult to kill. Maybe that was why the breeding grounds had to be here.

Endric had to change his plan. He couldn't risk himself, trying to slaughter all the breeding females. Injured as he was, he might not survive. What he'd discovered was simply too important.

He had to get this information to Nahrsin and to Gron, which meant he had to live.

He had to get back to the Antrilii.

29

A s he neared the end of the tunnel and could see out, Endric could tell the scene in the clearing was much different. The groeliin were awake. The patrols were more agitated. The creatures made their way around the clearing in pairs and triplets, all searching.

Endric stayed close to the rock, afraid to move. If the groeliin realized he was there, he would face more attackers than he could handle.

There still were probably a dozen different caves he hadn't reached. A dozen groeliin females that would continue to breed, and would continue to create offspring that would attack the Antrilii, and would continue to destroy.

Endric didn't move. There was no need to retreat—not yet. They didn't seem to know he was there.

But there was no good place for him to go, either. He could retreat deeper into the tunnels, but all that would do would place him away from the groeliin and keep him trapped. Endric needed an escape.

A grouping of four groeliin came in his direction. Two carried clubs while two seemed unarmed.

Endric realized the patrols moved into each of the cave mouths.

When they discovered the other females had been killed, how would the response change?

He focused on the groeliin coming his way. Why were two of them unarmed?

All of the groeliin he'd faced—all that he had fought for so far—had been armed in some way. Was there *another* kind of groeliin coming toward him?

He remained off to the side of the cave mouth. When they entered, Endric let them pass. Somehow, they hadn't noticed him.

He followed them, moving quietly as they went deeper into the cavern.

Endric waited until they were nearly toward the end of the cave when they were close to the discovering the dead female, then he lunged.

He stabbed, catching the first groeliin in the back. The other stepped away, and he missed as he swung through his form, but struck one of the lead groeliin, chopping off his arm.

The groeliin hissed, the sound painfully loud in his ears, likely gaining the notice of the others outside the cave.

Endric jabbed, catching the other groeliin in the gut, and it doubled forward, sliding up the length of his blade.

Endric's hand got caught, and he was forced to drop the sword.

He was struck in the back and staggered forward.

He managed to catch himself and turned quickly, noting that the remaining groeliin stood near him. He attacked bare fisted. The creature struck him again, catching him in the shoulder. Endric spun, not able to reach for either his sword or for the spear.

The groeliin kicked, catching Endric in the side.

He lost his breath and grunted.

Endric doubled over, and the groeliin kicked him in the head, sending him flying backward.

He tried reaching for a weapon, anything, but he lost the club somewhere, and he couldn't reach for a spear.

The groeliin kicked again. Endric managed to duck and avoid getting struck in the head once more. He spun, careful to stay out of reach. He felt to the side, and there he came upon one of the clubs the people had carried with them.

Endric jerked it free from their grip, not caring which one—the man or the woman—he took from.

When the groeliin kicked again, Endric swung the club and managed to catch his leg, striking enough that he spun the creature around.

It gave Endric a chance to remove the spear in his back, and Endric jabbed with it, connecting with the creature's shoulder.

The groeliin jerked and freed itself.

He lunged forward, slamming the club at the creature's head. He managed to connect, but the groeliin didn't fall, not as the others had.

Endric clubbed the groeliin again, and this time he connected with its nose, crushing it into the skull. Blood poured freely and the groeliin crumpled. Endric swung the club once more and collided with the side of its head.

Finally, the groeliin stopped moving.

Endric let out a shaky breath. He looked for his fallen sword and found it near one of the groeliin. He had to roll the creature to get it free.

There was something different about these groeliin. He was lucky to have killed the first one without it realizing he was there, but he didn't know why it had seemed stronger, possibly faster than the other ones he had faced. Maybe Gron's theory about the groeliin was correct. Maybe they did have some ability that gave them speed or strength.

Endric watched the cave, afraid that there might be more movement there, but he saw nothing.

He started forward and reached the entrance. There was a patrol near him, but they kept their backs to the cave mouth. Groeliin streamed into many of the other caverns before retreating.

They had to know someone was in the breeding grounds—especially after finding one of the females dead. What would they do now that he'd killed *three* of their females?

How many attacks would he be able to withstand? He had barely survived the last one, and his head throbbed where he'd been struck. His body ached. He didn't think he could tolerate another attack like that.

As Endric watched, one groeliin patrol turned toward this cave mouth.

Endric backed up, moving deeper into the cave mouth, and waited.

It didn't take long. The five groeliin entered, only two of them with clubs.

Endric hesitated.

If he attacked, would he be facing a similar creature like the last one that had nearly overwhelmed him? And worse, this time there were three. He might surprise one, which would leave two plus two more armed groeliin.

Endric didn't think he could survive a fight like that.

He remained pressed against the wall of the cave and waited for them to move past.

The groeliin passed him, and he didn't pursue this time.

Endric ducked out of the cave and stood exposed, waiting on the rock. Most of the creatures streaming into the cave mouths went toward the females, leaving them somewhat distracted.

If he were going to escape, he would have to do so now.

Endric inched toward the east part of the valley, toward the slope that wound up, ultimately away from the groeliin. There was at least one more cave he would have to move past, which meant that he would have to move quickly, but he would also have to be careful here so that he didn't get caught.

He still wasn't entirely certain whether they hunted by movement or by smell. Smearing himself with groeliin blood seemed to have concealed him, but he still suspected there was an element of movement that alerted them. Somehow, when he remained perfectly still, they didn't see him.

Endric inched along the rock. His heart hammered and he was afraid that the groeliin would notice him, that they would somehow hear his heart more than anything else.

He prayed to the gods to keep him safe.

The creatures seemed to overlook him. He reached the opening to the next cave mouth.

Part of him wanted to go in and take out another breeding female, wanted to destroy as many of the creatures as he could, but he thought back to a lesson his father had tried to instill in him. He couldn't let anger and hate drive him. He couldn't let emotion drive him. He had to think through things, had to become tactical in his decision-making. Emotion had been what led him to impulsive decisions before. It was possible that his emotion had been the reason he had agreed to the penance before understanding more about it and thinking through it.

A certain amount of emotion was necessary and good, but too much... too much would lead to his death. Already he'd been placed into situations many times because he let emotion motivate him. He could not let it happen again.

Endric glanced down the mouth of the cave and didn't see any groeliin moving.

As he searched the valley, he saw the patrols, but they weren't looking in his direction. Endric hurried across the mouth of the cave.

And then stopped.

Coming from outside of the cave opposite him, on the far side of the valley, was a groeliin unlike any he'd ever seen.

The creature was enormous, taller than any of the others, and as muscular as a blacksmith. Even from here, Endric could see the dark markings along its flesh. Flanking this groeliin were three others, much like the heavily marked ones that Endric had killed before. They seem to be regarding the much larger one.

Endric stood, unable to move, terrified. The groeliin was enormous, but that wasn't the reason he couldn't move. There was a distinct sense of power that radiated from it.

The Antrilii had suggested there might be another with power, one that might be something like the Magi, but Endric couldn't have imagined anything like this. This was a creature out of a nightmare.

As he stood there, not moving, not daring to even breathe, he prayed it wouldn't notice him.

Movement from within the tunnel startled him, and he turned.

Too late, he realized his mistake. That movement was enough to draw the strange, massive groeliin's attention.

It stopped, and the three groeliin around it stopped as well, and they stood almost perfectly still. They formed a triangle around the massive groeliin.

Dark power radiated from it and streaked toward him.

Endric couldn't describe it any differently. It was almost like the dark teralin lanced from it, practically summoned from within it.

Endric ran. He knew that it would draw the attention of other groeliin, but what choice did he have? If he did nothing, he was terrified of what would happen were that groeliin to reach him.

Endric hadn't even reached the end of the valley when he could feel a swarm of groeliin. There was no way he was going to be able to climb the rock sloping upward, and there would be no way he would be able to get himself free.

He turned, ready to fight. Resignation set in. He wasn't going to be able to deliver the information to the Antrilii. They would never know that groeliin used teralin in their breeding. And if they didn't learn, everything he had done would have been for nothing.

As the first couple groeliin approached, Endric noticed the powerful one standing back, watching.

He spun through, connecting with the first two, dropping them. Two more quickly surged forward, replacing them.

Endric sank into his patterns, into the familiarity of them, and embraced the emptiness within his mind that he would need to survive.

Distantly, he was still aware of the other groeliin watching him, almost as if it knew he had no chance of survival. Endric dashed forward, letting the groeliin surround him. He spun, falling through the patterns that he knew. Slicing again and again, bringing down one after another of the creatures. They fell before him.

Endric was struck, and he felt one of the groeliin clubs catch him in the back. The thick furs protected him, but he staggered forward, into the next attack. Between the two, he fell, managing to stay on his feet, but he slammed into one of the groeliin. Endric lowered his shoulder, wanting to knock the creature back to reset his position.

Endric darted back to get into his catahs, and as he did, he felt the groeliin squeeze around him, closing in. Endric screamed, no longer concerned about remaining silent, no longer concerned about anything other than bringing down as many as he could.

He was struck again and staggered to the side.

He charged forward, swinging his sword, forms essentially forgotten as he screamed, knocking down several more groeliin, and was again hit.

Endric fell to his knees.

As he did, the strange, powerful groeliin turned away, as if no longer concerned about him.

Endric stabbed, managing to connect with the nearest creature, and it fell, leaning toward him. Hot blood seeped around him.

He tried to get to his feet but was struck again.

Endric could no longer see straight.

Pain throbbed through him, pain too much like his first encounter with the groeliin.

The creature continued clubbing him, and Endric swung his sword, striking wildly, no longer thinking that he would even connect. He fought out of instinct, doing it out of nothing more than that, knowing that if he did nothing, he would fall.

Distantly, he was aware that he would die regardless. There was nothing that he could do to survive.

He was clubbed again, and as he fell to the side, he jabbed up with the sword, no longer aware when he connected and when he did not.

Pain struck him again, and he tried to swing but didn't know if he managed to connect or not.

His vision began to blacken, and Endric once more tried surging to his knees.

He swung again and knew that he had to have missed.

His ears were ringing. It sounded like a steady cacophony of violence, a slow and steady cry, one that carried with it a call that sounded in time to the throbbing in his head. It filled him, something like a bell constantly gonging around him.

As he lay there, he could no longer tell if it was his head throbbing or if it was something else. The ringing seemed to have a familiarity to it. He was struck again and again.

The ringing persisted.

This time, Endric knew he didn't imagine it.

Merahl?

Could they be coming?

He fought with renewed vigor, somehow managing to sit up again. He swung his sword, blood coating his hand, no longer able to hold the sword. He dropped it and began punching, using his bare fist, much like the groeliin that had attacked him in the cavern.

The steady calling increased, growing louder.

Endric had to continue to fight. He had to fend off this attack. He had to survive long enough for the merahl to reach him. This seemed to be a pack, and if that were the case, there might be enough for him to actually survive.

30

P ain continued, growing more intense with each passing moment. Endric didn't know how he managed to stay conscious, but he willed himself to remain alert. Having lost his sword and forced to attack with fist and foot, he was left weakened, uncertain whether his attacks did anything. Had it even mattered that he'd struck at the groeliin? There were too many for him to face as the swarm of creatures overwhelmed him.

The beating lessened.

Endric tried standing, but his body didn't respond as it should. His muscles didn't work. He fell backward, sinking toward the ground. The darkness seemed oppressive, full, and the rising heat reminded him of the teralin mines in Vasha.

Was he moving?

He opened his eyes but only saw blurred shadows.

Endric punched and was rewarded by a soft whine.

That wasn't groeliin.

Merahl? Had they reached him? Had he managed to stay alive long enough for them to get to him?

It seemed impossible, but then again, so was the fact that he lived. Facing that number of groeliin had been foolish. He should have run sooner—or should have remained in the tunnels until he found a way free or the groeliin departed the valley.

There was pressure against his skin, and it took a moment to realize what he detected.

The merahl licked him.

It was a painful sense at first, one that burned much like the Antrilii salves burned, before that sense faded, replaced by a steady throbbing. The pain in his head eased, and the ringing in his ears abated as well, leaving only the overwhelming body aches.

"Merahl?" The word came out as no more than a grunt, but his voice worked.

He was licked along his face, and the throbbing in his body eased.

Endric managed to open his eyes.

It was dark. The caves had the strange dark glow, that of the negatively charged teralin, and they were warm. How had he made it here?

He looked around him and saw seven of the merahl in a circle around him. They all sat on their haunches, watching him through eyes that glowed softly.

Not only their eyes glowed, but there was something of their fur that had a soft glow as well. Endric stared at it, trying to understand if it was something from his injuries that made him see the glowing—or whether it was real.

If real, it indicated a connection to teralin.

Was that why the groeliin and the merahl were such enemies?

Endric shivered. "The groeliin?"

The merahl watched him and one of the creatures—one with deep rims of dark eyes—stepped forward, lowering his head. The merahl approached and came close enough to basically look into Endric's eyes, meeting his gaze.

"This is the breeding ground," Endric said. "That's why you've been acting strange," he said, thinking that he understood. "You're connected to the teralin and… they did something to your collection of it."

The merahl began to howl softly, and the hackles on their back began to stand on end.

Endric wished he had some way of speaking to them.

No, he wished *they* had some way of speaking to *him*. It seemed that they understood him well enough, but there was no way for him to understand them at all.

The merahl nudged him with his nose.

Endric looked around the cave. What did they want from him? What did they think he could do?

There would be nothing that he *could* do.

"Why not let the Antrilii know what's going on?" he asked.

The merahl nudged him again. Endric stood, not knowing what else he could do and not knowing what the merahl wanted of him. The pain in his body throbbed a moment, and dizziness rolled through him, nearly sending him tumbling to the ground.

One of the merahl—a female with streaks of red fur mixed with silver—pressed against him and Endric leaned on her for support. He closed his eyes, letting the dizziness pass, and it finally did, leaving him with a sense of vague unease.

"Thank you."

The merahl barked softly, and Endric almost laughed. Here he was, alone and likely in one of the groeliin breeding caves, lucky to be alive, and he was talking to creatures that could understand him, but that couldn't speak to him. The idea that the merahl could understand him still shocked him, but not as much as the fact that he was still here. With everything that he'd been through, he *should* be dead. The groeliin had overwhelmed him, and swarmed over him, and had clubbed him to the point where he wasn't able to think clearly anymore, and could do nothing more than beat at them with his fists. Somehow, he was here. Alive.

The merahl took a step away. As Endric still leaned on her, he held onto her fur and was pulled forward. He stepped forward, still holding onto her back. The other merahl shifted their protective ring and maintained their presence around him.

She took another step.

The dizziness faded somewhat, but not entirely, and not enough for him to keep from wobbling as he walked. The merahl remained pressed against him, the heat of her body reassuring and her soft fur somehow soothing.

Endric took step after step, following the merahl, feeling like that was what she wanted of him. They had saved him— twice now—and he owed them.

Only, he didn't know what they would want from him.

The merahl led him deeper into the cave. The dark glow persisted, a steady, almost painful sense that pulsed against him. The air had the warmth from the teralin, but it was touched with a hint of a foul odor, one that reminded Endric of the stench that came from the groeliin's blood. Maybe it was him.

He'd coated himself with the groeliin blood and used it to conceal himself.

But he didn't think so. As he looked at his arm and the laca fur, he could tell that the merahl had licked the blood clean. Had that been all that they'd done? Was there any other reason for them to clean it from him?

The stink wasn't coming from the groeliin blood then.

Was it the teralin that he smelled?

The merahl continued guiding him along the tunnel. As she did, he began feeling stronger, less of the pain and dizziness that he'd been feeling following the attack. His mind began to clear, lurching forward. Should he be worried that he was in the cave again? Should he fear that the groeliin might return—and attack?

Would the groeliin attack with the merahl here? There were enough merahl present that Endric doubted they would. The merahl didn't struggle when facing the groeliin. Now that there were seven here, there should be more than enough to at least give him a fighting chance at getting free.

The merahl continued to push him down the length of the cave. Endric held on to her fur. There was a softness to it. It was not coarse or oily like the laca fur had been. This was soft, almost luxurious. He had held the cub several times but had never thought it quite as soft as he did now.

The cub.

Where had he run off to, leaving Endric behind as he had raced toward the breeding ground? Had the cub known this was where he'd find the groeliin? Was there a different connection here?

"What happened to the little one?" Endric asked the merahl.

The female continued to push him, guiding him along the

cave. Endric gripped her fur, unwilling to let go but feeling a rising concern for what might've happened to the cub.

"Did something happen? Is he okay?

They reached the wider opening, the place where Endric had found the female groeliin.

Endric was feeling well enough that he could stand on his own. He released the merahl's fur and continued into the cavern. His eyes pierced the soft, dark glowing, and he ignored the pressure against him, the soft pulsing that came from the negatively charged teralin. He was surprised to notice that there was a female groeliin here, and even more surprised to realize that she was still alive.

Endric turned, fearing that one of the heavily marked groeliin might be present, but there was no sign of it.

Had the groeliin abandoned this female here?

The merahl whined softly.

Endric glanced back, realizing that the others followed him. They no longer formed a protective circle, but they did trail him in a half circle of protection that guided him forward, giving him no choice but to continue onward, no choice but to continue toward the groeliin.

As he reached her, he saw her pregnant belly writhing much like he had seen with the other. She looked up at him with heavy lids, unmoving.

Endric looked down at the merahl. "What you expect me to do with her? I don't have a sword, not like I did with the others." He felt no remorse over the idea that he might have to kill the groeliin. They were horrid creatures, and they tormented the Antrilii, as well as the merahl.

One of the merahl barked softly, and Endric went back to him.

"I need my sword. Even a club would do." Using a club seemed almost cruel, but he would do it without remorse.

The merahl barked again.

The dark-eyed merahl turned and loped down the length of the tunnel, disappearing.

Endric didn't have to wait long. The creature returned, carrying something.

He stared, realizing that the merahl carried his sword.

He took a step forward, but the rest of the merahl prevented him.

The dark merahl approached, carrying the sword, hilt out so that Endric could take it. The blade was not his own, but it was teralin forged, though darkened.

Could he change the polarity?

He closed his eyes, focusing as he had when doing it before. Endric felt a flash, and a wave of warmth washed through him that he recognized.

When he opened his eyes, the merahl allowed him to take the sword. Relief washed through him.

Surrounded by the darkness, surrounded by the negatively charged teralin, he'd not realized just how much it had influenced him. Now that he held the sword again, one that was comprised of teralin, one that now flowed with the power of a positive charge that he had just placed on it, he was able to withstand the pressure from the negative energy.

He took a deep breath, drawing power from the teralin blade, letting the sense of it fill him. Now that he held the sword again, he looked at the merahl. "What do you want from me?"

The merahl nudged him forward.

Endric stood in front of the female, uncertain. The groeliin hissed at him, its voice dark, violent. Endric ignored it. He held the sword, ready to pierce the groeliin when the merahl nudged him again.

Endric glanced down, frowning.

"What is it? What do you need from me?"

The merahl seem to glow more brightly.

"Is it about the teralin?"

The glowing persisted, and now each of the merahl had a soft glowing to them.

"I know the groeliin rest on top of a collection of teralin. I saw how the females feed the young with the negatively charged teralin."

The merahl stared at him, eyes unreadable.

"I can't change the polarity of this much teralin."

The merahl bared her teeth, letting out a soft growl.

Two of the merahl slipped past him, and they grabbed the breeding groeliin, dragging her away, leaving the spot at the end of the cave uncovered.

Endric looked toward them, wondering if they were going to attack the groeliin, but they only pulled her away.

The female merahl nudged him again.

Endric stood, the merahl nudging him, and his gaze flicked from the pregnant groeliin to the merahl, before finally shifting toward the floor of the cavern.

There, he noted a patch of teralin. It was surrounded by rock, but the exposed area was oblong, and he realized that marks were made in the surface, and those markings resembled the same markings he'd seen on several of the groeliin. These were brood marks.

Endric turned to the merahl, shaking his head. "There isn't anything that I can do. This teralin is all negatively charged. There needs to be someone like Tresten to change the polarity." And even then, Endric wasn't certain whether Tresten would be able to change that much teralin.

The merahl nudged him again, and Endric staggered forward. He touched the surface of the negatively charged teralin, and it felt cold.

Not cold. This was a searing sort of sense, one that was almost wickedly hot.

Endric jerked his hand away.

Could he change it from negative to positive polarity? He'd changed the polarity of teralin in Thealon, but that wasn't nearly as much as what he found here. Could he even do this?

Another glance at the merahl showed that they watched him with what seemed like expectance. He might not think he was able to do this, but the merahl did.

If he failed, would he somehow disappoint the creatures? Would he somehow make it so that they continued to ignore the Antrilii?

Endric knelt in front of the teralin and then glanced at his sword. It was positively charged. Could he use that?

He stood and leaned over the teralin. How could he connect the positive and the negative? How could he change this much?

With sudden inspiration, he jammed the sword into the dark teralin.

Endric wasn't certain whether it would work. He wasn't certain whether the sword would be able to pierce the metal.

It sank in, practically to the hilt.

Endric held onto the hilt and pushed through it.

There was no other way to explain what he did. This was

something that he had felt before when trying to push away the darkness. He did the same now, using the bright energy—the positively charged teralin—to push out.

A trembling sense came through the sword.

Endric felt a rumbling through the earth. It came slowly, building an avalanche of power that began with a steady rumbling, one that shook him, deep within him.

He connected to it, recognizing the teralin. Endric continued to push, feeling the pressure as it shifted, sending whatever connection that he could through it.

The teralin in the ground began to glow. It shifted from a dark, almost painful sort of glowing.

Endric continued to push.

The dark glowing shifted, the shadows within it began to shimmer. As it did, Endric continued to press, continued to push on the power that he could feel. The rumbling around him continued.

Endric gave another push.

And then there came an explosion of color. Positively charged teralin burst beneath him, leaving him staggering with a sense of light and power.

Endric took a step back, releasing his grip on the hilt of the sword. As he did, he noticed that the darkened teralin that seemed to fill the space, that occupied the spot where the groeliin had lain, flickered. As it did, it surged, the darkness changing, shifting, and exploding in a brilliant white light.

That light stretched outward, streaking through the walls, flowing much like the avalanche that Endric felt within himself. As it surged past the groeliin female, she hissed, screaming. The light burned past her.

It reached the recessed area and then continued onward.

Faint white light now raced through the walls, leaving the teralin here now positively charged.

How had he changed the polarity of this much teralin? How could it be possible?

Endric reached for the hilt of the sword, surprised that he could withdraw it. The blade still glowed, the teralin flickering softly.

Endric pushed through it and felt as much as saw the intensity of the light burning more brightly once more.

The merahl howled again.

The female merahl began nudging him, and Endric followed, not knowing what else he could do. Where did she expect him to go?

When he reached the mouth of the cavern, he saw the carnage outside. The merahl had destroyed most of the groeliin. Bodies were tossed aside with huge gashes in their flesh, and these creatures that were so gentle to him had been ruthless when they hunted the groeliin.

Endric returned to the female still pushing on him. "What of the powerful groeliin?" he asked her.

She shook her head. It was a gesture that was so human, but this time he understood. The groeliin had escaped.

Endric sighed and started toward the east end of the valley, toward the mountains that would lead him up and back to the Antrilii. The merahl came around him, blocking him.

Endric frowned. "What do you want from me?"

The merahl nudged him. Endric looked up, saw where the remaining merahl were guiding him, and he understood.

With a sigh and a sense of uncertainty, he nodded and followed them toward the next cave mouth.

There were eleven caves in total. Endric hadn't known how many there would be, not having had a chance to count them when he had first tumbled into the valley. Eleven caverns, and eleven places with the dark teralin that infused the walls. There were eleven places where he repeated what he had done in the first.

Knowing what the merahl wanted of him made the process easier. It was still not a simple thing. The merahl guided him, showed him where they were, and Endric did what was required by sinking his sword into the teralin and pushing.

It felt like physical exertion, but the more he did it, the easier it became, though still not easy. By the second one, Endric was sweating and weak, barely able to stand.

But he went on. What choice did he have? If they did nothing, the groeliin could use the negatively charged teralin for more of the pregnant females. He wasn't certain whether he could stop that by charging these, but the merahl seem to think it was possible. That was enough for him.

Endric had found only one other remaining female. Like the first, they dragged her away, exposing the teralin void in the rock so that he could sink his sword into it. Each one was a struggle.

The merahl changed as he gradually changed the polarity of the caves.

They had been silent, almost somber, as he had started working, but that eased the longer he worked. The merahl began to bark from time to time, acting almost playful as they did. He found them nudging him, almost encouraging him, as he went.

As he worked, he came across the groeliin females he had previously killed. The heavily marked groeliin were missing. When he charged the teralin, the flash of bright white with each one caused the groeliin to burn, as if he ignited them through the changing polarity.

Endric staggered out of the cave, leaving the last one behind. He was exhausted from the effort of it.

He sunk to the ground, finally complete, and rested his head on his hands. His body felt weak, though not nearly as painful as he expected after the beating he'd sustained. The merahl, primarily the female that had been nudging him along, encouraging him, lay down next to him and rested her head on his lap. Endric scratched her ears, wondering whether that would be offensive to her, but she twisted her head so that he could get a better position.

All around him, he could see the entrances to the caves. They all glowed with a soft, almost faint light. The positively charged teralin pressed on him, and he realized that it felt right.

He turned to the merahl. "Now what?"

He'd found the breeding grounds, but he'd lost the Antrilii. More than that, he'd lost the cub who had been his companion through much of this.

So many had been lost. So many Antrilii sacrificed so that they could find the breeding grounds. From what Endric could tell, an entire tribe had been lost.

While sitting there, resting from the overwhelming sense of fatigue that came from somewhere deep inside him, a place that felt less like when he fought with the sword and more like a strange, not quite physical, exertion, he wondered if he would be able to find the Antrilii. Would he be able to reach Nahrsin and his tribe? Would the merahl accompany him, or would they abandon him again?

A soft howling drifted toward him, and Endric looked up to see a cluster of merahl making their way along the rock, coming from the west end of the valley.

The female that had been guiding him sat up. She barked once in response, and the merahl made their way toward him.

As they did, Endric noticed a small form among them.

The cub bounded over to him and jumped onto his lap, lapping at him, licking his face. Endric laughed.

One of the merahls with the cub began making a soft whine. The dark-eyed merahl appeared from behind some rocks and licked her face before trotting off and into the cavern where Endric sat.

He glanced back, wondering what he might be missing, when the female nudged him again.

Endric stood and followed the other two merahl into the cave. Once there, he froze as it sunk in that the female lay on the same spot that the groeliin female had lain.

Why would the merahl want the same place?

As he walked, the newcomer arched her back, and he understood.

She was giving birth.

Was this the reason the merahl had been unsettled?

But why the irritation with the Antrilii?

When the merahl gave birth, the cub that emerged was small and began slowly circling. When the cub settled, it began nursing. The mother's fur began to glow, taking on the same soft white glow that the other merahl had when he had gone with them through the caverns, slowly charging the teralin.

"Is she feeding the cub with the teralin's energy?" Endric asked.

He didn't really expect a response, but the merahl nuzzled against his hand. The smaller cub pushed on his other side, giving him two merahl, both competing for his attention. Endric crouched, petting both of them.

He turned away, leaving the female merahl and her cub to feed. When he stepped outside the other caverns, all had merahl heading into them, most waddling as they made their way in, likely as pregnant as the female who had entered this one.

Had this been nothing more than a competition for breeding grounds? Had the groeliin displaced the merahl? Considering how close this had to be to the Antrilii lands, the merahl would have been here first.

Had Nahrsin known?

No. He couldn't have known. Had he known, they would have not needed to search for the groeliin. They wouldn't have needed to question why the merahl had abandoned the groeliin. Endric didn't know why the merahl had grown angry, but it had to do with these breeding grounds. Did they blame the Antrilii?

What he needed now was to find the Antrilii. Did he share with them what he had discovered?

Endric didn't know if he could. The Antrilii fought the groeliin, and for that, he could explain that he'd found the breeding grounds, but maybe the merahl didn't want him to show the breeding grounds to the Antrilii.

But he could share with the Antrilii that the groeliin used teralin mines, and could explain how they were charged. Maybe he could even find those among the Antrilii who could change the polarity, allow them to hunt, and possibly prevent another similar attack.

Endric sat near the entrance to the cave, resting. He was exhausted, but he would take a moment to recover. And when he was, he would return to the Antrilii. It was time for him to return home.

Endric headed east out of the valley. He thought he would find Nahrsin, as well as the rest of the Antrilii, that day, but he did not. As he walked, he felt a growing sense of unease that made him think he would find the groeliin once more, but it faded, leaving him thinking that perhaps he had been mistaken.

He climbed, and the trail led him on a gradually sloping path that eased around the bend. After a while, Endric was forced to climb up the rock. He found the footing difficult but pushed on. He was determined to reach the Antrilii.

The cub followed him. Endric was thankful for the company but surprised that the cub would follow him now that the other merahl had returned. Then again, every so often, he saw flashes of fur and heard the occasional howl of merahl and knew they weren't alone as they made their way through the mountains. Other merahl were around him.

At the end of the first day after leaving the valley, Endric camped along the rocks. Snow and ice surrounded him, and he shivered, cold despite the laca fur. The cub curled up next to him for warmth. Endric debated starting a fire but decided against it. His stomach rumbled, and he realized that it had been days since he'd eaten. He missed the jerky the Antrilii had with them, and missed the comfort of having someone else he could speak to. As the night grew longer, a pair of shapes appeared in the darkness. Two more merahl came and joined him, curling up on either side of him, giving him warmth. Endric slept, drifting into the kind of sleep that came to him rarely, one that he needed after days spent on the move, never sleeping soundly. Knowing he had the merahl watching him gave him confidence that he could rest.

When he woke, the two merahl that had stayed with him through the night were gone, but he was left with a small rabbit. Endric glanced at the cub, smiling mostly to himself. "I take it you didn't bring this to me."

The cub nudged him, and Endric snorted. Using the sword, he skinned it and started a small fire. Then he roasted the hare until it was done. Endric tossed hunks to the cub, letting him get enough, and then he ate, thankful for the food.

They continued onward, heading east as he followed the trail. As the day went on, Endric still hadn't seen any glimpse of the Antrilii. He should have seen some sign of them by now, shouldn't he? Endric pushed himself, continuing until darkness spread, making it difficult to go on anymore. He camped again, and the cub once more curled up by him, sleeping soundly even before Endric had a chance to sleep. Three adult merahl joined him as he slept again.

When Endric awoke, he was less surprised that another gift had been left for him. This was another rabbit, and much as he had previous morning, Endric skinned it, roasted it, and shared it with the cub.

The days passed like that. After the third day and he still hadn't seen anyone, Endric realized he had to decide. He could either continue searching for the Antrilii, never knowing whether he would reach them, or he could attempt to turn south and begin his journey back to the rest of the Denraen.

There was another option, but Endric wasn't sure that he was willing to risk it. If he did, and if he weren't believed, the Antrilii would quarter him. He had little reason to doubt that the Yahinv wouldn't take that threat seriously.

And yet, the Antrilii needed to know about the breeding grounds. They needed to know how the groeliin used teralin. And they needed to know about the tribe that had been slaughtered.

He thought he understood why his father had made the choice that he had, why he had abandoned the Antrilii when he had embraced the Denraen. He couldn't do both. Endric couldn't serve the Denraen and serve the Antrilii. And he couldn't understand the Antrilii when he was pulled by the Denraen. As much as he wanted to understand who he was, where he had come from, and his ancestors, it simply didn't seem possible.

"What should I do?" he asked the cub. Endric didn't think the cub could answer, especially since the merahl had made it clear that they no longer supported the Antrilii. To his surprise, the cub nudged him in a direction that surprised Endric. The cub wanted him to go north.

Endric said, inhaling deeply of the sharp, cold air, "Are you sure?"

The cub nudged him again, and Endric veered north.

E ndric reached the base of the mountain after two weeks of travel. During that time, he saw no sign of the Antrilii. There was no sign of anyone. He came across tracks, but he was guided by the cub, which led him in a different direction than where those led through the mountains. Endric wasn't certain where he would appear, not knowing where he would emerge from the mountains but trusting the cub—and his nose—to lead him in the right direction.

The mountains gradually changed, slowly sloping northward. The path through the mountains became clear, and he walked with increasing speed, a greater sense of certainty pushing him forward. By the time he emerged from the mountains, he was not nearly as tired as he would have expected. He had eaten reasonably well, fed by merahl as they provided him a morning meal. Early on, it had been rabbit every day. As he neared the base of the mountains, there was a little more diversity, with some squirrel and even a few small creatures he didn't recognize.

While in the mountains, he'd been more comfortable with the merahl joining him each night, providing not only protection but warmth, and now that they had left the mountains— and the merahl—he started feeling more unsettled. It was a natural sense, one that had nothing to do with what he'd felt of the groeliin and everything to do with the sense that he risked himself by returning to the Antrilii. And yet, in the time that he'd descended from the mountains, he had grown increasingly certain he was making the right decision.

Endric was surprised that the cub had remained with him, especially with the other merahl coming along. When Nahrsin and Gron had claimed that the cub bonded to him, Endric hadn't been certain what that meant. He still wasn't, but he did believe that there was a connection between them. It was one that he found comforting. He didn't know what would happen as the cub grew older, or whether it would even follow him when he made his return to the south and back to the Denraen.

He reached the flatter grounds and paused. From here, the mountains stretched above him, but toward the north, they flattened out, rolling into a gentle plain that led into the Antrilii lands.

He didn't know where to find the Antrilii, but now that he was out of the mountains, he had a sense that he *could* find them. He could follow the steady rolling plains until he reached either Farsea or the Antrilii tower, and from there, the Yahinv.

"Are you going to remain, or will you return to your pack," Endric asked the cub.

The cub barked at him and nudged him forward. In the two weeks they had traveled together, the cub had grown. Endric wasn't sure if it was his imagination or whether it really had grown as much as he thought it had. The cub was nearly twice the size it had been when he first encountered it.

Every so often, Endric thought he noticed the cub's fur glowing softly. Most of the time, Endric thought it was nothing more than his imagination, but there were times when the glowing became impossible to ignore. Teralin. He didn't understand the connection, but it was there, and real.

They started off, heading toward the plains. About midday on the first day after leaving the mountains, he encountered someone else. A pair of Antrilii, one man and one female, were in the distance. As he approached, the male Antrilii watched him with a question on his face.

The woman wore orange woven into her hair, braided heavily, much like he'd seen of the women before he was exiled.

"Who are you?" the man asked. He eyed Endric, taking in his Antrilii boots, the sword strapped to his waist and likely noting the quantity of his laca furs.

"I am Endric, son of Dendril, general of the Denraen. I have served my penance, and I have returned."

The man and the woman looked at each other with wide eyes.

The woman answered, "Come with us."

He arrived at the base of the tower, tired and with rising uncertainty. There had been no talk during the walk toward it. After a while, the couple had been joined by others, and they spoke quietly to each other. At one point, someone had brought in horses, and they had ridden. Endric worried the cub wouldn't be able to keep up, but he had proven faster than Endric could've imagined. The horses thundered across the plain.

Endric spent the time worrying about what he would say. He had already claimed his penance had been served but was that true? He hadn't slaughtered an entire brood, but he had destroyed three—no four—females, which meant that he had destroyed four broods from continuing. Likely it didn't even matter. Likely the groeliin would continue to breed and would continue to create new broods, but if nothing else, he had slowed it. He had disrupted the breeding grounds. That had to be worth something.

When he reached the tower, he was met by the seven women of the Yahinv.

All of them regarded him with an open distrust. Endric met their gaze defiantly, thinking that he could do nothing else.

Nessa stepped forward, and Endric climbed out of the saddle. One of the other Antrilii led the horse away. As he did, the cub bounded up to them and sat on its haunches next to him. The women of the Yahinv glanced from him to the merahl, and he noted that a few faces softened.

"Rumor has it that you claim to have served your penance?" Nessa asked.

Endric nodded. "I was given a penance on behalf of my father, Dendril, general of the Denraen. It was only after I was sent from the Antrilii, exiled into the mountains, that I learned that the penance was meant to be impossible." Endric glanced from Nessa to Isabel, and then to Melinda. All watched him, and Isabel wore defiance in her eyes.

"A penance must be difficult for it to matter," Nessa said.

"Difficult I understand. Sending me into the mountains naked and unarmed, forcing me to survive. That is difficult.

Telling me that I must destroy a brood of groeliin when no others have ever killed that many, that is impossible."

"You are not Antrilii. What do you know of what is possible and what is not?" Isabel asked.

"I might not be Antrilii, but I understand the purpose of what you do possibly better than you do."

His words were icy and did not match the heat boiling within him, the anger that surged. These were the women who had exiled him, who had sent him to serve a penance on behalf of his father, one that they knew he would not survive. They seemed disappointed by the fact that he had.

"You would dare—"

Melinda raised her hand, cutting off Isabel. "How is it that you've returned?"

"How? I fought off a pack of laca during my first few days. That allowed me to clothe myself. I broke a branch from trees and used that as a club, along with a spear I fashioned and used those to defend myself against the first three groeliin I encountered."

"The first three?" Nessa asked. She looked at the other women before turning her attention back to Endric. "How far out were you when you first encountered the groeliin?"

Endric shook his head. "I don't know. A week? Maybe less."

"That's too—" one of the women started before getting cut off by Melinda, who raised her hand once more. The woman she cut off had yellow woven in her hair.

"You said that was the first time you face the groeliin," Nessa went on.

Endric nodded. "The first time. The second time, there were five."

"Five?" Isabel asked, the incredulity in her voice plain. "Few

Antrilii could survive five groeliin. And none armed only with a club and a spear!"

Endric turned toward her, anger still boiling within him. "The second time I faced five, I barely survived."

"I doubt he faced even a single groeliin," Isabel said.

Endric fished into the pocket he'd fashioned into the laca furs. He pulled out the groeliin skins that he'd cut free and tossed them to Isabella. All were marked with the same brood mark.

"Then I came across something surprising. I discovered this cub, bound by a rope of flesh made from a dead Antrilii. The groeliin used him to draw out the merahl."

Melinda met his eyes. "What happened then? How did you save this creature?"

"You don't seem surprised," Endric said.

Melinda stared at him, blinking.

Endric's heart hammered. He had been struggling with what had happened, struggling to understand. The merahl felt abandoned by the Antrilii, enough so that they had stopped hunting with them, and the Antrilii knew that groeliin were breeding. Could there be a connection?

"There would have been too many groeliin..."

Endric tipped his head, studying Melinda. "There were. There were dozens of groeliin."

"Dozens?" Isabel asked.

"You wouldn't have survived against dozens of groeliin," Nessa said. She had a more measured response. He glanced from Isabel to Melinda.

"No, I wouldn't have. But I had help."

Isabel grinned darkly. "You cannot serve a penance with help."

"No? And if the merahl choose to help me?" Endric asked.

Endric debated what else he should share with them. Did he mention the fact that he had come across Nahrsin? They needed to know about the tribe that had died. That much, they did need to know.

"Which tribe is the blue?" Endric asked. He looked at the women, trying to determine if he could tell from the ribbons in their hair, but it was not obvious which of them favored blue.

"Blue?" This came from a mousy-looking woman who stood toward the back of the line of women from the Yahinv. "Why?"

"Don't encourage him, Rebecca," Isabel said.

Endric turned to Rebecca. "I came across your hunters. The groeliin slaughtered them."

Her breath caught. "How many?" she asked.

She glanced at Isabel, but the woman didn't look in her direction. "They were supposed to travel with the Aram tribe. They were hunting, convinced they would find the—"

"Enough!" Isabel said.

"You knew the groeliin were breeding when you sent me out. And you were responsible for the merahl losing faith in the Antrilii, weren't you?" Endric asked, looking at Isabel. Could she have intended for him to find the breeding grounds? Could she have even wanted him to be captured by the groeliin? That seemed too harsh, even for someone who hadn't seemed to care for him from the moment he first came to the Antrilii lands.

Isabel looked at him, anger flashing in her eyes. "This was an attempt to end this conflict," Isabel said. "This was an attempt to finally allow us to stop fighting."

"What attempt?"

"It doesn't matter, Nessa."

Nessa crossed her arms over her chest in an expression that

told Endric that it *did* matter. She turned her attention to Rebecca. "And you were in on this. You knew about this?"

Rebecca met her eyes, shaking her head. "I wasn't in on anything. I agreed to send hunters from our tribe after the Chisln, the same as the rest."

Nessa looked from one woman to the next. Melinda met her gaze, but she carried with it a certain defiance.

Nessa frowned. "And you? Is that why you didn't want Endric going? What of your tribe? Did you involve them as well?"

"Do I need to help when the plan is as foolish as what she intends? Do I need to help prevent that kind of folly?" Melinda met her eyes, shaking her head. "No. She chose her path. Her people chose to follow her. Anything from there that happened is on them."

"But we are all the same people," Nessa said. "We all serve the same purpose. We all have taken the same vows. If you're willing to let other tribes be sacrificed simply because you don't care for them..." Nessa fell silent for a long moment. "And now we've lost a tribe of hunters. We lost men who are meant to help protect our people, to carry out the vows that we made to the gods long ago. Without them, what are we?"

Melinda crossed her arms over her chest. "As I said, she made a choice. Her people chose to follow her. That is not my fault."

"And when the groeliin breeding destroys another tribe? Whose fault is that?" Nessa asked.

"The groeliin have never stopped breeding," Melinda said. She turned her attention to Rebecca. "That is on her. She knew the history of our people as well as I. She knew how futile such an attempt was. That is not on me."

"But if we could," Isabel said. "Think of what we could—"

Nessa jabbed the other woman in the chest with her finger. "We have never managed to stop a breeding. The best we can do is prepare for the next hunt."

Endric looked at both of them. "I stopped a breeding."

Melinda looked at him sharply. "You were barely able to survive in the mountains. Why would we believe that you were able to stop a breeding?"

"Did you know why the merahl were upset with the Antrilii?" Endric asked.

Nessa turned to him. "What is this?"

"The merahl. They were—*are*—upset with the Antrilii. They refused to hunt with them."

"The merahl never stop hunting with us," Nessa said.

Endric looked at Melinda. He saw something in her eyes, something that told him that she understood.

"What did you do?" he asked. "How are you a part of this?"

"Enough. You have returned to the Antrilii despite your penance," Isabel said. "You have returned without proof that your penance has been paid. You have violated this custom."

"No. I found the breeding grounds. I killed three breeding females. Those are three broods that will not attack the Antrilii again."

Melinda glared at him. "You might be my grandson. You might be the son of Dendril, the man who should have been heir to the Scroll tribe, but you do not know the Antrilii way. You do not understand what we've faced over the years. You do not understand what we've prevented over the years."

"I understand more than you realize," Endric said.

Nessa shook her head. "What happened with the merahl?"

"I don't know. All I know is that when they showed the

orange painted tribe to me, they did not want to go any further. They were angry with them."

Nessa turned to Isabel. "That is your tribe."

Isabel pinched her lips together. "I am of all the tribes."

"But of the Aram tribe most of all. What did you do?"

"Nothing other than finding a way to discover the breeding grounds," Isabel said defiantly. "Melinda knew—"

Nessa turned to her. "Melinda knew? What is it that you're keeping from the rest of us? What is it that you believe that you could have done?"

When she didn't answer, Rebecca stepped forward. "What did you know?" She had been mousey and quiet, but learning that her tribe was lost had changed her. She could have been broken, but instead, she seemed to be stronger.

"You wouldn't understand," Isabel said. "You don't have the same responsibility—"

"I am responsible for my people, the same as you. Don't downplay the responsibility for any of us." She looked at Melinda. "And you," she said, focusing on Melinda. "Haven't you lost enough? Haven't you seen enough of our people harmed because of these creatures?"

"Which is why I thought we needed to take this risk."

"Enough!" Isabel said. "He is not even Antrilii. He should not even be here as we discuss this."

"No?" Rebecca said. "From what I can tell, *you* shouldn't be here, especially if you allowed an attack to take place and allowed our people—my people—to be sacrificed."

"For the betterment of all," Isabel said.

"Are you so certain? Do you really believe that losing an entire tribe is better for our people? Do you really believe that losing so many in such a way without discussing it with the rest of us is what the gods would have wanted?"

Rebecca continued arguing with Isabel and Melinda, but Nessa touched his arm and guided him off to the side. When they stopped, she looked at him, a question in her eyes. "Did you really see the breeding ground?"

Endric nodded.

"What happened? How were you able to survive?

"The merahl. They came when I had the greatest need."

"Do you know why?"

Endric's gaze drifted to the sword. "I think they knew something about me that even I don't fully understand."

"And what is that?"

"I can charge teralin."

Endric watched her face, wondering whether she understood, but had the sense from Nessa that she did. She had knowledge, and she had been the one to save him when he had nearly died coming to these lands.

Her eyes widened slightly. "The groeliin use it?"

"You knew?" Endric asked.

Nessa shook her head once. "Not known. But we have suspected. We have long suspected that the groeliin somehow have access to the negatively charged ore."

"Do you know how to change the polarity?"

Nessa glanced at the other women, all of whom were still arguing. "Only a few do."

With the comment, Endric understood. "They drew them, didn't they?" he asked.

Nessa frowned, staring at the other women. "Gods, I hope that wasn't the case."

"That's the reason the merahl abandoned the Antrilii."

Nessa looked back, surprise widening her eyes. "Why do you say that?"

"Because the merahl use the positively charged teralin."

Nessa gasped.

The sound caught the others' attention, and they all turned to her.

Nessa turned to the others. She stared at them, heat growing in her eyes. "The Yahinv must convene. We must discuss the leadership of the tribes."

"I called the Yahinv," Isabel said.

Nessa shot her a heated stare. "After our meeting, it is likely that you will no longer even sit among us. Come," Nessa said, motioning to the others.

E ndric sat outside of the tower, waiting. The rest of the Antrilii who had accompanied him back this way remained near, practically guarding him, almost as if they were suspicious of what he might attempt. Endric didn't mind. He wondered what would come of the Yahinv meeting, now that he thought he understood what it meant.

Isabel and Melinda had thought to draw out the groeliin, knowing the breeding season was near. They must have suspected that teralin was involved, and had negatively charged it. This had, in turn, angered the merahl, who then had abandoned the Antrilii and caused the groeliin to converge on the lands they used for breeding.

Melinda had sent her tribe, and but had done so in a way that wouldn't put them in direct conflict. She had made certain that it was Isabel's tribe that went first. Somehow, Isabel's tribe hadn't reached the breeding grounds first; it had been Rebecca's, and they had all been lost.

It made his head swim.

Yet Endric had changed the polarity of the teralin, and he had hopefully ended the conflict with the merahl. He hoped that in time, the enormous cats would once again work with the Antrilii.

And as much as he resented what had happened, and as much as it had nearly led to his death, he still understood. The Antrilii wanted to end the fighting.

The door to the tower opened, and Nessa came out. She was the only one to emerge.

She saw Endric and made her way toward him. She took a seat, settling next to him, smoothing her long, colorful skirt and staring at the cub sitting at Endric's feet. After long moments, she sighed. "Does he have a name?" she asked.

Endric grunted. "I'm not certain I should name him."

"He is yours, and you are his. You will need to give him a name."

"I can't remain with Antrilii," Endric said. "I'm not certain that I deserve to have one of the merahl accompany me. They need to continue to hunt, fighting the groeliin."

Nessa looked up, pulling her gaze from the merahl up to Endric, and she smiled. "When you first came to Farsea, you wanted to know about the Antrilii. You wanted to know what it would take to prove that you were descended from them."

"I understand that I can't be a part of both the Denraen and the Antrilii. I think my father understood that as well."

"Perhaps," Nessa said. "Yet you have satisfied his penance. "

"You believe me?"

Nessa shrugged. "Gron sent word ahead. They came upon a valley littered with dead groeliin. They counted almost two hundred gone. They were of several broods, unusual for the groeliin."

Endric nodded. He hadn't known how many broods there were, but two hundred groeliin? The merahl really were impressive creatures.

"I wasn't responsible for most of them," he said.

She chuckled. "No, I wouldn't think that you were. But you are responsible for enough of them. And the merahl fought with you. That, to the Antrilii, is the same."

"The Yahinv agrees with you in this?" he asked.

Nessa shrugged. "The Yahinv required that you serve a penance. They required that you eliminate a brood. Considering most broods are no more than fifty groeliin, two hundred would be equivalent of four broods. That doesn't even take into consideration the fact that you removed several queens as well."

"I didn't think you believe me."

"I believe what you say, Endric, son of Dendril. You have been true to your word."

"What will happen to Isabel and Melinda?"

Nessa chuckled softly. "They will be stripped of leadership."

"No penance?"

"Do you think they require penance?" she asked. There was an earnestness in her voice, and it seemed she truly wanted to know his opinion.

"They wanted to destroy the groeliin. They thought to draw them into a Chisln."

"That is what they claim."

Endric sighed. "I think they both acted in ways they felt would help the Antrilii. I don't think either of them intended to risk their people. I don't think either of them intended for Rebecca to lose her people."

"Rebecca felt the same way."

"There's something I still don't understand," he said.

"And that is?"

"Someone had captured the merahl cub and used flesh from one of your warriors to hold him to draw the groeliin."

Nessa's eyes narrowed. "That troubles me as well. There are several possibilities, including that Melinda and Isabel were more involved than they admit. It will take much questioning to discover the answers."

Endric had hoped for more clarity, but he would have to be satisfied with whatever Nessa could learn. "I am sorry you lost the hunters that you did. I hope the gods have welcomed them back."

Endric still didn't feel devout, but it felt right to say. It felt right to think that the Antrilii, especially the men who had never forsaken the gods, who lived every day in service of them, should return to them.

"I find you interesting, Endric, son of Dendril."

"Why is that?"

"You come to the Antrilii, seeking to understand your ancestors. Yet it was you who helped remind us what it means to be Antrilii."

Endric shook his head. "I thought I could come and under-stand what it meant to be Antrilii and what that meant for me as Denraen."

"And what have you learned?"

"I've learned that I can't be both."

Nessa watched him, studying him. "Are you so certain? It seems to me that Dendril managed to serve both the Antrilii and the Denraen. You're more like him than you give yourself credit for." She stared at the merahl cub for a moment longer. "You really should give him a name."

Endric smiled. He didn't have a name, not yet, but if the cub was to remain with him, perhaps he *should* name him.

"How long will you stay?" she asked.

"You're asking this time?"

"You have proven that you deserve to know your people," Nessa said. "And I think your cousin would appreciate more time to spend with you."

"I would like that."

"Besides, one of the tribes came upon a man in the mountains and brought him to me. He was injured, near death, but I've been nursing him back to health, much as I did with you."

"Brohmin?"

She nodded. "He was most concerned when he heard that you accepted the penance. He was even more concerned when he heard what that penance entailed. I think he will be pleased to learn that you returned. He can be most persistent. If he had his way, he would have gone after you into the mountains."

"Can I see him?"

"Soon. There are some things we must discuss first."

"Such as?"

"Such as which tribe you would claim."

Endric frowned. "Which tribe?"

"You are Antrilii, Endric, son of Dendril. You have been away, but you have proven yourself. All men get to choose their tribe."

He thought about the tribes, thought about what he knew of them, but it was very little. Without spending any time with the Antrilii, how could he make such a decision? He could join Nahrsin, be a part of his tribe, but that meant Melinda or her successor would lead. He thought about Nessa. He respected her and thought that she would treat him fairly. Yet, something else came to him. A tribe that needed him perhaps more than any others.

"Do you think Rebecca would welcome me to her tribe?"

Nessa watched him, a sly smile spreading across her face. "I think she would." Nessa stood and smoothed her skirt. "I think... I think that I am disappointed you would not choose my tribe. I think that you will make a great Antrilii, Endric, son of Dendril. I think that Dendril knew what he was doing when he sent you north." She looked at the mountains in the south, squinting slightly. "I believe your cousin approaches. He will be pleased to see you alive. But I would like to visit with you more while you remain in our lands."

Endric smiled. "I would like that as well."

"You are welcome among us, Endric, son of Dendril, Denraen soldier and Antrilii."

As she walked away, Endric smiled.

Maybe it *was* possible for him to be both Denraen and Antrilii.

Check book 4 in The Teralin Sword series, Soldier Saved:

Endric returns to Vasha after discovering his connection to the Antrilii and how they serve the north but finds that much has changed, including his relationship with Senda and Pendin. As he struggles to understand how he can serve the Denraen, he learns that the Denraen hold Urik—and that his father has granted him the freedom of the city.

Urik isn't done plotting and Endric fears that whatever he intends is the reason Mage Tresten has disappeared. Discovering those answers will put Endric at odds with the Denraen and sends him on a journey that leads to even more understanding about his role in the Denraen—and the Conclave.

ALSO BY D.K. HOLMBERG

The Teralin Sword

Soldier Son

Soldier Sword

Soldier Sworn

Soldier Saved

The Lost Prophecy

The Threat of Madness

The Warrior Mage

Tower of the Gods

Twist of the Fibers

The Lost City

The Last Conclave

The Gift of Madness

The Great Betrayal

The Cloud Warrior Saga

Chased by Fire

Bound by Fire

Changed by Fire

Fortress of Fire

Forged in Fire

Serpent of Fire

Servant of Fire

Born of Fire

Broken of Fire

Light of Fire

Cycle of Fire

The Endless War

Journey of Fire and Night

Darkness Rising

Endless Night

Summoner's Bond

Seal of Light

The Shadow Accords

Shadow Blessed

Shadow Cursed

Shadow Born

Shadow Lost

Shadow Cross

Shadow Found

Stolen Compass

Stone Dragon

Made in the USA
Lexington, KY
01 February 2018